Déjà Vu

Susan Fraser was born in Newcastle and grew up in Sydney. She studied English literature and languages at Sydney University and later taught English and French. She then studied law and worked as a lawyer before moving to France in 2000. Susan lives south of Paris, with her French husband and fifteen-year-old son.

Déjà Vu

SUSAN FRASER

VIKING
an imprint of
PENGUIN BOOKS

VIKING

Published by the Penguin Group
Penguin Group (Australia)
250 Camberwell Road, Camberwell, Victoria 3124, Australia
(a division of Pearson Australia Group Pty Ltd)
Penguin Group (USA) Inc.
375 Hudson Street, New York, New York 10014, USA
Penguin Group (Canada)
90 Eglinton Avenue East, Suite 700, Toronto, Canada ON M4P 2Y3
(a division of Pearson Penguin Canada Inc.)
Penguin Books Ltd
80 Strand, London WC2R 0RL England
Penguin Ireland
25 St Stephen's Green, Dublin 2, Ireland
(a division of Penguin Books Ltd)
Penguin Books India Pvt Ltd
11 Community Centre, Panchsheel Park, New Delhi – 110 017, India
Penguin Group (NZ)
67 Apollo Drive, Mairangi Bay, Auckland 1310, New Zealand
(a division of Pearson New Zealand Ltd)
Penguin Books (South Africa) (Pty) Ltd
24 Sturdee Avenue, Rosebank, Johannesburg 2196, South Africa

Penguin Books Ltd, Registered Offices: 80 Strand, London, WC2R 0RL, England

First published by Penguin Group (Australia), 2007

1 3 5 7 9 10 8 6 4 2

Design by Elizabeth Dias © Penguin Group (Australia)
Cover photograph by Yasushi Kuroda/Getty Images
Quote on page 85 from *Madeline* by Ludwig Bemelmans, © 1939 by Ludwig Bemelmans,
renewed © 1967 by Madeleine Bemelmans and Barbara Bemelmans Marciano. Used by
permission of Viking Penguin, A division of Penguin Young Readers Group, A Member of
Penguin Group (USA) Inc. All rights reserved.
Typeset in Fairfield Light by Techbooks, India
Printed and bound in Australia by McPherson's Printing Group,
Maryborough, Victoria

National Library of Australia
Cataloguing-in-Publication data:

Fraser, Susan, 1960–.
Déjà vu.
ISBN 978 0 670 07076 3 (pbk)
ISBN 0 670 07076 9 (pbk)
1. Fourth dimension – Fiction. 2. Life change events – Fiction. I. Title
A823.4

www.penguin.com.au

For Molly and Jake

Prologue

Prologue

We were on our way back from Toulouse, driving along the auto-route in the rain. It must have happened somewhere along that section where the road tapers down to two lanes, two very narrow lanes. I always used to hold my breath as we overtook the convoy of trucks travelling up from Spain, from as far as Portugal even, thundering alongside us in the 'slow' lane, within a hair's breadth. And that evening it was particularly bad, what with the rain and spray off the trucks as we came up alongside them, even with the windscreen wipers swishing frantic. Travelling blind.

It must have happened then.

I remember speaking to Charlie on the mobile – telling him we'd be home in about an hour, and that he should stop playing on the computer, check the windows were shut and have a shower. That was the last time I spoke to him, and it was only briefly. I could tell he was in the middle of his Age of Empires game, because he had that 'Got to go' voice – distracted – which always riles me. So I don't think I called him 'darling' or anything particularly endearing.

I don't even think I said goodbye, which of course upsets me. I wanted him to get off the computer. I was worried he'd been on it all day, even though he told me he hadn't. I always know, though, when he's lying. It's something about his voice. I can't explain it. I can just tell.

'Give him another five minutes,' Marc had said.

That's when it hit me. What did it really matter, after all? He was having a good time. We'd been gone the whole day and he'd been fine. He'd said 'Cool!' when we told him that morning we were leaving him alone for the day. So we'd laughed and asked how he'd like it if we left him alone for the night, for the week even. 'Cool!' he said. 'Oh *sure!*' we said, and joked about how he'd have to leave all the lights on for fear of aliens and how he'd get pretty sick of toast and Vegemite all week. Then I reminded him not to stick a knife or anything metal in the toaster if the bread got stuck and to make sure he kept the door locked and not to answer if anyone came by that he didn't know, and not to eat more than three pieces of chocolate. 'I *know*, Mum.' But he wasn't listening.

The thing is, I could see him – we *both* could – just as he grunted 'Bye' to me, his eyes trained on the computer screen as he hung up the phone, missing the receiver at first, then clunking it into place finally, clumsily. Yes, that's when it happened – we were home with him again.

Though I don't remember ever arriving...

We were standing in the doorway watching him, his hair thick and messy, the colour of sand, flopping over his eyes as he punched at the keyboard with his grubby eleven-year-old fingers. He hadn't even looked up.

'You see, Marc?' I said.

'Five more minutes, Charlie, *c'est tout.*'

But he was too immersed in his game to even grunt our way.

Ah, what *did* it matter? So Marc uncorked the *Colombelle*, our favourite, which we'd been lucky to find that day in some back-street wine cellar in Toulouse. And we sat on the couch, sipping our wine, savouring the moment, listening to Charlie upstairs as he made his crash and boom sounds, fighting battles in some far-off field in medieval times. It had been a good day, even if he *had* eaten nearly the whole block of chocolate.

It was strange, because we didn't hear the knock at the door. And looking back, I often wonder if it was the wine that had numbed our senses. We were both feeling so relaxed. Charlie had finally turned off the computer and was under the shower. I heard him shut the water off suddenly – too suddenly as usual – the clank of old pipes resounding throughout the house like those shots through the valley in the hunting season. And when he called out 'Who is it?', Marc and I looked at each other and smiled, wondering what he was on about. Marc called back '*Qui, cheri?*', but Charlie didn't answer. Maybe he hadn't heard. *We* could hear *him* though, shuffling around on the floorboards upstairs. I was thinking he'd hardly been under long enough to wash himself properly when suddenly he came bounding down the stairs, missing the last four steps – as always – and crashing to the floor. He was barely dry, with his hair dripping wet, and half-dressed in just his shorts.

We watched him thunder past us as he moved towards the front door, leaving a trail of footprints, puddles on the floorboards.

'What's the matter, Charlie?'

He didn't answer. He reminded me then of when he was little, when he'd sleepwalk, his eyes open but glazed, their crystal blueness misting to cloudy grey, unseeing. But now his hand was on the lock, turning it over, his bare back with its tiny brown birthmark, the shape of Africa, twitching between his shoulderblades.

We both jumped up at the same time, each with a glass in our hand, wine spilling over on to the rug. There were two of them, a man and woman, immaculately starched blue uniforms, police officers, standing out there on the doorstep, rain pummelling the glass portal.

They were only young, the woman particularly – just a girl, with her hair pulled back tight from her round, ruddy cheeks. She was obviously fresh out of the academy, or whatever it's called in France. I remember her eyes – very dark, *very* grim – although it may have been the fact that she was focusing all her attention on Charlie, *staring* at him actually. Even though I'd put my glass down and pushed past him to ask her what was wrong, she was staring at him still. And then I realised it was the man who was doing the talking. I should have known – she was obviously his offsider, being so young, with her uniform barely out of its packet. He had stepped into the room, slipped past me somehow and was talking to Charlie. I tried to cut across him, but he kept going, talking over me, a hand on Charlie's bare shoulder, as if I wasn't there. He was speaking in French, naturally, and because I'd missed the beginning, I couldn't work out what he was saying. I could hear the words, but for the life of me couldn't put them together to give them meaning.

Charlie's mouth, his lips frozen, fixed open – a perfect 'O' – and a shudder rolled through his body, like when he was a baby, when his temperature shot up to 39.8 and his ears turned to crimson.

'What's wrong, Charlie? *Tell Mummy what's wrong!*'

And then I looked back at Marc. He was still standing over by the couch, transfixed, glass in hand, but tipped up so that his wine was spilling on to the rug.

He'd heard it all.

Chapter
one

We have argued about it many times since, about how the story goes. Marc tells it differently. But I guess that's to be expected, even though we were together in Toulouse, in the car coming back, then finally home again with Charlie.

Or so we thought.

We do agree though, we'd had a good day – significant in one sense, ironic in another. First, we'd come to the end of a pretty rough week, a week of fighting over nothing, over everything. So in a way we'd reached a crisis point, that moment you ask yourself where your life is going – or more to the point, where the hell your life has *gone*.

Marc disagrees with me there. He says I'm exaggerating *comme d'habitude*, and that he wasn't thinking that at all. Ah, but *I* was. We'd left Australia and were back living in France. The problem wasn't France, though. It was *where* we'd ended up – in some tiny forgotten village called Lherm.

We were lost. *Lost in Lherm.*

Déjà Vu

Through a magnifying glass, it's just a speck on the map, in the middle of nowhere. You drive and drive up long winding roads, roads that taper down to bumpy overgrown tracks bordered by green fields and hills, bucolically green, and finally you are in Lherm – end of the road, last stop. The only way out is back the way you came, for there's nothing beyond but woods. Paradise, you say?

True, when we first drove up that narrow dirt track late one evening in early May, rounding the corner of an open field bordered by apple trees, and pulled up in the centre of the village, I admit I said it too.

Time, it seemed, had stopped in this peaceful little backwater. The cluster of houses, their old stones bleached a rosy white, shutters faded to a washed-out steel blue – the colour of the sky on a cloudy day – and ramshackle gardens with apple trees and roosters strutting proud. The medieval church set on high like a tiara – the pride of the village. We'd wandered in and out of passageways lined with hollyhock, giant single-stemmed flowers, standing tall and majestic, their blood-red petals wooing swollen bumblebees, buzzing lazily from one flower to the next, blissfully drunk on pollen.

We were searching for an old stone house, the one in the photo the agent had given us – the house, he explained, that used to be the village café and post office, with the pink and purple hydrangeas out the front, and where the locals would come seeking old

Madame Rosière's herbal remedies or, failing that, a Ricard at the bar. '*C'est la meilleure de tout façon,*' the best remedy anyway, he'd chuckled. And there it was, tucked in beside the church – its stone glowing pink in the twilight.

We'd been looking for months.

We made our way up the track leading out the other side of the village, towards the woods, past an overgrown cemetery at the top of the hill where some of the headstones had long toppled over, partially buried under a mound of untamed grass. Their inscriptions were hidden by centuries of lichen, the stone tinged a motley green and white. We sat up there on the wall, and looked back down over the village, over the *whole* valley basking in its brilliant blood-orange glow as the sun slid behind the hill. It was like looking through a stained-glass window – like cellophane paper at Christmas.

That's when I turned to Marc. 'This is it.'

He nodded. I could tell he felt it too – both of us drawn in by Lherm's sleepy magic, a spell cast over us.

The trouble is, there are good spells and bad spells. And sometimes, when you're looking too hard, looking for something you've lost, you can't tell the difference.

But I am jumping ahead. I should explain how it was that we came to be there, how we'd ended up in Lherm, in the middle of nowhere.

Chapter
two

I never knew my father. He died before I was born – something my mother never really got over. The pain of his loss made her tough, staining her outlook on life, on *my* life.

'It's no use talking about fate, or bad luck,' she used to say. 'You make your own bed, Annie MacIntyre.'

But with age, I learnt there are some things in life you have no control over. Some things just *happen* that have nothing to do with what you may or may not have done. Like Marc losing his job.

That's how it all started. We were in Australia. Marc was made redundant. I remember it well – exactly two years earlier to the day that we were on our way home from Toulouse.

'*S'il te plaît,* Annie, I didn't lose my job,' Marc likes to claim. 'Alsttel made me an offer. They made us all an offer, and I accepted. *C'est tout.*'

As Charlie would say, 'The man's in denial, Mum.'

However he wants to put it, Marc was made redundant. Yet in the first few weeks following that news, we were on a high.

Marc had been with Alsttel from the very first year I brought him out to Australia, some ten years back, so the redundancy package was a hefty one. This was it then, we told each other, our chance for a sea change had arrived; it was our ticket back to France, where we'd first met.

Where we'd been happy.

We began to make plans, like excited kids with a big bag of lollies. We were so optimistic, just like we used to be. It was to be the start of something wonderfully new. We'd buy a house in the French countryside, somewhere in the south-west where the River Lot winds through the villages like a shiny silver dragon's tail. A life in the country, in France – *another world*, away from it all. Our second chance.

So each night I would lie awake, thinking about what we should do. We'd sell our Sydney apartment, our car, and have a garage sale. I'd finally get rid of that old couch, turf those boxes of junk piled up in the garage; maybe even sort through Marc's old clothes while he was out sometime. It was time for his cowboy boots to hit the road, and for me to quit my job. Yes, I'd even quit my job. Now that decision was hardly heart-rending. I'd never liked the law, never liked walking into court with a trolley-load of files, standing before His Honour with stomach churning and heart pounding, bowing my head: as the court pleases, Your Honour, three bags full, Your Honour.

I remember one night as we lay in bed, I wouldn't let Marc go to sleep; I wanted to keep talking about it.

Déjà Vu

'*Tu es comme Perrette et le pot au lait,*' he moaned, pulling the pillow over his head. '*Oui*, you are just like Perrette. Let me sleep.'

He often likens me to her – the girl in some fable the French love to quote. She was on her way to the markets to sell a jug of milk, excited about the prospect of how much she would get for it, planning what she would spend it all on. But in her excitement Perrette dropped the jug. Poor girl. Still, at least she'd had a good time thinking about it.

Marc reckons I've missed the point. But isn't the fun in the planning?

So, in the year following, we moved into that old stone house in Lherm, in France's south-west, deep in the provincial heart-land. *Truly* away from it all. We'd bought our new home for next to nothing, a real steal, we thought gleefully. Sure, it needed a lot of work – water put on, electricity connected, the roof mended. But what fun it would be! I'd find a teaching job and Marc would work full-time on the house. Compared to law, teaching would be a breeze. 'I can do it standing on my head.' I laughed. We'd be doing it rough, but that would be the fun part.

But then, with no crystal ball, we weren't to know.

And yes, in that first summer we moved to Lherm, we were happy. We used to bike ride down to the river at Castelfranc, the village some ten kilometres down the road, where the River Vert meets the River Lot, water gushing into water, that clear crystal green – the stones worn away into smooth, flat pebbles under our bare feet.

We'd ride over the old stone bridge spanning the Vert, the locals perched along its walls like seagulls on a pier to fish, to talk, nodding their *Bonjour Messieurs,'Dame*, to us *étrangers*. And we'd ride on past the old water mill with its shutters long closed up, past the tiny railway track for the local goods train, grown over now by lavender and rosemary bushes, their pungent perfume following us down to the river.

We'd strip down to our Speedos, walk barefoot along the river's grassy edge, under the shade of the weeping-willows, and up towards the floodgates where the current swirls mad. Then laughing, screaming, we'd jump in.

Face up to the sky, arms spread like Christ on the cross, we'd float down, fast and out of control, about 200 or so metres towards the bigger, modern, wagon-green and crimson-edged steel bridge spanning the Lot – the three of us floating in its shade, Marc, Charlie and I, like kids, all three of us. There'd be no one but us in the water, even though there were groups of sunbathers, picnic-makers at its edge, French dogs barking mad at us. We were Australians, foolhardy Australians, plunging into perilous waters.

That's how I liked to picture it – that the river was ours because we were big, bold Australians who could swim like Ian Thorpe, who could swim against the current.

'Like salmon.' Charlie would laugh. 'Pink salmon.'

Chapter
three

$\mathcal{W}$e enrolled Charlie into the local primary, a small country school about ten kilometres down the road from Lherm. From the outside it looked surprisingly austere, an ugly 1970s brick building with a bitumen schoolyard behind. I had pictured something more romantic – an ex-convent perhaps, with high-ceilinged classrooms set in an open field of green grass, giant fig trees and lush paddocks beyond. I imagined a couple of chestnut mares loping up to the school fence, where the kids would feed them apples every day and ride bareback after school.

But there were no horses.

I knew this was going to be the hardest part of the move. On the surface, Charlie looked and sounded like a French kid – he could *speak* French. But that was it. He couldn't read or write. And he *was* different. He was Australian – still a foreigner, despite the French father.

La rentrée rolled around, that mad period when all the French arrive back home from their summer holidays, when the autoroutes are classed as *rouge* – jam-packed with caravans, four-wheel drives and roof-racks chock-a-block. It was September, the start of the new school year – D-day for Charlie. But as I sat at the breakfast table watching Marc dunk his croissant and Charlie shovel down his Weet-Bix, a thought occurred to me – he'd be eating at the school canteen from now on, a hot meal every midday. And I had forgotten to warn him about mad cow disease.

'Charlie, whatever you do, don't eat beef, *boeuf,* okay? Or veal, that's *veau,* all right? Or spaghetti bolognese. And steak tartare is right out, because that's raw —'

'But I *like* spaghetti bolognese!'

Marc was giving me 'the look', like *I* was the mad cow. 'Annie, *s'il te plaît! La vache folle, c'est fini!*'

'Oh no it's not, Marc – it's not over at all. That's just what the French government and the meat industry want you to believe. It's like the hunters!'

Marc's croissant splashed into his bowl, coffee spilling over the sides. 'The hunters?'

I reached for the baguette and Vegemite: I'd make Charlie a sandwich, just in case. 'Yes. The hunters are too strong for the government to ever rule against hunting in France... and it's the same thing with the meat industry and mad cow!'

'What noise does a mad cow make?' asked Charlie, giggling.

'Charlie, *please*, I'm serious —'

'*Ba-hhh!*'

So I realised the conspiracy theory and mad cow disease were issues *way* too complex to explain then and there. We didn't have time.

'Just don't eat it, all right, Charlie?'

'Not even spaghetti bolognese?'

We drove him down together. It wasn't like the time we started him in kindergarten back in Sydney, at Paddington Public, when the parents huddled together, nervous, giggling, as we watched our children in their fresh school uniforms, three sizes too big, and their shiny black shoes, trail off like ducklings. They were *so* trusting, following their new 'mother' in pairs, holding hands – that wonderful age when it's okay for a boy to hold another boy's hand and not be taunted with cries of 'You're gay!'

Of course, Charlie was older now, all of nine – a *big* kid. I could tell by the way he was standing as he waited for his name to be called out: his shoulders hunched, eyes not flickering my way, but focused straight ahead – that he was saying, 'Don't acknowledge you're my mother, *or else*.' He had a look to maintain: Mr Cool, standing at what he obviously considered a respectable distance – a metre from Marc and me – with his hands shoved into his jeans pockets. So that meant I had to play the part, act like the big kid's mother, behave and not say anything embarrassing, like 'Do you want me to come into the classroom and explain to the kids that they should be extra nice to you because you're from another country?' Besides, I was a mother with a funny accent now, and a ridiculous way of putting things.

The principal, a Gitane-smoking hard-edged sergeant-major type, was barking out each and every student's name in the school, one by one, to sort them all into their new classes. So we waited in silence, watching the boys saunter over to join their new class-mates, dragging their feet, hands shoved deep into their pockets as if they didn't give a damn; the girls letting out excited squeals and throwing their hands out Hollywood-style as they hastened across to join their *bestest* of *bestest* friends, kissing each other on both cheeks.

And without school uniforms, they all seemed older, certainly older than Charlie: the girls sporting low-cut jeans, tight T-shirts and bare midriffs, and the boys with every label under the sun written across their chests, and enough gel in their short spiked hair to sink a battleship.

I looked over at Charlie. No, he didn't have the same look at all, with his hair cut in soft layers, *forever* flopping over his eyes. It needed a cut, but he wouldn't be going to the same barber as this lot.

I'd noticed a group of boys whose names hadn't yet been called, leaning against the fence on the far side of the schoolyard. They were significantly bigger, so obviously older than Charlie by a year or two, and sniggering at anything that moved, particularly any-thing smaller. Their hairstyles were different again – cropped close all over except for a long bit on top hanging over their foreheads. They were making me nervous, making me wonder if we had done the right thing, bringing our son to this strange new world over which I now had no control. So I momentarily forgot the rules – the code of silence among cool guys.

'You okay, Charlie?'

'Fine.'

But he didn't look my way as he kicked at the ground.

'*Arrète*, Annie. You are making him anxious!' whispered Marc.

He was right, of course. But I wondered if he'd noticed the tough guys.

'*Every* school has them, Annie. *Ce n'est pas unique à la France.* You see them in Australia too.'

So he had noticed, and he was right again – toughies were everywhere. Besides, maybe it was just the haircuts. I was letting their appearance cloud my judgement. And they were only kids, after all – other mothers' sons, not much older than mine.

Suddenly the sergeant major barked out Charlie's name, or words to that effect.

'*Sharlie Muucinntiire-Morvan!*'

Charlie didn't budge.

Marc slid over to his side, a hand on his shoulder. '*C'est toi, mon lapin.*'

'*Non, non*... that's not me!' He hadn't understood this strange pronunciation of his name, the French version.

Marc nudged him forward. '*Si, si, Charlie! Allez!*'

I could hear the panic in his voice. *Now* who was making Charlie anxious?

'*Sharlie Muuccinnntiiiire-Morvan!*' came the call to action again.

This time it clicked. Charlie began to move off, shrugging his father's hand from his shoulder as I whispered 'Bye!' after him, resisting the urge to remind him about the mad cow.

But the mad cow would be the least of his problems.

Chapter
four

*I*n the autumn, the drive through the countryside was magical. I'd never really appreciated how many colours go to make up a tree, a leaf even – how many varieties of greens, reds, oranges and browns. Unlike the locals, who'd rip through the valley in their four-wheel drives, I used to take those roads very slowly, fearful that a deer, rabbit or even a wild boar might leap out in front before I had a chance to brake. My biggest fear was the boars. 'They can do your car a lot of damage,' our neighbour, old Monsieur Martin warned.

What can they do if you're out walking, I wondered?

If you head south along the River Lot, another thirty kilometres on from Charlie's school, you hit Cahors, where the river loops and where all the kids from the local villages end up to finish out their schooling – like fish caught up in the river. Those who plan to go on to university choose the *Lycée Général* in the centre of Cahors. Or, if they're into mechanics, they head for the *Lycée Technique* on the outskirts of town, to the sprawling mish-mash of hard-edged buildings set in among the council estates, in *La Zone Industrielle*.

That's where I landed a job teaching English, a few weeks into the new school year.

Day one, I started out so enthusiastically, despite the deputy head's warning that these kids were more into car engines than grammar lessons. As the bell rang out for the first period, I walked across the schoolyard, through the scattered groups of kids, their puffs of smoke rising like a scene from a spaghetti western – an open prairie of teenage smokers. Where had I landed?

But as I nudged my way up the corridor, through the long-legged, lank-haired teenagers slouched against the walls, stepping over their barrage of bags thrown every which way but out of my way, I imagined myself as the Australian version of Sydney Poitier. *Yes-siree*, I was going to make a difference. I had stories I could tell them that would be sure to get them in, about Australia: stories beyond their boring textbooks and their cars.

Each morning, I'd drop Charlie at his school and then head off for mine, a pile of *Sydney Morning Herald* web-page articles stashed in my briefcase – the scariest, goriest and most morbid I could dig up. Australia had become a minefield of fatal disasters since we left, it seemed: a vast open desert where you could drive for days and never see another living soul (and heaven help you if you ran out of petrol); an island surrounded by killer sharks; a myriad crocodile-infested rivers; not forgetting the giant, hairy huntsman, the red-back and funnel-web spiders; the flying greasy-brown cockroaches as fat as your thumb and as long as your index finger; and the slippery red-belly black snakes that could slide out from under your pillow and bite you dead before you'd even got a chance to reach for your rifle!... Of course, I'd always been a city girl, but the kids didn't need to know that.

I loved those drives into work, Charlie sitting next to me.

'Tell me if you see something on the road, Charlie.'

'*Careful*, Mum!' he'd screech, pointing up ahead. 'I see a frog.'

'That's not funny, Charlie.'

But I'd swerve around it anyway, that tiny bump on the road, to save a life and make Charlie laugh, to hear that rolling giggle from deep within his chest. His lovely unselfconscious little boy laugh when no one else was around, when he would turn his face to me, his blue eyes meeting mine.

'You sure that wasn't a stone, Charlie?' I would say. Just to hear him giggle.

I always thought I could tell, merely by looking into those eyes, that I could see into his soul and know what he was thinking. That I would know if something was troubling him – always.

But then, boys must become men. They must learn to fear nothing, or at least not to show it. Even at nine.

Déjà Vu

I remember in that first summer, we'd gone down to the river one hot and sticky day. Steam rose from the mud under our feet. The river was higher than usual, churning wild and brown. It had rained non-stop for a week. So I hesitated, looking out at the water, measuring the risk, my attention drawn to a log hurtling past us, towards the bridge, too fast.

'No.' I was shaking my head. 'Not today. *No way.*'

But Marc and Charlie had already stripped off, running keen, already halfway up the track, heading towards our jumping-off point. I called to them, but they didn't seem to hear me. I watched Marc for a moment, thinking he would stop, but he didn't turn around – not once – not even to see if I was following. And I thought, isn't he going to think about this? Is he just going to let Charlie do this? They were nearly to the point when I screamed out, louder this time.

'Marc, *stop!*'

He turned, but only to smile at me, motioning for me to come as I held up my hand, fingers outspread. But he must have taken it for a wave, as he waved back. Crazy French fool. Then he jumped.

And there was our son, poised on the river's edge, about to do likewise.

'No, Charlie!' I screamed.

But it was too late. He had obviously heard me, sensed the panic in my voice and decided to follow Marc, that bigger kid, his father. In he leapt without even so much as a sideways glance in

23

my direction. So I broke into a run, panicked, thinking I would jump in after them, save them somehow – haul them out, then kill them both. But then I stopped dead in my tracks, having caught sight of Charlie coming up level with me, hurtling like that log down the river. I could see his face – just his face – bobbing up and down in the water. And my heart froze in my throat when I saw the look in his eyes.

'Charlie!' I yelped like a wounded dog.

I jumped, fear like a vice clamped to my heart. I hadn't time to stop and look for Marc. And when I hit the water, I swam hard, driven, a mad woman swimming against the current, like Charlie's pink salmon.

The thing I remember most vividly is the sensation as I grabbed hold of him, his cold flesh against my hand, my nails scratching his flesh, pinching and gripping his shoulder, frantic. I had him. Down the river we hurtled together – together. But I had him.

We were travelling fast towards the bridge. It loomed over us, a giant metal spider spanning the river. And in its shadow I thought, this is where we should be getting out. But we missed our stop, and went right on. And on.

Dislocated images passed through my mind like tapestries, intricately detailed, unravelling. They say your whole life passes through your mind when you think you're about to die. But I was thinking about something else, about *someone else's* life, about Marc's childhood friend, Serge. They were from the same village, Ozouer le Voulgis, a tiny medieval town surrounded by forest with the River L'Yerres slicing through it. He was a fisherman – a big strong guy, *une force de la nature*, as Marc said. He'd gone down to the river one Sunday afternoon with his dog. It was the middle of a particularly cold winter so the water would have been no more than about five degrees, and the dog had fallen in. So Serge had lain across the old stone bridge, stretched his giant torso out over the water to try to get a hold of his dog, somehow grab it by the collar. But he leant out too far and fell in. He drowned, but the dog survived, having managed to struggle up on to the embankment just a few hundred metres down from the bridge. I wondered what went through the man's mind as he was swept away by the river – his wife, his four children, his regret, I wonder? And his wife, what must she have thought once the dog, stringy and wet, returned home? Who did she curse, the dog or her husband?

The river was pulling us over, forcing us to one side, tired of us at last. I felt soft earth under my feet. We were safe. I struggled, pulling Charlie with me. We were crawling, spluttering our way to the embankment.

The first thing I saw was his feet. Marc was standing at the edge of the embankment, hands on his hips, waiting. So he'd survived. Now I'd kill him.

'*Alors?* That was fun, *non?*' he said.

Still crouched in the water, still struggling against its pull, my knees pressing tender against sharp stones in the river's shallows,

I looked up at his face. I don't think I will ever forget it – that look in his eyes: wide and wild with excitement. That's when it hit me – I've married a madman.

'Marc.' My voice was low as I struggled to my feet, unsteady. 'Charlie nearly drowned.'

But I don't think he could hear me over his laughter. Yes, he was laughing – at me. 'But Annie, you are still in your clothes!'

I looked down at myself, my dress transparent, clinging to me, muddied and bedraggled.

'Well of course I'm still dressed!' I shouted, crying now. 'I had to jump in and save our son!'

Marc stopped laughing suddenly. Perhaps the weight of my words had hit him, finally – the gravity of what might have happened. But *no*.

'*De quoi tu parles,* Annie? You are being melodramatic.' He shrugged, dismissive, looking past me to Charlie. 'Wasn't that fun?'

Seething, I turned to our son, who was standing shakily, arms crossed over his heaving chest, lips purple, teeth chattering, his face a shade whiter than white.

'Yeah, Charlie, tell Papa just how much *fun* you had!'

For a moment he said nothing, looking from me to Marc, then down at the water. We waited, tense. It is a cruel thing to do to your child, to force him to choose, to make him take a side. But, in my mind, this was different – a clear case of Marc being a total moron. The wonderful thing about kids, though, is their unpredictability.

'It was cool.'

And that was all he said. Like I said, boys must be men.

It was only after I'd pulled myself up on to the embankment, having refused Marc's outstretched hand, that I noticed the blood, oozing rich and red around my foot, staining the grass. I must have cut it when I jumped in.

'*Mais*, what have you done, Annie?' asked Marc, alarmed suddenly as he bent over and grasped my ankle.

'*Oh là!*' he clucked. 'You really should be more careful. Better to keep your sandals on next time, *non*?'

Chapter
five

*B*y the winter, the hunting season was in full swing. We could hear them in the forest surrounding Lherm: the cries of the hunters, their dogs barking excited as they homed in on their prey, the rifle shots.

So how are we meant to go out walking without getting killed? I wondered.

Every Sunday evening the mayor's son, André, and his mates would pull up in the centre of town, the thrill of the chase making their ruddy cheeks ruddier, their bloodied, chafed hands clapping together, ready for a beer. They'd earned it – with a deer or, if they'd *really* been lucky, a wild boar, lying dead in the back of the four-wheel drive, alongside their pile of rifles. André was a great beast himself with a booming laugh that could wake the dead; a hairy, dark-haired giant with hands like swollen jelly blubbers, *so* big I wondered how he managed to fit his finger through the trigger. Charlie nicknamed him *le Géant*.

By the winter, our finances were just about drained dry. Yet there was still so much to do on the house. And we were in for a winter without central heating. Monsieur Martin shook his head and laughed his toothless laugh as he waved his finger at us. *'Attention hein, les australiens. Ca va geler!'* There was no way we could endure a winter without central heating, he warned, not if temperatures were to go down to minus fifteen as they had the year before. 'Minus fifteen?' I whispered. 'Is he serious, Marc?' Apparently he was.

So we bought a big old wood burner. Marc enlisted the Giant and his hunter mates to help him carry the thing up the front steps. As André lumbered through the house, the floorboards creaked and shuddered in protest. He could have carried the burner by himself, if pushed.

'Voilà!' cried Marc, once they'd finally eased the thing into the fireplace. 'That should keep us warm for the winter!'

The Giant's booming laugh made the windows rattle.

It was around that time I came to the painful realisation that my teaching career wasn't going to be a remake of *To Sir, With Love* after all. I was fighting a losing battle. My students were nice enough kids as far as teenagers went, but really all they wanted was to be out in their cars, puffing on a *'clope'* and talking on their mobiles. *'A quoi ça sert?'* What's the point, they'd whine whenever I'd try to strike up a conversation in English. So eventually, like them, I began to wonder, what *is* the point? There were only so many stories about Australia I could tell before they lost interest, before they needed their tobacco fix. Text messages on their mobiles were obviously *far* more captivating, so much so that at one stage I considered giving them English lessons over the phone, via text. The system had failed them a long time ago. And I was merely a bit of light entertainment on their way out the back door – more a Mary Poppins than your Sydney Poitier.

Even the drive in and back had become a bit of a nightmare. Of course, the countryside was still beautiful, but in a stark, mystic way – the trees with their twisted bare branches, black against the twilight sky. And Charlie would sit beside me, silenced by the darkness. I remember one evening, when the sun had already well and truly turned in for the night, we were headed up the road leading into Lherm.

'*Whoa!*' he cried out suddenly, startling me so my foot hit the brake, bringing the car to a screeching halt. '*Look!*'

It was there, *right there* before us, poised motionless, eyes staring blank back at us, dazzled by our headlights. I'd never seen a deer up close like that – kangaroos, yes, *lots* of kangaroos back home, but never a deer. It was a delicate thing – limbs poised like fine springs. And I thought of André and his mates, those crazy dumb bastards roaring through the village in their mud-splattered four-wheel drives, decked out in their military greens, horns blaring, trigger-happy macho morons.

I turned and looked at Charlie, watching silent, as still as the deer. He shot me a look back, eyes sparkling in the dark.

'I know how he feels.'

'*Who,* Charlie?'

He nodded at the deer. 'I know what he thinks about, when they chase after him…when they come looking for him.'

Why hadn't I seen it coming?

When I was a girl, Grandma told me, 'You can make anything happen, Annie, if you just wish hard enough.'

'You mean, like not having to go to school?'

'No…' She shook her head. 'You have to wish for something good, something *positive*.'

But, as a kid, I didn't really understand what she meant by this. Not having to go to school seemed like a pretty good thing to me. I was quite *positive* about that. So there *had* to be a way round it. 'But what'll happen if I wish and wish and *wish* that I didn't have to go to school?'

'Mmm…Let's see.' She paused, as if my question was indeed something to be considered with great seriousness. 'If you wish and wish…*and wish*, you say?'

'Yep,' I nodded, excited, jiggling my legs up and down as I sat next to her on the couch. I could always count on Grandma to find a solution.

She snapped the book shut on her lap, and I looked into her

face. She had a beautiful face. Her skin was like a fine translucent cloth. The delicate veins beneath the surface were like brush strokes, the tips of the brush dipped in blue. Light brush strokes on fine white cloth.

'Well...' Her blue eyes focused on mine over her reading glasses. 'I suppose it *could* happen too, if you wished hard enough.'

And I smiled, like a smug Cheshire cat. But she'd held up her hand then. 'Be careful, Annie MacIntyre,' came her warning as I jumped up and started dancing like a hula girl around the living room. 'You should always choose your wishes wisely. Otherwise you *might* find that what you wished for is something that you *never* should have wished for at all.'

I didn't get to ask her what she meant by that, because Mum then came into the room, dragging the vacuum cleaner behind her, clearly cross. We were obviously conspiring again.

'Why do you fill her head with all that *rubbish*?'

She couldn't possibly have heard what we had been talking about over the blast of the vacuum, but that was what Mum always said, whether she heard us or not.

It snowed during that first winter in Lherm. Our toothless soothsayer, Monsieur Martin, claimed it wouldn't: 'It hasn't snowed here in twenty years!' So Charlie and I *willed* it to happen. And it did – the heavy grey sky let forth just tiny light white droplets, so that we weren't sure at first. Then they came – big, wet flakes falling soft on our faces as we stood outside, Charlie's arms spread, mouth open, to greet them.

The next morning the roads were lined with a thick wall of snow in the drive down to the main road leading into Cahors. It reminded me of arriving on the ski slopes in Thredbo when I was a girl – that wonderful buzz, the thrill of all that whiteness, like icing on top of a Christmas cake, on top of our wedding cake.

That was until one morning, when Marc was scraping ice from the windscreen and he just happened to mention in passing, 'Watch out for *verglas*.'

I had already started the engine to get the demister going, warming up the car. 'What's *verglas*?'

'*Glace*.'

At first I imagined ice-cream, until I realised.

'You mean ice on the road?' My breathing had quickened suddenly. '*Black* ice?'

He nodded. '*Oui*.'

'Cool!' said Charlie.

'Don't look so *scared*, Annie.' Marc had reached my side window by this time with his scraper – the screech of its blade on the glass making my skin creep. 'You just drive slowly, *très lentement*, especially round the bends, and whatever you do, *don't brake*.'

I wondered if he was joking. That seemed like a lot of things to remember for something I shouldn't worry about. Don't brake. So how do I stop? I wondered.

'What happens if I brake?'

But I shouldn't have asked. '*Tu vas déraper*. You'll slide.'

'Whoa!' Charlie had buckled up his belt, ready for action.

So I instantly pictured it – my foot on the brake, Charlie and me disappearing over the side of the road where it drops away, hurtling downwards through the trees, sliding on and on, coming to rest at last against a massive snow-covered rock.

I got into work very late that morning, maximum speed just twenty kilometres per hour. As for my co-pilot, he thought it was great fun, the best and scariest ride he'd ever been on, even better than that one at the Easter Show, watching out for black ice all the way.

But when I think on it now, that was the thing – we had already begun our slippery descent a long time before. And I hadn't even seen it coming.

That insidious black ice.

Chapter
six

The hardest part is piecing it together. I can remember it all – the details in my head like reams and reams of pages filled with words. But it's as if a sudden breeze has scattered them, so I can't tell you now which bit comes when. Marc reckons *that's* the easy part. It's the *why* of it all that escapes him. Now that's funny, because that's the part I *do* get.

If I can just piece it all back together, maybe he'll see it too.

According to Marc, it was after, just after they spoke to Charlie, those two sad and sorry police officers, that we were alone again. It didn't dawn on me straight away. That's the scary part. It was only when I said something to Marc, something like 'I could do with another drink' and turned to recover my glass, wondering where I'd left it – perhaps on the coffee table, or on the mantel over the fireplace – that it hit me.

We weren't in the living room any more. No, we weren't any-where remotely related to that room, nor any other part of the house, for that matter. And when I looked over at Marc, I noticed he was saying something to me, only at first I couldn't hear him. And then I could.

'What?' he was shouting, and I wondered why. 'What did you say, Annie?'

That's when I realised he hadn't heard me over the din. Yes, I remember the din. It was like a cloud, just a distant rumble at first, muffled voices and laughter, a tinkle of glasses rolling in, ominous, from some place far off.

Then suddenly it was upon us.

The air smelt of stale beer and cigarette smoke, thick and warm with sweat. We were standing together, jostled up against each other by a crowd, a bunch of raucous merrymakers. Only they weren't making *me* merry. I reached for Marc, my hand gripping his arm, my voice a whisper, inaudible over the noise, this incredible noise.

'Oh my God, Marc...Where *are* we?'

His eyes met mine and I saw it then – the panic. He obviously didn't know either. It had all happened so fast – a rush, a wave crashing over us. And as I turned to try to get my bearings, some guy with cropped red hair and a flattened nose bumped heavily against me, knocking his schooner glass against my shoulder, splashing frothy black beer, cold across my chest.

'Sorry, love.' But he was smiling, *leering* like he wasn't sorry at all, his red eyes resting bleary on my chest. 'Can I wipe that off for you – give it a bit of a rub, maybe?'

Who were these people?

But when I turned back to Marc, I was struck by something stranger still. His face, his face so familiar, now had something different about it, something *very* different, only I couldn't work out *what* exactly. I reached my hand up to his cheek.

'Marc?'

He was staring back at me, silent. That's when I noticed his eyes. My fingers moved up, tracing that soft part underneath his lower lashes. There was something not quite right *at all*. And then I realised what it was. The crinkles, those funny criss-crosses at the edges of his eyes, had disappeared! And his eyelids seemed tighter, as if the skin had been pulled back, as if...

'I don't understand —' My hands cupped his face, my fingertips pressing into his cheekbones, moving in a flurry now, softly pressing, feeling under his jaw – that soft part under his chin... his jawline was firmer. And all the while he just kept staring back at me, his mouth open, dumb-struck as my hands held his face.

'Marc, what's happened? Talk to me!'

'*Annie!*'

But his voice was just a croak as his hands gripped my elbows, leaning his weight into me as if to steady himself. My eyes moved over him, from his face down over his body. It wasn't only his face. He was bigger all over, squarer in the shoulders, meatier somehow. He had changed, though I laugh when I say this, as in fact it wasn't that he'd *changed* but that he *hadn't* changed at all.

It was Marc as he was when I first met him, some fifteen years back.

We met in Paris, in an Irish pub of all places. I saw *him* first, across a crowd, standing over by the bar. He was with a mate, sipping a Guinness, this dark-haired man with eyes as clear as an April sky – Easter in Australia – that blue so crisp it makes your skin buzz. He was obviously a Frenchman judging by the way he was taking his time over his beer, his lips pressed together, unaccustomed to its bitter black strength. And I remember thinking *Nice* as I looked over at him, checking him out – his square-set solid chunkiness, the way he moved, the way he held his beer, his fingers on the glass, an unselfconscious confidence in his movements – shame about the clothes, though. I don't think he noticed me until he was well into his third schooner, *well* on his way.

'*Pas vrai*,' he says. 'Not true at all. I noticed you the moment you walked through the door.'

But *I* was there before him.

He was wearing an old denim jacket, obviously his favourite. I could tell, even from across the room, the fraying, faded blue cotton was on its last legs – he was not exactly dressed to impress. To be fair on him though, later he would tell me that he'd never intended to pick up anyone that night, that he hadn't wanted to go out at all; Yves, his mate, talked him into it.

'It's *the* place to pick up Irish girls with red hair and cute accents,' Yves had insisted. So I guess Marc lucked out in a way. At least that's what I thought until... But I will come to that.

I was there with Beattie, who actually *was* a red-headed Irish girl. Beattie and I went back a long way. We met in the early days, when I first came to Paris. I had arrived in the middle of a snow-storm, having thrown caution to the wind and left Australia, left my mother. I was seeking adventure – that silly, self-indulgent thing she had warned me against as a girl, but which a young woman of three and twenty is wont to yearn for.

My mother had raised me to believe that life is a battle, so you had best arm yourself against it. But despite my mother I had remained an incurable romantic, a girl who still believed in fairytales and Mr Right. My grandmother reckoned it was inevitable – in my blood. She was a romantic too, having married four times. And my mother *had* been – until my father died.

And so, barely off the plane at Roissy Charles de Gaulle airport, I was crossing the Quai D'Orsay, slipping and sliding, knee-deep in snow with only a trench coat and frivolously thin-soled shoes to weather the storm and an ice-cold wind whistling over the Seine and through my hair. I was headed for the American Church, where all the English-speaking backpackers gather to find work and a place to stay.

I found Colangue's ad high up on the pin-board, in the top right-hand corner, the soles of my feet slipping out of my squelching-wet shoes as I strained to get a better look. They were looking for an English teacher.

Beattie had already been teaching there for a year. So I landed a job and a friend all in the one day. She taught me about thermal inner-soles. And, within the month, we had become flatmates.

Two years on, one Saturday night, we'd come out, hoping to pick up someone who'd at least shout us a second round. Having just paid the rent on our apartment for the month, we were broke again. Teaching in Paris holds few financial rewards. But back then we were young, both of us single and still in love with the idea of living in Paris, so it didn't really matter.

That is how we met, Marc and I. *He* paid for that second round.

So it was a shock, to say the least, *déjà vu* in its purest sense, to see Marc as he once was again, those blue eyes, *Charlie's* eyes, staring back at me, his hair still thick and so black – the silver threads all gone.

But I'd barely the chance to say anything before I felt a sharp jab to my left side – an elbow in my rib cage. I turned and there she was, this young woman, this *other* familiar face, with her wavy mass of red hair, a ball of fire enveloping that finely chiselled face like an Elizabethan queen, her sharp green eyes level with mine.

'Have you *completely* lost it, Annie MacIntyre?'

It was Beattie – only younger. So I knew then, we were back, back at Kitty O'Shea's, that funny little Irish place in a back street behind the Opéra.

I turned to Marc, searching his face, desperate for him to come up with some logical explanation, to make sense of it all – a trick of the light maybe, or a bad joke, like the ones he used to play. But I could see it in his eyes. This was no joke.

Charlie would call it *virtual reality*. Yes, it was in a way. For we were still together, having a drink, but we'd moved from our living room into a different place, a different time – like watching an old home video, watching us as we were. But we were right in the thick of it, back *here*, in 3-D. And we couldn't turn it off. We were both lost for words, our senses dulled by the shock. But not Beattie.

'I mean, I leave you alone for a minute —'

Her attention had shifted, her eyes fixing on Marc. He'd been staring at her – in a daze. So her eyes met his, then moved downwards. She was giving him the once-over, taking in his jacket, his jeans – pausing on his shoes.

'*Love* the boots!'

She always did have a wicked sense of humour. There they were, his old cowboy boots, tanned leather, the real McCoy, long and pointy with heels, the kind Neil Diamond used to wear – the kind *only* Neil Diamond should wear – but that Marc used to wear all the time back then. I had forgotten about his taste in clothes, if it can be called that. And it worries me that *even* now he doesn't think it was *that* bad.

'*Beattie* liked my boots,' he says.

It must have been the sight of them, those old boots that later Charlie used to strut around in when he was four with his plastic pistol and cowboy hat and that I'd finally managed to get rid of, *finally* when Charlie had long grown out of them, even though his father hadn't... Yes, it was the sight of those ridiculous old boots that triggered the first real wave of panic.

I needed air. My hand reached over for Marc and clutched his jacket sleeve, my voice barely a whisper as I mouthed the words, 'We have to get out of here!'

Meanwhile, Beattie was looking on, eyes wide, speechless – but only for a moment.

'Hold on, Annie. Who is this cowboy?' Her hand was on my wrist. 'You're not leaving with him, surely?'

But it was too late for that, wasn't it? I already had.

Chapter
seven

$\mathcal{W}$e were walking the back streets, in the cold, grey light of Paris, the familiar dank smell rising from the pavement making me shiver as we tried to retrace the path we'd taken that first night when Marc had offered to drive me home. But we weren't sure of it now, turning in circles, round and round along the dimly lit pavements in the shadow of the old stone buildings, past hotels, bars and cafés – noisy, Saturday-night revellers jostling past us. We were back where we had been twenty minutes earlier, walking past the same old theatre *again* with its elaborate nineteenth-century stone façade, in rue Daunou – a narrow little street around the corner from Kitty's. It's not easy trying to find where you parked the car fifteen years back.

Perhaps it was the cold of the night air, a crisp March night, brutal in its impact on our senses, cruelly sobering – like waking in Recovery after an operation, with the groggy gas-induced numbness wearing off way too fast. We had woken, only we were still in this murky timelessness, still in Paris.

And where, oh where, was Charlie? His face was there in my head, that look in his eyes, his body trembling, making me tremble now.

Marc was up ahead, his pace increasing. I was trying to keep up with him, but my shoes were too tight and too high, my skin rubbed raw by the straps around the back of my ankles. And there was something in his stride – a young man's energy. Or was it panic pushing him forward in a frenzy? Yet we weren't getting anywhere, and I was *so* cold, my arms crossed tight across my chest.

'Marc?'

He didn't turn around.

'Marc, *please! Stop!*'

He turned then, stopping dead in the middle of the pavement, and threw his hands up. *'Je n'sais pas!* I don't know the way.'

I wondered what he meant – the way back to his car, or back home to Charlie? 'Where *is* he, Marc?'

He was staring back at me, shaking his head. *'Je ne sais pas, Annie!* I don't understand any of this!'

My teeth were chattering now, out of control. It was all too much – hot tears pricked my cheeks as I stared down at the pavement.

'Allez…Come on, Annie.'

It was only a whisper, but I could hear it in his voice too – the fear. I didn't want to look at him, to see it in his eyes. So I focused on the pavement. 'I need to go to the toilet.'

Déjà Vu

He stepped towards me. 'Ah... *D'accord.*' This was obviously something he could deal with. 'There's a café across the road. *Viens.*'

By the second cognac I had begun to feel it, the fiery magic as the warm amber liquid worked its way through my system – a cloud forming around my brain, numbing my senses. By the third, I had stopped shivering. The cool giant glass ballon resting in the palm of my hand, as I swilled the last drops round and round, was comforting.

In the eye of the storm.

We sat opposite each other in the corner by the window of the dimly lit café, like lonely stragglers waiting at a train station in the middle of the night, without a train to catch – staring out at the street in silence, trying to take it in. We were alone, save for an old guy hunched over the bar, lost in drunken reverie, and the waitress in her crisp white apron and high-heels standing in the doorway smoking a cigarette, waiting for us to leave.

But where were we supposed to go?

I'd caught a glimpse of myself in the grimy, cracked mirror over the washbasin, out the back of the café. She took me by surprise, this young woman, in the brutal honesty of the harsh fluorescent light, with her long hair falling sleek and dark, and her brown eyes shining back at me. And I remembered the deer that had crossed our path on the road leading into Lherm – eyes wide and innocent, caught in the glare of the high beams. I moved in closer, staring at my face, white skin like alabaster glowing smooth. And there they were – the freckles, a cluster splashed across my nose, those tiny golden-brown dots that had faded away in my thirties. I had forgotten... his first words to me before offering that second round, before I'd even said *Bonjour*: '*J'adore tes tâches de rousseur.*'

'My freckles?' I'd laughed. I hadn't the heart to tell him then: they were a dime a dozen back in Australia.

I reached up, my fingers running through my hair, searching for the narrow strip to the left of my forehead where it had only recently turned to grey – Zorro's silver slash, as Charlie called it. It had disappeared. The girl in the mirror looked *so young*, this girl from my past in her funny clothes... the black velvet waist-jacket with its fake diamond buttons that I'd bought one Sunday at the flea market in Porte de Bagnolet. And I realised then, everything was as it was, *exactly* as it was. Why, even the jeans I was wearing – faded blue 501s, the *only* jeans to wear in Paris, as Beattie and I used to say. Right down to the shoes, these *things* clamped to my feet that were causing me so much pain now: black stilettos, perilously high and pointy, the kind my mother would never have approved of. I had bought these with Beattie only that day. *Today!* We had gone shopping together, in Galeries Lafayette.

'There they are!' she'd cried as we stepped off the escalator. 'They'll go with your princess jacket!'

But it was only as I was reaching down to adjust the straps at my ankle, leaning back with one hand over my stomach, that I noticed something else: the round tummy that had never *completely* gone away after Charlie's birth was now perfectly flat – as hard as a washboard. And I wasn't even breathing in.

Marc was obviously feeling it too, this temporary calm. Unlike me, though, he had slugged his cognac back like there was no tomorrow. Maybe there wasn't. I was aware of his eyes, glassily focused on my face. '*Tu es si belle.*'

I shook my head. No, I didn't want to hear this right now. Besides, I wasn't sure I liked the implications. I reached across the table, my hand gripping his.

'I need you to tell me about the policeman – what he *said*, Marc, what he said to Charlie.'

But he turned from me, staring back out at the street, making my heart start up fast again, struggling against the cognac.

'It was about us, wasn't it, Marc?'

He shook his head and started to chuckle, low and soft – that out-of-control laugh he gets when he's had a little too much to drink. The waitress was glaring at us as she made her way back to the bar. I could feel Marc's knee jiggling up and down under the table as he signalled to her. '*Un express, s'il vous plaît.*'

He was stalling. 'Marc?'

And he wouldn't look at me. '*Il a dit que nous étions…*'

'They said that we were *what?*' Why wouldn't he look at me? But then he did – straight in the eye.

'*Que nous étions morts.*'

I heard the glass shatter, but didn't realise what I'd done, not until the waitress was upon us, cursing out loud as she gathered up the broken bits and cradled them in her apron, her cleavage hovering over us.

'*Dead?* They said that we were *dead!*'

My raised voice had attracted the attention of the old guy as well, his hand coming down heavily on the bar. '*Hé ho!*' We had obviously woken him with a start. '*Du calme!*'

My hand gripped Marc's, so tight he winced. Tears blurred my vision. Yet the terror on Charlie's face, his body shaking under the policeman's hand, was clear in my mind. 'But *why* would he say that, Marc? Why would he say such a thing to Charlie?'

'*Tu ne te rappelles pas,* Annie?'

'Remember? Remember *what?*'

Whenever Charlie used to lose the one piece of Lego, the tiniest of pieces that he *absolutely had* to have right then and there, within that *very* second, because if he didn't it would mean the end of the world, I used to say, 'You have to think backwards. You have to go back over where you were last, and then keep going back until you find it.'

'Like walking backwards?'

'Yeah, I suppose – a bit like Michael Jackson moonwalking!'

'But what if I'm on a cliff? What if I'm walking backwards and —'

That's how it felt now – as if we were on a cliff. There was a great gaping hole behind us, and one big blank in my mind.

I remembered this – we'd gone to Toulouse for the day, to get away, to clear the air...

We'd sat down by the Pont Neuf, looking out on to the Garonne, a cool wind blowing in off the water, brushing the hair off my face, stirring the leaves at our feet. And for the first time in a long time, we'd talked calmly about what we should do. And I'd realised that, what with work and Charlie and all the house crap, we hadn't stopped to talk – until then. That's the irony: we'd come to a decision finally, without threats, screams or even tears – those raging blowouts where I'd tell him I couldn't take the dour deadness of village life any more, and he'd say there was *no way* he was going back to *Métro, Boulot, Dodo*, the 'stinking race of the rat city'. He never could say it right.

Yet this time, it was different. It was settled – Charlie and I were leaving. And Marc had offered no resistance. 'We're just testing the waters... *un essai, c'est tout,*' he said.

The real irony is that at that moment, as Marc smiled at me, anxious, his blue eyes crinkling at the edges, I thought to myself, he's a nice bloke, a really nice bloke. But his hand didn't reach over to mine, nor mine to his, as we sat on the bench looking out at the river – neither of us willing to bridge the distance between us.

So I turned away then, looking up at the old stone bridge hovering over us, my gaze resting on a couple, just a boy and girl, students perhaps from the local university, standing together in the centre of the Pont Neuf. They were leaning over, looking down at the river, their hands trailing over the wall like kids, the sky a Van Gogh painting, a swirling purple mass of clouds behind them – the storm brewing. Her hair, long, dark billowing silk, was blowing over his face. The little mermaid and her prince, I thought. They were laughing, kissing, her dress flying up, licked by the wind as her body pressed against his so that from where I watched, their silhouette was just one, their bodies indistinguishable. And I thought, no, it's more than that. We both knew it was much more than merely testing the waters this time. I was going to find a job in Paris, settle Charlie into a new school up there, and leave Marc to finish the house in Lherm. We'd be some six hundred kilometres apart.

We were going to separate.

Déjà Vu

I found an old photo of my father once when I was a girl, while vacuuming under Mum's bed. I'd pushed the big old base away from the wall to get right under, just as she'd told me to do. 'No point in doing a job,' she'd say, 'if you don't do it properly.'

It was hidden, wedged in behind the wooden skirting board at the base of the wall, a yellow corner, once white, peeping out. At first I'd tried to get at it with the nozzle head, thinking it was just a loose bit of paper that had floated there. But then, when it didn't budge, I flicked off the cleaner, knelt down and pulled at it. And out it slid.

I'd never seen my father. She'd kept nothing. Once, when I'd asked her why, she became agitated. 'Because the house burnt down!' she screamed, so I didn't ask her again. But I knew right away it was him.

It was a close-up of his face and upper torso. He was bare-chested, lying on his back, obviously somewhere out in the open. I like to think it was by a river under a tree, taken as they picnicked there together. But I really have no idea. He was smiling at the camera, a lover's smile for a lover's photo. His arm was flung behind him, supporting the back of his head. He was very, *very* handsome – dark eyes and hair, thick and black as a raven's. It was his smile that I recognised, *my* smile. And he had a dimple in his left cheek, only the one, like mine. So I knew.

I kept the photo. I know I shouldn't have. But it was my way of getting back at her. She never asked for it. How could she? She'd kept nothing, she said.

The waitress rapped the metal coffee doser hard against the side of the bar. The old man stirred. I glanced over at Marc, aware he'd been watching me.

'But we're not *dead*, are we, Marc?'

His grin was like that first lightning flash at the end of a stifling hot day – the first promise of rain breaking through the heat, through the tension. I had forgotten how much I loved that grin. I realised things were all too crazy, all too impossible, to get worked up about. We just had to stay calm and let it ride over us. It would all be over soon, *surely*.

'If you ever get caught in a rip, Charlie, whatever you do, don't fight it. Stay calm and swim across it, not against it.'

We just had to wait it out. I glanced around the café, looking up at the imitation Rococo walls, and remembered then. 'This is it!'

Marc raised his eyebrows, confused.

'This is the *same* place.'

He followed my gaze, unsure. '*Peut-être*...I don't know, Annie.'

'I'm telling you, this is where we came after Kitty O'Shea's that night. Don't you remember?'

'*Non.*' He nodded in the direction of the waitress heading towards us with his coffee, her breasts swaying like swollen pendulums. '*She* wasn't here. I'd have remembered her. *Ca c'est sûr!*'

That grin. 'You always were a creep, Marc. *Seriously*, I think we even sat at this table.'

'Well, I *do* remember the coffee was crap.' He took a sip, then gagged in that exaggerated French way of his. '*Et oui*, it's *still* crap. Just like pees.'

'You mean *piss*, Marc.'

'Oh *sheeet*, Annie. Yes, pees, if you like.'

And to think when I'd met this man, when he'd walked up to me in the bar, he could barely manage more than a heavily accented hello. Now here he was, sitting opposite me in this *same* café, swearing like a trooper, albeit a trooper with an unmistakably French accent.

'You exaggerate about my accent,' he says.

I don't think so. Again, as Charlie would say, 'He's in denial, Mum.' I studied his face – that funny thing he did with his mouth, the same downward movement, so Gallic, but less ingrained some-how, not yet set in stone. I'd never seen the likeness with Charlie as clearly as now. And then I remembered.

'Take a look in your wallet.'

He looked back at me, one eyebrow raised, puzzled as he reached into his trouser pocket. Obviously he'd forgotten.

'*C'est fou, tu sais!*' He was shaking his head, contemplating the tattered old brown leather thing he used to carry around. 'What-ever happened to this?'

'Dunno,' I lied. It had actually gone out with his boots and matching denim jacket, secreted into a Salvos bin somewhere down at Bondi one day while he wasn't looking. Besides, that wasn't what I was getting at. 'Look inside, Marc.' I had to change the subject, quickly. 'How much money do you have on you?'

'Nothing.' He was riffling through it, nervous suddenly. '*Merde*, I hope *you've* got some cash on you!'

'Well, *yes*, Marc.' I smiled at him. 'That's just my point. Don't you remember how you'd invited me for a coffee, and then you discovered you didn't have any money on you?'

'*Oui, mais* I didn't do that on purpose, Annie.' It could have been Charlie talking. 'Anyway, why bring that up now, at a time like this?'

I reached over, grabbed his hand and looked directly into his eyes. 'Because, Marc, don't you see? Everything is as it was – exactly as it was! *Tu vois?*'

He shook his head. '*Non*, Annie, I *don't* see. I don't see this at all.'

We both sat silent for a moment, forlorn, looking out on to the street, that same street. And then I saw it – his rusty little white van, just across the road, parked where he'd parked it all those years ago. We'd been standing right next to it before crossing over to this café, frantically searching. Looking without seeing.

I pushed my chair back and dropped three ten franc coins on to the table. 'Come on. Let's go back to your place.'

'*Oui.*' He was distracted as he fingered one of the coins. 'Still francs. Not euros.'

True. And I'd only *just* got used to the changeover to those new funny little brown coins, the one and two centimes, that first made me realise as I headed towards my forties, I needed reading glasses.

Chapter
eight

'*Le problème,*' Marc began slowly as he negotiated the traffic, up towards the Champs Elysées, heading north towards his old apartment, 'if we go back to *my* place, then it *will* be different.'

I considered his profile, this perfect, regular profile like a paper cut-out – the strong, straight line of his nose, the firm line of his jaw, stirring something in me that I had forgotten about. Such strength in his features, yet *so* young again, this man that I had loved.

The massive arch at the top of Champs d'Elysée loomed over us as Marc edged the van into the tangled mess of cars swarming like wasps in the roundabout at its base. True, that first time we met he had dropped me back home to my apartment in Porte de Bagnolet, in the 20th arrondissement, east of Paris. We hadn't ever gone back to his place, not in the beginning anyway. Well, we could hardly go back to mine *now* – not with Beattie there, no doubt ready to fire off a barrage of questions, an Irish inquisition that I just wasn't up for.

That *first* time, I had watched his hands on the wheel as he cut a path through the traffic like a true Parisian, past Place de la

République, the great bronze lady towering over us with her olive branch extended to the heavens; on and through Place de la Bastille with its golden *génie*, this glorious spirit of liberty flying high and proud atop his tarnished green brass column; past the swanky new glass Opéra as we rounded the square.

On and on, taking me home.

I had fallen in love with his hands then and there – those beautiful square fingers, their touch on my knee as I sat with him in the car outside my place, making the blood shoot up my inner thigh. The *thrill* of his touch – his lips close to my ear, in my hair, as I reached for the door handle.

'*Ne pars pas*, Annie. Let me come in – we can just talk.'

But I knew if he did, I couldn't *just* talk.

The warmth of the van and the familiar purr of its motor, like a fat asthmatic cat, had lulled me into a semiconscious oblivion. For now, I didn't want to have to think. I wanted Marc to work out the rest. If I could just go to bed, then everything would be fine. I was convinced of it – come morning, there we'd be, back home with Charlie. There was no point in fighting it.

'So, what are you suggesting we do, *Marc?*'

It must have been the way the tone of my voice rose, wavering on his name, the cognac beginning to wear off, because he shot me a look – something resembling concern. Or at least, that's how I read it at the time.

It's interesting how, even after fifteen years together, we can still misread each other – a passing comment, a look.

He reached a hand over to my knee.

'*D'accord.*' He was obviously trying to sound positive. 'Let's just see what happens. *On verra.*'

We'll see. I looked out the window, too tired to argue. But it did occur to me then, well that's what we'd always done – just played it by ear.

And look where it had got us.

We stood together, awkward, like two strangers, trespassers in his living room. It was as it had always been – a colourful, frantic mayhem filled with bric-à-brac he'd found lying abandoned on street corners here and there around Paris, odd bits and pieces that he'd dragged into the back of his van, then fixed or converted. I knew all their stories – the worn, brown leather club armchair that he'd patched with bits of leather and ruby-red velvet, its springs still poking through the base. Against the wall, over by the record player, was the wooden filing cabinet that he'd found in a back street behind the Boulevard Haussman. La Banque de Paris was renovating, throwing out the well-worn oak to bring in the new, pristine hard-edged steel – the modern look. And over in the corner by the window was his antique Singer sewing machine with its black iron base and foot pedal that had always worked perfectly well. He'd bought it for twenty francs from an old lady who had once worked for Coco Chanel in rue Cambon, in her *atelier* in Paris.

I'd definitely had a Zen influence on him since. And I remembered the first time I'd come here. He'd poured us some wine and put on a record, Herbie Hancock's *Takin' Off*, I recall, which I'd thought was rather poignant. Up until then, we'd always gone back to *my* place. So it had been new, even though we'd already been seeing each other for some time – for well on a year.

'Dance for me,' I'd said that first time as he stood opposite, his fingers rapping the rhythm out against his thigh, his eyes looking into mine.

'*Non!*'

'Dance for me, or I won't go to bed with you.'

His grin '*Et donc*, if I dance for you, what will *you* do for me?'

So here we were again. Except all I wanted *this* time was to go to bed – to sleep. To wake up back home, with Charlie.

'Oh Marc, this is *so* —'

But there were no words to describe it, not *now*, with my body aching and my brain a blank. Fatigue had set in with a vengeance – the worst case of jet lag, like the time we travelled from Australia to France with Charlie as a baby, when the plane was held up in Singapore for six hours on the tarmac, and he'd howled *all* the way, from Sydney to Paris.

Marc nodded, silent as he stood at the entrance to the living room, his eyes scanning, taking it all in. I kicked off my stilettos, letting them fall, letting them clunk heavily on to the floorboards – just like we used to tell Charlie never to do with his runners – and slipped an arm out of my jacket as I made my way towards the bedroom. Even after all these years, I knew the way well.

'*Attends*, Annie. What are you doing?'

He was whispering, and I wondered why. I turned back to him. He hadn't moved.

'I'm going to bed, Marc. Don't you want —'

'*Non.*' He seemed very edgy. And he was whispering still. 'I don't think we should be here. I think we should go. *Viens!*'

He was holding his hand out for me to come, flicking his keys over in the other, impatient.

'*Marc*, are you serious?' I could feel the tears rising again. '*Where* are we meant to go? We *have* to stay here!'

He was gesturing for me to calm down, actually 'shooshing' me, which of course only made it worse, because in French they say 'sshht'. It's that 't' at the end that always gets on my nerves.

And that's when *she* appeared – out of nowhere, it seemed.

She was standing in the living-room doorway behind me, naked except for a T-shirt, staring at us. Now, I'd have preferred to describe what she was wearing (or more accurately, what she *wasn't* wearing) as baggy and long, unflattering if you like. But it wasn't, unfortunately.

'Marc?'

She spoke softly, so softly I thought for a moment perhaps I had misheard her, that she'd somehow got the wrong place, stumbled into this apartment through a window maybe, even though we were up on the fourth floor. After all, how would she have known my husband's name?

'Marc?' But this time there was no mistaking it. *'Qui c'est, Marc?'*

The thing I hate most about French women is that, generally speaking, they are petite. So when they speak in that soft, babbling-brook way of theirs, they are like small twittering birds. But – and this is the really annoying part – they are twittering birds with curves nonetheless. Despite the match-stick wrists and ankles *and* size thirty-six-and-a-half high-heeled shoes, they still have breasts, bums and hips – which, when I think on it, must be where the term 'sexy bird' comes from. And, in this case, the blonde curly locks did nothing to contradict this irritating Frenchwoman thing.

I had no idea who she was, never having laid eyes on her before, not back then, not ever.

Marc had though.

He says I should tell it straight. Well, this is the only way I can tell it – how *I* saw it. He can tell it any way he likes, until he's blue in the face even, but it won't change the fact that *he* was the one who should have told it straight in the first place, all those years ago.

She was Frédérique, of course, his *supposed* ex, except that she was less 'ex' than he'd always led me to believe.

Actually, I *had* seen her before. I found a photo not long after I first moved in with him, hidden in an old trunk at the end of his bed, right at the bottom in an envelope, underneath a pile of folded sheets. At this point I *could say* that I'd wanted to change the sheets and just happened to come upon it, but I won't bother.

She was lying on a blanket under a tree, eyes closed, *supposedly* asleep. But judging by the sensuality of her pose, I had the feeling she was wide awake. She was stretched out on her side, as if she'd landed there weightless in mid-flight, one leg bent languorously over the other, accentuating the curve of her bum, a perfect bum (not even the hint of a dimple), her feet pointed as 'naturally' as a ballerina's, arms outstretched like the lead in *Swan Lake* – choreographed to a tee. Her skirt had flown up, perhaps with the breeze, or his hand? Either way, it was up.

The girl really didn't go in for underwear.

Chapter
nine

I remember one evening, out on our first real date, meeting Marc after work, at the entrance to métro Saint Germain des Prés. I was late. He was waiting for me, squinting in the rain, on the corner – that magical corner with the Eglise Saint Germain des Prés, where Sartre and de Beauvoir also once stood, on those same pavement stones. I had reached out to him, squeezed his arm – his wet jacket sleeve – and run my hand down to his. My lips touched his cheek, savouring his moist skin, the taste of rain on his lips and on mine as he kissed me back under my umbrella. The thrill of his warm palm, sliding wet in mine...

We'd sat in the corner of the café in Les Deux Magots across the road, eyes shining under the sepia light, sharing Tarte Tatin and *une coupe de Champagne,* watching gold bubbles rise in our glasses as the rain fell outside, tiny drops kissing the window panes. My fingertips traced his lips, still moist. I wanted to kiss him again, to taste the salt on his skin, to breathe in his smell. And I had looked into his face, into his beautiful blue eyes, and seen my own face in their black centres, my soul reflected in his, shining back at me.

Fresh cream slid over apples, warm plump slices piled over fresh pastry. 'Better than sex,' I'd said as I slipped a spoonful into my mouth. 'Ah,' he'd murmured, running his hand along my thigh with a grin. '*On verra ça.*' We'll see.

So we'd taken the métro together, back to my place – *just to see*. And later that night, he'd told me about *her* – about Frédérique. I was lying on top of him, my arms crossed over his chest. His hands held my hair back, his fingers threaded through my hair, sliding through, pressing into my scalp, rubbing – my scalp tingling, putty in his hands. I wanted him to keep going, to never, *ever* stop.

'Do you have a girlfriend?'

He smiled as he pulled on my hair. 'You are very curious.'

I giggled. 'Well, it's not like we're two strangers sitting on a bus here!'

His eyes, staring straight into mine – not a flinch, not a sideways glance. '*J'en avais une. Mais c'est fini maintenant.*'

I did, but it's over now. Those were his words. *It's over now.* Funny, because I'd have thought it was a given, then – that she'd be gone.

'But it *was* over, Annie. We weren't together any more, *pas comme ça*, not like boyfriend and girlfriend,' Marc likes to claim.

So why was she was standing in his living room in a skin-tight midriff and nothing else?

Déjà Vu

I didn't learn the truth about my father until I was nineteen. By then, Mum and I had long stopped talking. We had crashed and banged into each other all through my teenage years, colliding and reeling like bumper cars at the fair, until finally one day when I was eighteen and through my HSC, we stopped talking altogether. Her 'grin and bear it' outlook on life had become a yoke around my neck. So I came home from my ancient history exam, my last, packed a bag and left – for good.

And as I zipped up my travel bag and slammed the door shut behind me, I had the feeling she was quite relieved to see the back of me.

It was my grandmother who told me, 'Your mother wasn't always this way, Annie.'

The beautiful man in the photo and my mother had an argument one evening. She had spent the morning in the city, shopping. It was lunchtime on one of those sweltering hot days, so she had stopped off for a vanilla ice-cream from a Mr Whippy van, parked on the corner of Pitt and Market streets. As she stood in the middle of the bustling city she was feeling happy, light-headed – in love. She was young, just twenty-one, and only recently wed.

So when she spied him through the crowd, sitting by the window in the coffee shop across the street, she had smiled. She hadn't expected to see him there at all. It was a nice surprise. All morning, she had been thinking about him.

It was only as she started across the street, waving her ice-cream at him, that she noticed the young woman sitting opposite him, her knees pressed into his.

So that evening, when he came home from work, she told him to leave – just to pack up his stuff and get out. My father had pleaded with her over and over, 'It's not what you think!' But my mother wouldn't listen. She didn't want to hear his excuses.

And so he had left, without even packing his bag. He'll be back, she'd thought. *He'll be back to say he's sorry*. But he never came back.

When the police came to tell her about the crash, my mother collapsed in the doorway. They were worried she'd lose the baby. She didn't, of course. I was born three months later.

Though she did lose something else.

According to Grandma, she blamed herself for his death. If she hadn't screamed at him, hadn't told him to go, he wouldn't have driven off in a blind rage like he did. And he wouldn't have driven straight through the red light.

And so my mother's guilt turned this beautiful man in the photo into a hero.

'But he was cheating on her, Grandma!'

My Grandmother just smiled and nodded. 'You'll understand one day, Annie dear.'

My feet barely touched the ground as I flew down the stairs. As I hit the first-floor landing, pausing to slip my arms back into my jacket and to pull on those stiff, unyielding stilettos, I heard his voice – an echo down the stairwell.

'Annie, *attends! Waaait!*'

But that was just the thing. I *had* waited. I'd waited and waited some fifteen years to discover this! I looked up through the polished-wood banisters at his face perched over the handrail. The young man that I had loved was hovering above me now, on the top floor of this old building. In the space of this crazy day, the whole world had turned upside down. A door creaked open somewhere on a floor between us. We were creating a scene.

'*S'il te plaît*, Annie! It's not what you think!'

My heart froze. I had heard those words – Grandma's story about my father...*His* words!

I reached for the handrail to head for the ground floor, to escape this madness, this world that no longer made any sense. But my knees gave way underneath me. And I heard a woman crying, 'No! I don't want to hear your excuses!' – a low baleful wail, eerily familiar.

Another door creaked open on the landing behind me as I sank down on to the top step. An old man was hissing at me, '*Hé ho là! Shhttt!*'

Then I realised, this ghastly cry, this pained howl, was *mine*.

Marc was calling to me still. 'Annie, *attends!* I'm coming.'

I looked up. But his face had disappeared from the stairwell. And then I heard *her*.

'Marc, qu'est-ce qui se passe? C'est qui, cette femme?' Who is that woman?

I could hear it in her tone. The robin's twitter was now a magpie's caw, raised and menacing. This was no *ex*! But it was his reply that made my stomach turn, made me wonder if I would make it outside as I sat doubled over at the top of the stairs. His words were incoherent, a low sing-song floating down the stairwell. But I heard him nonetheless – *how* he spoke to her. He was trying to calm her down, gently murmuring, to placate the magpie.

So now *I* had become the ex.

If I could just get some air, if I could get down this last flight of stairs, I would be okay.

I took the métro at Simplon – that station practically outside his door – and jumped on the Porte d'Orléans line without thinking, a knee-jerk reaction, even after all those years. 'This line,' I used to say back then, 'is my lifeline.' It was the one I'd always taken when I was headed into work or briefly back home just to grab some more clothes. We used to take it in the evenings too, back into Paris to go out to a restaurant, to the cinema – wherever, just out.

But for now, I had to change trains at Réaumur Sébastopol to take the Porte de Bagnolet line. It had been a long time, but I still remembered the way back to my old apartment without having to stop and look at the métro map. I wandered down the warren of underground tunnels leading to my platform, the noxious odour of piss off the dank walls making me nauseous, claustrophobic, just like it used to. And as I stood on that crowded platform, watching while an old homeless man opposite screamed at us all for being there, it hit me – I might never see Charlie again.

When you stand on the platform of a crowded métro station in Paris and cry out loud, when you cannot stop the tears, when you can't even find a tissue in your handbag to wipe them away and blow your nose, no one even looks your way.

You're just another eccentric standing on a platform.

When Charlie was born, he was a bit of an ugly duckling. Of course, everyone said how beautiful he was – friends, family, strange women in supermarkets even. But I knew he wasn't. And even later, *much* later, Marc and I would take out old photos, shake our heads and laugh. He'd had something, yes – those clear blue eyes and that wide toothless smile. But he was such a scrawny, long thing, his red toes like octopus tentacles – not at all like those seductive roly-poly babies you see in the ads. And he was born with a bump on his small downy head that refused to go away until many, *many*

months later. Now it's funny, because I'd always thought that mothers were supposedly oblivious to such things.

But I wasn't.

It wasn't until Charlie hit about fifteen months that it happened, and almost overnight. We have, or *had*, I should say, a video of him then.

Bath time: his chubby, dimpled hands slapped at the water, splashing bubbles on to his round tummy. He was making those funny little boy sounds, voices for his Duplo toys as he lined them up on the edge of the bath. I had slicked his hair back, up off his face. His rosy cheeks glistened, his wet lashes stuck together like black kohl outlining the blue of his eyes.

He was *so* beautiful.

Chapter
ten

That was the straw that broke the camel's back for me in Lherm. Charlie.

I had come to pick him up after school, like always, except this time he was standing alone on the corner, some distance away from the school gates, waiting for me. I was surprised. Usually he'd be mucking around with his friends at the gate. I'd always have to wait a couple of minutes as they said their goodbyes, showing off like boys do. But that day, I'd barely had a chance to pull off the road before he grabbed at the door handle and jumped in.

'Hi mate.' I smiled at him. 'What's the rush?'

He shrugged and didn't look at me. 'Can we just go home please?'

'Sure.' I drove past the school and waved over at his group of friends. They didn't wave back. I would wait until we turned the corner before trying again. 'What's the matter, Charlie?'

'Nothin'.' The mumble was barely perceptible as he looked the other way, out the side window.

I decided to let it ride for the next few kilometres as we drove alongside the river. The sun had only just come out after two weeks of solid rain, so the water had turned a muddy tea-tree brown. Time to give it another shot.

'River's up.'

Nothing, not even a grunt.

We turned off on to the bumpy road leading up towards Lherm. 'Look, Charlie, you're going to have to tell me what's eating you, you know. Otherwise —'

That's when he lost it. 'Leave off, Mum! You *can't* help me!'

His holler was so loud it startled me, my foot pressing down on the brake too suddenly. I flicked on the indicator, an automatic gesture having grown up in the city, even though there was not another soul on the road, and pulled over.

I turned to him. '*Right*. Supposing you tell me what it is then, just so I know what it is that I can't help you with.'

He shot me a look, a frown. That's when I noticed it for the first time: his nose, swollen red around the bridge, and the dark circles under his eyes.

If there's one person that can holler louder than Charlie, it's me. '*Shit!* What the hell did they do to you?'

I reached over to turn his face towards me, but he jerked it out of my grip. 'It's *nothing*. Don't be *hystérique*.'

'Hysteri-*cal*!' I snapped back. *God*, how I hated this new term he'd picked up from his mates. He was using it a lot since we'd

72

arrived in Lherm. 'I'm not being hysterical, but I will be if you don't tell me this instant *exactly* what happened!'

That got his attention. He was staring back at me, measuring my mood. To be honest, I think I might have been pretty close to hysterical as I studied his nose, running my finger lightly over the bridge as he tried to pull away from me. Well, it was certainly swollen, but luckily not broken – just bruised, *very* bruised. My eyes met his. I could see he wasn't about to give in lightly. Time to pull out the big guns.

'And if you *don't —*' I paused, contemplating what threat I could conjure up this time. 'I'll turn this car around *right now*, march you back into that school and demand to speak to the principal. Then you'll see just how *hystérique* I can be!'

I could see it in his eyes – the flicker. So I waited.

I had to lean in closer when it finally came. 'There's a kid in *Cinquième.*'

I nodded, remembering those bully-boys standing by the fence sniggering on that first day. 'The year above you, right?'

'Yeah,' he breathed out. 'He's always going on about how Australians are losers, and that I should go back to where I came from.'

'And?'

'Today I was coming out of the toilet and he was standing just outside the doorway with his friends, and he started calling me a loser again.'

'Were you alone?'

He nodded.

'He's a big kid, right?'

He nodded again.

'Did you hit him?'

'*Mu-um!*' Obviously I'd said something ridiculous, *again*. 'Of course I didn't! He's too big!'

I smiled. He was no fool, my boy. 'So what happened then?'

'I told him *fous le camp*, to get lost. So he came up and grabbed me by my jumper.'

I sucked in my breath.

'And then he gave me *un coup de boule*.'

'A *what*?'

'*Un coup de boule*.' He jerked his head forward suddenly, violently, to show me.

'A *headbutt!*' I cried, horrified. 'The kid gave you a headbutt?'

But the rage I felt right at that moment was nothing compared to the next morning when the sergeant-major principal suggested I might be overreacting to the incident. '*Après tout, Madame,*' he'd said, throwing his hands up. 'It was just a common playground fisticuffs.'

In French, there is no word for *bully* – funny, that.

His smile was as sincere as a snake's as he steered me out of his office, his hand on my elbow. '*Franchement, Madame, ne soyez pas hystérique!*'

74

Déjà Vu

It was the *hystérique* that did it. I knew then, it was time to go.

When I was in third grade at school, just the thought of facing Mr Payne each day was enough to set my stomach off. I'd double over in agony, cramps shooting sharp and fast every morning as I pulled my uniform over my head, full of dread.

So I wished I didn't have to go to school. I wished so hard for it that one morning it actually worked. I remember Dr Gruinsite looking over his glasses at my mother as I sat beside him on his great worn wooden desk, nervous, my fingertips scratching the surface, his stethoscope cold on my tummy. 'It's just stress. *Something's* worrying this little lady.'

I knew as soon as I heard the word 'just' and Mum grunted 'Hmph' that I was doomed.

'What are you *stressed* about?' she asked me as we walked back to the car.

'School,' I told her, tears running down my cheeks, ashamed that Dr Gruinsite hadn't found something abnormal, something I could put a name to that all the kids would be impressed by – that would mean I would never have to go to school again, *ever*.

I'd been hoping for appendicitis. I had no idea what it was at the time, but it sure sounded pretty spectacular as far as illnesses went. Rumour had it that's what Mary Malloy had – an attack of *appendicitis* – just as Mr Payne was in the middle of asking her for the answer to 'What is the capital of Lithuania?', his squeaky voice making our hearts pound faster as we all sat rigid in our chairs, holding our breath as Mary screamed out loud.

They'd rushed her to hospital, the ambulance siren flashing and blaring just outside our classroom windows. And Mr Payne had screeched at us to all get back to our desks *or else*.

I remember my mother's words as she drove me to school, her eyes staring into mine in the rearview mirror as I sat miserable in the back.

'There are some things in this world, Annie MacIntyre, you have to face up to – that you just have to grin and bear.'

But I remember wondering why – *why* did I just have to grin and bear it? There *had* to be a way around it.

Chapter
eleven

I had made my way – hobbling like a wounded soldier come home from the war – in my stilettos, up the narrow street, unsure at first. Was it this street or the one after? It was so long ago, and I was tired and cold and so *lost*. Then I noticed the *boulangerie* with its Easter decorations already frosted around the edges of the window pane, and I remembered. Beattie and I would come here on our way home from work. The baker, an indefatigably jovial man with a white apron stretched across his great round stomach and flour sprinkled over his forearms, would huff and puff behind the counter, short of breath but never his sense of humour.

'Je vous aime!' I love you! he would cry when we walked through the door. But that's what he told all the young girls.

A little further up, on the next corner, I found it: the three-storey nineteenth-century stone building with pretty cornices under each window, where Beattie and I had lived for three years. Our two-bedroom apartment was on the second floor.

I rummaged through my old tanned leather saddlebag, searching for my keys, cursing all the paraphernalia that had no meaning for me now – bits of scrap paper, loose coins, used métro tickets, bobby pins, gritty Tic-tacs and old lipsticks. *Everything* except the damn keys. So I didn't see him, the dark figure lurking in the shadows by the main entrance. A dog barked from somewhere up in the building, stirred by my scream as the shadow lurched towards me. He'd been waiting for me.

'Annie! *Shhttt!*'

There it was again – his *shhttt*. But I was too tired to say anything, too tired to protest now.

I slept, an alcohol-induced unconsciousness, so that in those first few seconds of waking, before opening my eyes, I was untroubled – sweet oblivion. I hadn't yet noticed the absence of doves chortling just beyond our bedroom window in that tiny village, Monsieur Martin's rooster with its French '*Coccorico*', and Charlie's cartoon show, the *Rugrats* speaking French, the volume turned up way too loud downstairs. I had forgotten.

It was the sound of a hairdryer that made me wonder, in that split second before it all came back to me, before my eyelids flew open. And someone's whistling – high-pitched and waffly – confirmed it. Beattie had always whistled, and not terribly well.

Déjà Vu

There was a sudden break in the tune. Perhaps my long, low groan, like a bloated cow come home for milking, had startled her. I bit my bottom lip, sucked in my breath and pulled the covers up over my mouth. The body lying motionless next to me stirred and turned over. I didn't want to look at him – not yet.

I had wanted to simply sleep and wake up like Dorothy back home in Kansas, even if my Kansas was Lherm – to put this ghastly nightmare behind me, wash it away with one good, strong cup of coffee. But here we were, *still* – Sunday morning in Paris, some fifteen years back.

How could this be happening?

The whistling had resumed. I lay still, unwilling to move, desperately waiting for my breathing to slow, for my heart to quit banging so hard, to be back in our bed at home and for Beattie to maybe move on to another tune. And as I contemplated the ceiling of my old bedroom, the crack that used to make me homesick because it was shaped a bit like a flattened Australia if you squinted hard enough, I thought about what he'd said on the way to his place, about how maybe we'd be making it different by going *there* and not here. What I'd said in the café, about it all being exactly as it was that first time, had obviously got him thinking, hence the look he gave me in the car – worried. He'd put two and two together and thought maybe *she'd* be there, his 'ex'. Maybe he didn't know for sure because he had, after all, come back with me to my place that first time.

Of course, if we *had* played it like back then, I'd never have known about her, just like before. I wondered then, about my mother. Had she thought the same thing? Had she thought, if I hadn't gone into town, if I hadn't gone shopping, hadn't stopped off to buy that silly vanilla ice-cream, then I wouldn't have seen him sitting with that woman. I would never have known... and he'd never have died. It was funny, I thought, because my mother never ate ice-cream – not in my lifetime anyway.

I turned then. He was lying on his back, staring up at the ceiling. It was eerie, looking at that profile, back here in this room. I have, or *had*, a photo of him lying there, just like this. And I sighed, remembering how I'd felt as I'd taken it.

I closed my eyes to stop the tears coming, and thought about the time we went away – our first summer together. We'd got up at dawn and jumped in the van with a tent in the back and not much else. We headed west, driving all morning until we hit the coast at Quiberon, in Bretagne – a funny little grey town with crepes, lots of crepes and cider. That's all I remember about it because then we'd taken the ferry out to Belle Ile. And it was as if we'd passed into another time zone, another place so far removed from the rest of France, from *anywhere*. When I think of it now, I think of the colour blue, brilliant blue. It was just like all those postcards you see of tiny fishing villages – quaint wooden boats moored in the bay, colourful toys bobbing in the water, like Charlie used to play with in his bath.

Déjà Vu

We'd pitched our tent – an enormous lopsided thing that Marc had kept from his military service days – and headed off on our bikes down to the beach. God, when I think about it, we hadn't a care in the world... or so I thought. And I wonder now, did we realise that then, as we fooled around together in the water, and later, when the sun was low in the sky, as we made love, frantic and sandy, behind the rocks?

Where was it now – that passion?

'It's not there any more,' Marc said.

'What?' The adrenaline was making my heart pound. Had he read my thoughts?

He pointed up at the ceiling. 'Sydney.'

I pulled myself up, resting my weight on one elbow, and looked down at him, searching for a clue of what he was on about.

'*Tu ne te rappelles pas?*' He was staring back at me. I really had forgotten how beautiful his eyes were – that intense blue, their black centres, like my old bottle of Yves Saint Laurent perfume.

'Remember what?'

'We pulled that desk across, put the chair up and I stood on top,' he replied, pausing as he watched me, pulling on a strand of my hair that had fallen over his face.

Yes, I remembered then. I lay back down and looked up. He was right, it wasn't there any more. He'd marked Sydney on my map, stood naked on the chair, whiteboard marker in hand, trying to find the spot as I directed him from the bed, laughing as he flailed about, unselfconscious, like a statue of David. He hadn't any idea where to mark it then – it could have been at the top of the Northern Territory for all he knew.

'You lied to me.' I was still looking up at the ceiling.

He didn't move. *'Je ne me rappelles plus, tu sais.* It's so long ago now. I don't remember *what* I told you, Annie.'

But *I* did: *J'en avais une. Mais c'est fini maintenant...*

'Hah, very convenient!' I sat up, my back to him now, not wanting him to see how much it hurt, even after all these years. We'd been on the brink of separation just yesterday, yet it hurt. He had stirred something in me, this young man. Memories of what we'd had. What I'd *thought* we'd had.

I'd left my clothes in a pile at the end of the bed, dumped them there before passing out. I had no idea what time it was, having lost my watch somewhere along the way. I'd had it in Toulouse, but after that...I reached for something to pull on and retrieved something black and lacy, a bra I used to wear back then. Such a frivolous thing, I thought as I slipped the straps over my shoulders, trying to work out how the hell it did up, fumbling with the catch. My hair, falling halfway down my back, was getting in the way. I hadn't had it this long in years. My hands had lost the knack, that special gesture all those young girls have, to flick it out of the way *just so.*

'Funny how you remember the Sydney thing, though.'

He reached up to help me with the catch. He was always good

at those fiddly things. 'Even better at undoing them,' he'd say.

'Annie, *t'es sérieuse?*' One hand rested still and warm on my back. 'What does it matter now?'

His fingers rubbed softly, working their way up towards my neck. I wanted him to keep going, to run his hands all over me, to ease away the tension... and the thoughts of that woman.

But I pulled away. It mattered to *me*.

'It was *over*, Annie!'

I reached for the rest of my clothes. 'Let's get up.' I didn't want to hear his excuses, his lies, not now, not *ever*.

The stilettos were lying over by the door, where I had obviously flung them, though I had no recollection now. No, I would not be wearing those ridiculous instruments of torture today, or ever again. I would have to try to dig out something more practical. Hopefully there'd be some semblance of that in the cupboard.

I shivered. I was even starting to *think* like my mother.

Chapter *twelve*

Beattie was standing by the kitchen window in her grey tracksuit, looking down on to the leafy central courtyard, her back to the doorway. It was where she'd always stood when she made herself a tea in the morning, leaning against the kitchen sink. In the clear light of day I noticed her figure – this young girl with her slender hips and slight shoulders, not yet the more mature Beattie I had grown older with.

That morning after I first met Marc, Beattie and I had stood here in the kitchen, laughing together about his boots as she sipped her tea by the window. But this morning, I had hoped to slip by without her seeing Marc. She must have heard us in the bedroom, murmuring through the wall, because she turned just as Marc reached the doorway behind me.

'Good morning, cowboy!' she smiled. I noticed how radiant her face was, her clear white skin and her green eyes, without the slightest trace of make-up. 'Tea?'

Marc smiled awkwardly back at her, silent.

'Sorry, Beattie.' I ushered him on past the doorway and up the corridor towards the front door. 'We're off out!'

We walked from the apartment towards Père Lachaise, with neither of us suggesting we go there. We used to wander up there on lazy Sundays, pulling ourselves out of bed so late in the day sometimes that afternoons would melt into evenings, and the week-end would be gone, all too quickly.

For now, I just wanted to sit under a tree, somewhere green, somewhere calm. We were a long way from Lherm.

We were standing before a small gate covered in vines, a side entrance to the cemetery – the closest thing to a park in this part of Paris. As Marc reached down to lift the catch and push open the gate, I remembered how he used to stand *just* there, how he'd hold it open and wait for me to pass through. And I'd recite that first line from the story of *Madeline*: 'In an old house in Paris that was covered with vines…' I wondered if he remembered too, although I don't think he ever really understood why I used to say it, or what the words actually meant.

The gate creaked as he pushed it open. 'Lived twelve little girls…' I waited, wishing for him to be thinking the same thing. Then he looked at me and smiled as he stepped back, waiting, his hand against the open gate. But I didn't say it. Why should I say it? It wasn't the same any more. He'd lied.

I stepped forward. But he slipped his free hand around my neck and I felt his lips brush against my ear, then kiss my cheek. Perhaps he'd remembered after all. I wished then that I'd said it, but it was too late now – we were already through. Then the gate clanked shut.

We walked up the narrow cobbled path under the bare, twisted branches of the sycamore trees, spread over our heads like giant spindly fingers. We used to sit somewhere further up on a stone bench, but I couldn't remember exactly where.

He stepped ahead of me suddenly, across my path. 'Here.'

There it was. It's funny, because I'd half expected it to be grown over, or for some modern fixed metallic thing to be there in its place – for that ancient worn stone to have disappeared, as we had. But no, it was here still, as if we had never gone away at all.

He kicked at the ground as we sat there together on the stone, a cloud of fine dirt settling on my shoes. 'She says she's going to move out, *dès qu'elle peut*, as soon as she finds a place.'

I held my hands up, fingers spread like a shield. In my mind's eye she was there, still in that T-shirt. 'Don't tell me! I really *don't* want to know.'

But I did, and he knew it. He laughed softly and shook his head. That was the thing, he knew me too well now. '*Tu sais*, Annie, when you think about it, this is *so* silly.'

I watched him run his fingers through his hair and I wondered, had he run them through *hers* last night as he tried to calm her down – through those curls?

Perhaps he read my thoughts. 'She's not important. She doesn't exist in our lives any more. *C'est le passé.*'

My heart leapt up into my throat. '*Any more?*' These words gave her importance; an existence I had never known about. 'So how long was it going on, Marc, after you met me?'

He shrugged. 'Oh, Annie, I don't know!'

But these weren't the words I wanted to hear. I'd wanted him to deny it – to tell me it wasn't going on *at all*, even though the fact that she was there, standing in his living room, said it all.

'You don't get it, do you, Marc? She *did* exist! And she *does* exist. But you lied to me about her.' I leant forward so I could see his face, to *make* him understand. 'So she *is* important *now*.'

He brought his hands down, heavy, rubbing them back and forth against his thighs, uneasy.

'*Mais de quoi tu parles*, Annie?' His breath was white steam in the cold. 'Nothing happened last night, if that's what you're thinking, *rien du tout*. I followed you in the van, straight after...'

But I wondered how many nights he had been with her back then, in the first year that I had known him, when we'd never gone back to his place. A bitter wind stung my face. My hair whipped my eyes. 'It's not about *that*!'

'Well, just *tell* me then, Annie, *enfin*.' His voice was low now, his patience giving way to exasperation. 'What *is* it about?'

I was cold. The damp off the stone was seeping through my jeans, through to the backs of my thighs. I stood up, hugging my arms around my chest, moving my feet up and down off the pavement like a child, restless.

'It's about the past – it's about what happened back then —'

'But what does it matter *now*, Annie?'

I looked down at him, stunned. Had he ever loved me at all? But pride wouldn't let me ask this question now. Besides, it was more than that – much, *much* more.

'It's about Charlie.' It was hard to pronounce his name.

'*Quoi?*'

I bent towards him, my face so close to his I could feel the warmth of his breath against my skin, on my lips. '*Charlie*, our son, remember?'

His eyes met mine, as if searching for a clue. '*Oui?*'

I pulled myself up straight, glancing at the sky, still heavy with thick winter clouds, and thought, how I am going to make this make any sense?

'Us going back to your place – *her* being there. It's all different now. You should have just told me in the car.'

He shook his head. '*Non*, Annie, I couldn't do that. You were so tired. How could I have told you then?'

'You had fifteen years to tell me, Marc. If I'd known, I'd *never* have suggested we go back there. We were meant to go back to my place for a reason. Now it's too late.'

'What are you talking about – *too late?*'

'We've changed the way it went, changed how it's meant to be, so now the future is going to be different, don't you see?'

A low and distant rumble rolled through the sky.

He stared at me then, so I think that's when he *did* see it, finally. '*Tu*...You mean —?'

A young couple was heading towards us, pushing a pram up the hill together, laughing with the effort. 'Yes,' I replied, nodding. 'I don't want to lose him, Marc.'

'*Mais attends*...' His hand reached out, gripping my elbow, pulling me towards him. 'This doesn't mean we won't have Charlie!'

But how could he know? How could we be sure of anything? Our lives were now destined to take a different path.

There are those moments in your life when you feel it: happiness in its purest form. Of course, it doesn't last forever, but that's what makes it so good, I suppose – the high of it compared to the rest.

When Charlie was born, I cried when they brought him to me – the sheer ecstasy of seeing this tiny, funny thing with his hand clasped around my finger, his wide toothless yawn and his small, downy head with that bump.

After Charlie, they told me I wouldn't fall pregnant again. I didn't believe them – I'd had Charlie, so I would have another. We tried and tried for years, and I still didn't believe them. It's only now, looking back, that I think I finally accept it.

He was, like they said, 'just a chance in a million' – my miracle baby.

Chapter
thirteen

I've never liked Mondays, and without a doubt this one was the pits. Sunday, both of us merely floated. But Monday fell hard. Six a.m. and the sky was a purple–grey, like squid ink splashed thick across my bedroom window, its murkiness staining my thoughts as we lay there together. Let it stay that way, I thought. If time has stopped, let it stop here. We had to go back to work, pick up where we'd left off that last Friday before we'd met.

'I can't do this,' I whispered.

'We don't have a choice.' His tone was as bleak as death, which didn't help.

I could tell he hadn't slept – the voice, and his silhouette like a corpse next to me, flat on his back, one arm slung over his eyes. But then, he'd never been a great morning person and I guess this time he had a good excuse. I didn't want to think of him going back to his apartment, maybe seeing *her* as he changed for work. I hoped by now she'd managed to find some clothes.

'Say something nice.' My fingertips skimmed his bare chest,

firm skin under my touch. 'Say something to get us through this.'

'*Ca ira*. We'll be fine,' he said lamely. 'Just don't think about it.'

That didn't help either. He was standing in my bedroom doorway, about to go, to leave me there. *Don't*, I wanted to tell him as I moved towards him. I might never see him again, never see *us* again, *us three*.

'Meet me at Julien's?'

His eyes met mine, soft like Charlie's. Could he see him too – somewhere, somewhere in *my* face? Where was he now?

'I'll book a table for seven-thirty.'

I nodded, thinking *yes*, that would help. And as I reached up to touch his face, that face so young, so open, I remembered that expression, his eyes smiling soft, watching me across the bar at Kitty's, across the table at the Deux Magots that first Friday after we'd met...the next morning. I had woken with his face over mine, those blue eyes, his black hair. Our first time, our first night together, drunk on champagne, on Tarte Tatin at the Deux Magots, drunk on passion.

'I want you to meet my friends,' he had said. 'I want them to meet *you*. *Ce soir*.'

Such conviction in his words. I remember wondering how long he'd been staring at me like that, as I reached for the glass by the bed. Had my mouth been hanging open?

'Will they like me?'

'*Non*. They will think you are very 'orrible.' His hand had caressed my cheek. 'You should always wash your face before sleeping, *non*?'

In the bathroom, I'd screamed at the mirror – the black smudges under my eyes. I heard him laughing as he lay there in my bed, that wonderful deep laugh penetrating the wall, penetrating my skin.

I was in deep, right from the start.

I'd arrived at the party late that night, entering an apartment full of cool-looking people standing in a dimly lit, smoke-filled living room. There was a woman over in the corner with a chic haircut cropped close to her skull, gamin-style, sitting on the edge of a couch, perched there like an elf. I touched the back of my hair, nervously pushing at the wisps that had fallen loose, suddenly feeling very *passé*. She was talking to a man sitting beside her with his cap on backwards, throwing her head back, laughing at something he'd whispered in her ear, her cigarette held *just so*. That blasé chic I envied in French women.

I knew no one, no one except Marc, and I couldn't see him anywhere. He had told me to meet him there; he had a couple of things to do, I remember him murmuring as his lips moved down my neck, and down further, making my skin tingle, my hips rise. Great, I'd thought, it would give me the afternoon free to shop for something to wear.

But now I wondered, was he with *her* that afternoon all those years ago? Funny how at the time it never occurred to me that there might be someone else. I'd had such faith.

It was that look in his eyes.

I had chosen something daring – a low-cut little black dress, *too* little for comfort, but passion had given me confidence as I shopped that day.

I scanned the room for his face, desperately self-conscious. A couple of guys standing by the door fell silent and gave me the once over. I yanked at my dress, wishing I'd worn jeans. The taller of the two, his lank wavy hair flopping over his eyes, had moved in closer, standing over me. He probably had a bird's-eye view right down my front. I held my hand out.

'*Bonsoir. Je suis* Annie.'

He grinned and extended his hand as his mate smirked behind him. '*Bonsoir! Je suis* Gilles.'

Then someone turned up the music just as Gilles moved in closer, so I couldn't hear what he was saying. I smiled and shrugged. His lips brushed against my ear and his hand touched my shoulder. I hadn't noticed his fingers slip under the strap of my saddlebag until it fell heavily to the floor.

'*Viens danser.*'

His hand had moved down to find mine, his sweaty grip pulling me further into the room. I wanted to tell him *Non, merci*, that I didn't feel like it right now, that I really wouldn't mind just hanging back a bit with a drink until I could get my bearings, to at least give my dress another yank. And a thought had occurred to me suddenly: what if this wasn't even the right party?

He was dancing close to me, moving in *too* close, as I tried to look back over my shoulder to locate my bag.

And that's when I saw him.

He was leaning against the door frame opposite, arms folded, smiling over at me. My heart did that silly flip it used to always do back then.

'Help!' I mouthed.

But Marc didn't budge. Well, at least I knew then I'd found the right party, so I didn't mind so much after that.

His eyes watching me – that look. I was dancing for him.

Chapter
fourteen

*E*ven at the best of times it's rotten returning to work after a break, getting back into the swing of things. You go away, fall into another rhythm – another *world* – so that first day back, it takes very little to become unravelled, to lose it.

With me, that morning, it would be little more than a *bonjour* that would do it.

I took the métro with Beattie. I felt strangely removed from myself, like a fly on the white tiled underground tunnel, as I stood on the platform at Porte de Bagnolet, watching as I moved as part of the crowd, grabbing a seat on the crowded carriage, sitting in among the dour French faces as it rocked us gently back and forth, pulling in and out of each station and whirring like a plastic salad spinner. Beattie sat opposite, taking off some woman perched to her right with thin eyebrows, skinny knees and a chihuahua in her handbag. I shook my head and smiled. I had forgotten how she used to be – the pranks she used to pull.

She grinned back. 'So who is he?' She was gathering her things together; next stop was ours. How was I ever going to do all this?

'Who?' I was playing dumb, following in her wake as she pushed a path through the crowd. *'Pardon, pardon, s'il vous plaît. Merci.'*

She turned and rolled her eyes at me. The doors slid open on to Gare St Lazare, the grand central station, with another round of commuters pushing their way in before we'd even got off. 'Oh, *merci beaucoup,'* Beattie called as we shoved our way through and on to the platform.

'Always let the people off first, Charlie.'

The warning signal sounded and the doors banged shut behind us, up the length of the platform – there was no turning back now.

We'd reached the main exit, a massive series of archways leading out on to la Cour de Rome, when Beattie grabbed my elbow and pulled me over to the side, the flock of commuters surging on past us, as if all this was normal and I was just part of the crowd.

'What's got into you, Annie? You're acting *so* weird.'

I shrugged. She'd always known me well. But not *this* well. 'Not sure... Mondayitis, I guess.' But she didn't look convinced. 'I'm just tired.'

'Yes, I'm sure you are!' She was fixing me with one of her stares, eyebrows raised, obviously waiting for me to explain. But I couldn't.

We stopped off at our café at the entrance to Gare Saint Lazare, the place we'd always come to before work: a bustling, noisy coffee stop for Parisians working locally, on their way in to the office, to the Banque Nationale de Paris or Société Générale perhaps, or down the Boulevard Haussman to take up their positions behind the counters in the large department stores, Galeries Lafayette and Printemps. And as we stood at the bar, it hit me how we'd been right at the hub of it all – that 'race of the rat city' as Marc would say. The bartender, cigarette planted permanently behind his ear, winked and served us our *grands cafés crèmes* and croissants from the basket on the silver counter – even flirted just like he used to – while the other regulars looked on and smirked.

'When will he ever give up?' said Beattie, too loud. Never, it seemed.

We were running past the pharmacy on the corner when I stopped suddenly, remembering – there used to be a weighing machine, right *there* underneath the flashing green fluorescent cross. *Pesez-vous et découvrez votre avenir:* Weigh yourself and have your fortune told. I remember the first day it appeared on the corner – a particularly cold day. Beattie and I were running late for our eight o'clock start, yet she insisted we have a go – a competition to see who weighed less. So we'd stripped off our coats and our shoes in the middle of the square – foolish young girls! – and Beattie's grin was victorious, because she weighed point three of a kilo less than me. I had kept it – that tiny slip of paper, long after the numbers and letters had faded to a washed-out purple. It was the prophecy that intrigued me, not my weight: *Si vous marchez dans les pas de votre mère, attention* — If you follow in your mother's footsteps, beware — But the bit at the end had jammed in the machine, so the rest of the sentence had remained a mystery. 'It's a sign,' Beattie reckoned at the time.

Yet now the machine wasn't there. Strange… everything else was as it was, except this.

We were barely out of the lift and through the door to Colangue when it started – my unravelling. It was Murielle who sent me spinning. Murielle, otherwise known as Mademoiselle Ice Maiden back then, was a tall, blonde Swiss–German, a grown-up version of Heidi turned mean. She was top dog at the school, the director's personal assistant, a *very personal* assistant. Rumour had it she'd started out as filing clerk. But being very competent, very efficient and, like I said, very tall and blonde, she'd soon worked her way to the top and stayed there – literally on top, because that's supposedly how the director liked it. Everyone was wary of Ice Maiden, even him. No, it didn't pay to cross her.

He was married, of course, the typical Frenchman with his bit on the side. His wife would come in every Friday for lunch, converse and laugh politely with Ice Maiden, her husband's lover. She knew, of course. Unlike Ice Maiden, she was just a petite thing, impeccably dressed in her Chanel suits, Chanel handbag, bob and poodle, picture perfect. She had everything she wanted. Why rock the boat?

'*Bonjour*, Annie.' Ice Maiden's face beamed efficiency at me, like it always had, her grey eyes as warm as steel in snow and with a smile that would crack glass. 'Your Monsieur Vitali is here. I've put him in *salle* eight.'

Ah, Monsieur Vitali. . . I was coming to him.

'Interesting. *Ca t'arrange en fait*,' says Marc, 'that you should forget to mention him. Very convenient.'

Carlo Vitali had signed up for 'one-on-one' lessons. He'd wanted to *perfect* his English with his own private teacher, preferably a woman, he'd told Ice Maiden. Now this was a pretty reasonable request, given that his company would be picking up the tab, that he was its deputy director *and* he liked women. Yes, he liked them *a lot*.

So that is how I came to meet Carlo.

I'd been teaching him for around a year before I met Marc. Though, to be honest, I can't say that he made much progress in English.

'*Non, mais* certainly he did in other things,' says Marc.

It is difficult to put the extent of Carlo's charisma – his irresistible charm – into words. To meet him was to fall in love with him. He was Italian, originally from Milan – beautiful looking, tall and dark with an animated face and a smile as wide as. . . I don't know. Even a photo would never do him justice.

He'd come to Paris twenty or so years back, in his twenties, but still spoke French with an Italian accent. When he spoke it was like poetry, carefully measured, rhythmic and melodic. And when he pronounced my name, it was A*nn*a, which of course is a different thing altogether from Annie. A*nn*a: tender in the middle, the tip of his tongue resting on the *nn*s, my consonants, savouring them in his mouth, making them swell and ache like —.

'*Ton clitoris?*'

No, Marc. He gave my name sensuality, making it swell and mature like a girl maturing into a woman, making my knees go weak, my... It's important to appreciate the extent of Carlo's charm in order to make sense of the rest: why I fell in love with him, why *any* woman would. Why, when he clicked his fingers, I would come, to his house in Italy, to some tiny, exotic restaurant on the other side of Paris. *Wherever!* I was, after all, barely twenty-four back then, still so young, so naïve. That's why I haven't yet mentioned one thing which, according to Marc, is quite significant. *Yes*, I will come to that.

But then, *he's* one to talk.

It wasn't until we'd been seeing each other for quite a while that I found out about *her*, about Carlo's wife. It hadn't occurred to me that he would be married. He'd never mentioned her, so I had just assumed he wasn't. Though you think it would have clicked after a while, the fact that he could very rarely see me on weekends, that we'd never been back to his place, and that he always chose out and away places for us to go to, yes, the kind that weren't in the Michelin – the kind where he could be sure he'd never run into *her*. When I think about it now – the fact that he was married – and when I think about Marc and Frédérique, it sort of makes me wonder: *exactly what planet was I on at the time?* I was young, yes, but how could I have been so naïve?

Of course, it upsets Marc that I should compare his situation with Frédérique to Carlo. 'Our relationship was over,' he says. 'How could I have still been with her, when I was coming over to your place nearly every night?'

It's his 'nearly' that niggles at me.

Chapter
fifteen

$\mathcal{H}$e was waiting for me in the classroom, sitting with his back to the door and looking out the window as if I had just stepped out to get something – a dictionary, or a whiteboard marker, perhaps. He was humming. I'd been gone fifteen years, and he was humming.

I paused in the doorway, silent. But he must have sensed my presence as I took in the silhouette of his shoulders, his hand on the table, fingers tapping softly on the surface, content.

'Anna!'

He had turned, getting up to greet me, *so* delighted – like Charlie when he was three, when I'd come to pick him up from day care, jumping out of the sandpit, running across the yard…

'Mummy!'

Carlo stepped towards me, his arms open, before I'd even clicked the door shut behind me. I heard footsteps in the corridor, pausing, then moving off quickly – Ice Maiden's, perhaps?

Over the years my image of this man had blurred. I had remembered him in parts, his features like pieces of a puzzle that

I had taken apart and packed away – the blackness of his hair, the silver flecks at his temples, the playfulness in his dark eyes, his eyes as black as kohl...his smile. But I had forgotten the impact he once had on me, the complete picture, this three-dimensional Carlo from my past – the sheer unadulterated beauty of this man, his imposing stature and the strength in his hands as he gripped my forearms and pulled me closer. The impact he *still* had on me. Nothing, not even age, can make you immune.

I'm no saint.

I felt the red rising and my body stiffen as he pressed against me, his hands working their way round to my back, moving lower, then lower. He took me by surprise – the urgency in his movements, his frenzied touch, his pelvis pressed hard against mine, the way it made me feel... I pulled away quickly, squirming in his grip, my hands on his chest pushing him off, awkward. I wasn't prepared for this intimacy with a man I no longer knew, with a man other than Marc.

'*Carlo!*'

'I have missed you!' He reached out and pulled on a strand of my hair as Marc had done only yesterday. I wondered what he meant. Did he know how long it had been?

'You should have come with me, *Anna!*' His arm was around my waist, drawing me over towards the table. 'I have brought you something back.'

Come with him *where*? And then I saw it, and remembered.

It was on the table – a small, slim package, wrapped in gold. He'd gone away to Italy – to his villa in Tuscany. He had wanted me to go with him for the week. But this time I'd resisted, sick of playing the mistress.

'Take your wife, Carlo,' I had said.

So he'd gone without me. And I'd wished he hadn't. I'd wished I'd gone after all.

'Come on, Annie, get over it!' Beattie had said, fed up with me moping around all week and all day Saturday. 'Forget him. Come out to Kitty's.'

So I did – and met Marc.

'Open it, Anna!' His hand on my back pushed me forward.

But I didn't need to open it. I had recognised it instantly.

'You shouldn't have got this for me, Carlo.' That's what I'd said back then as I handed his present back to him without opening it. 'I can't accept this.'

He'd laughed, pushing it into my hands 'What do you mean?' His hand touched my cheek. 'Silly, funny Anna! How do you know until you open it?'

'I don't want presents – no more presents, Carlo.'

I had met Marc.

And he'd nodded, disappointment in his eyes, taking it and putting it back in his briefcase, silent. He'd understood then. Or so I'd thought.

I'd found it in my locker, after class. The watch.

Déjà Vu

I was late. It had been a long day – eight hours straight teaching. Like I said, I can teach standing on my head, but that first Monday back it felt like I actually had.

It is difficult to describe what I felt without a Barbara Cartland slant to it, that moment when I pushed on the heavy glass door and the maître d' rushed over to me, smiling wide, holding it open, ushering me into Julien's. What is Paris if it's not romantic? And as far as Parisian restaurants go, Julien's, with its rich velvet curtains – ruby red – draping the entrance to a grand, sepia-lit dining hall, is the epitome of those starry-lit backdrops in the French classics, with lovers looking steamily across tables at one another. We had always loved to meet there after work. How could I have felt anything but uplifted, goose bumps rising on my skin? Yes, it was like walking onstage, re-enacting a scene we'd played out so many times before – the clink of heavy silver against porcelain, voices resounding around my ears like ghosts clapping, welcoming us back as I weaved my way through the tables towards him.

He was sitting in the corner, our favourite spot, his back to the wall, underneath one of the grand old mirrors. Its speckled tarnished pane once reflected blurred images of us, of others, dining, kissing and sharing *crème caramel* as waiters in long, starched white aprons rushed between tables, carrying buckets of ice and silver trays, pouring champagne, crisply folded white serviettes draped over one arm.

They were all here, still.

Marc had seen me and was smiling, watching as the maître d' helped me with my coat and I thought, just fleetingly as the cloak-lady stepped forward and whisked it away, maybe we'd be okay. Maybe we would get through this, and somehow find Charlie after all.

I had made an effort tonight, pulled on some long-lost dress I'd found in my wardrobe – pure chance, for it was hidden at the very back, intentionally hidden. And as I pulled it out, I gasped, remembering. It was a beautiful thing, soft jersey silk, a present from Carlo, yet I had never worn it. I ran my hands over the dark soft fabric and slipped it over my head, slid it down my body and smoothed it over my hips. It clung like a second skin. I looked at the young woman in the mirror, holding my hair up off my neck, and thought about the silly thing I'd been, too self-conscious, not knowing what I'd had. He'd handed it to me one evening in a white box tied with silk ribbon, that box so beautiful in itself. I'd never been given such a thing. And when I pulled on the ribbon and lifted the lid, the dress lay like a delicate rippling wave of fabric, wrapped in tissue paper and tied with string. It was too much. It wasn't me.

'You should give it to your wife,' I'd whispered.

'Oh, Anna!'

I'd never worn it for him, nor Marc, for that matter. Till now.

As I approached he stood up, pushed the table out and stepped aside to let me take his place, *my* spot looking out on to the restaurant floor. He seemed happy, surprised.

'I don't remember that dress. And your hair. . .' His lips brushed against my ear, an accident, my bottom against his pelvis as I slipped in front of him to take up my position. 'You've done it like you used to.'

I looked at him as we sat down opposite one another and waited for him to pass judgement. I guess I still lacked confidence, even now.

'*Tu es belle.*' He was studying my face, his eyes scanning my features like a critic contemplating a painting.

'Yeah, well, that's why I'm late.' I reached up and touched the back of my hair, pushing the stray strands back into place as I felt the red rising, treacherous, up my neck. 'It took me forever to pull it up – all those *bloody* pins.'

And he laughed. I guess I may have *looked* like that girl back then, but I don't think I sounded like her any more. But then, when I thought about Carlo and how naïve I'd been, it was surely for the best. Marc was still looking at me, the critic. That's when he noticed – his eyes flickering on my wrist. 'You found your watch.'

'Let's order,' I said quickly. 'I could eat a horse.'

Chapter
sixteen

When I hit about seventeen and started going out with boys, my mother would often say, 'Just remember one thing, Annie MacIntyre. There's no such thing as a free lunch.'

Like I said, my mother was not a romantic.

When I first started teaching Carlo, I was ill at ease. He would sit opposite me in the small sunlit classroom up on the fourth floor at Colangue and smile, following me with his dark, playful eyes as I got up to go to the whiteboard, watching my hands as I tried to explain a grammatical point, making me self-conscious as I pretended not to notice. It unnerved me. No man had ever given me such attention. It made the blood rise to my face. I couldn't teach him English. I couldn't teach him *anything*. Yes, it was difficult.

'Foolish girl,' as my mother would say.

He asked me out just after our second lesson, his hand on mine across the table, turning it over, his fingers running along my palm, moving upwards towards my fingertips, pressing them flat under his. I pictured his body, his pelvis, pressing into mine – lying under him on the floor right there in the classroom, flesh on flesh. But I clamped my hand shut and said no. The lesson was over. I don't know why I refused. After all, at that stage I had no idea he was married. When he spoke about his life during our lessons together, it was strictly in the first-person singular sense, 'I'. He never slipped up, not once.

'*Un professionnel*,' says Marc.

Yes, I suppose he was. I was wary at first, my mother's daughter after all. I was twenty-four. He was older, *much* older than me – in his forties. Of course, that doesn't seem so old now, but it wasn't his age that held me back. He was deputy director of one of the biggest companies in France. He was handsome, intelligent and powerful. There was power in his every gesture, in the way he had run his fingers along my hand. And he made me laugh. But I had a feeling he'd made others laugh. He could have anything he wanted. *Why me?*

Then one day he didn't come. I sat in the classroom waiting. No one came to tell me he'd be late or that he wouldn't be coming at all. So I sat there and thought – about him. And I realised I was disappointed. I wouldn't see him now until the following week. I had run the kohl pencil along my eyelids with a little more precision than I usually did for a Monday morning, and he hadn't come.

The following week, 8.20 a.m., once more he hadn't arrived. I sat in the classroom, watching the clock, afraid he wouldn't turn up again, not today, and perhaps *never* again. 'Never wait for a bus or a man,' Grandma would say. 'There'll be another one along in a minute.' But I thought, no, he wasn't like any other man. He was Carlo.

Then suddenly in he strode, suit jacket swung casually over his shoulder. '*Bongiorno,*' he said, and sat down.

Nothing more – no explanation, nothing. So I stood up and got on with the lesson. I was, after all, just his English teacher and, as Ice Maiden warned when she first allocated him to me, he was Colangue's most important client. But then she *would* say that.

Finally, at the end of the hour, right on the dot, he stood up to go. He had never done this before, never once glanced at his watch or the clock on the wall behind my head. I was always the one to bring the lesson to a close, to usher him out of the room, apologetic, embarrassed, saying I had another class to teach. And he would laugh, feigning disappointment.

'Is that all I am to you, *Anna*, just another lesson?' His hand clasped my elbow, my skin hot under his touch.

But today he was obviously in a hurry, barely managing a 'See you next week'. Smiling briskly, he took up his jacket from the back of the chair, slid his arms into its sleeves, picked up his briefcase – polished black and impeccable – and turned to leave. As he reached the door I almost went to ask him, 'So am I just another teacher to you?' But I didn't.

And he left.

It was only about halfway through my following class with a particularly boring inanimate group of five electrical engineers from Dumon Aviation that I noticed it – a folded slip of paper tucked into the plastic sleeve of my teaching folder.

It was marked *Anna*. I smiled, nodding encouragement as one of the Dumon guys pronounced in his monotone, faltering and heavily accented English, 'I am learning English since a very long time.'

'That's wonderful!' My cry was perhaps a little too enthusiastic. Simultaneously, all five students looked up from their worksheets, eyes trained on me like fighter pilots, suspicious. Up until that moment I had barely managed more than a grunt of encouragement, even on the rare occasion that one of them had actually got something right.

I didn't open it until after they left, when I'd closed the door behind them, finally alone.

It was a simple message. He wrote:

Meet me for dinner. Tonight. Café de la Paix, sur Les Grands Boulevards, 8 p.m. I will be punctual this time.
Carlo

True, he was *very* professional.

It was my mother who convinced me to go that night, even though we hadn't spoken in over a year, since my grandmother's funeral. But in the twenty minutes I'd waited for Carlo that morning, sitting at my desk as the clock ticked relentlessly and as I clicked my pen over and over *and over*, thinking about him, I had thought about her.

My mother had never approved of my choice in men, the straggly string of boyfriends I'd brought home in my teens, often comparing them to my father.

'Your father,' she'd say, 'wasn't like that.'

Then Grandma would say with a wink, 'No, of course, your father was perfect.'

Ever since I could remember, Mum had held him up as the perfect man, the perfect lover – his sin forgotten. He was her *constant* point of reference.

Clearly, Carlo would not fit the mould. And that is precisely what attracted me to him – the devil streak. He was dangerously exciting. I knew that from the moment he walked into my classroom.

He took me to a concert once – a string ensemble in a tiny cathedral, set in behind the Paris Town Hall.

It was raining heavily, a Thursday evening in April. I was waiting for him on the Boulevard Haussman, underneath the entrance to Colangue. The wind was driving the rain up against my bare legs, my skirt sticking to my skin like a wet paper bag, making me

shiver. When he pulled up finally – late again – stopping cars behind him, I ran out, holding my jacket over my head. But it was
no use – I was soaked through anyway.

He didn't move off straight away, even though the drivers were
honking mad behind him. He didn't care. He *never* cared about
that sort of thing.

'He was rich, *très riche*,' says Marc. 'He could afford not to
care.'

No, it wasn't that. Life was a game to him, just a game. So with
the traffic stopped behind us, he just looked at me, ran his hand
through my wet hair and said, 'You're very wet.'

'Well, it's raining cats and dogs.'

And he'd clapped his hands together, obviously delighted by
this expression. 'Cats and dogs! *Really, Anna?*'

And that was part of his magic, turning the mundane into
fun – even my words, this silly, simple expression, to poetry.

We sat on fragile wooden chairs that squeaked under our weight
up in the transept of the cloister, partly hidden, looking down upon
the ensemble as their music reached up to us, bouncing off the
stone walls, off the bodies of saints.

I watched them draw their bows, passionate, fingers pressing
like frenzied insects up and down the strings, making music, as
Carlo's hand reached under my wet shirt, sliding softly, up and
down my back, my skin damp, making my nipples hard.

Sinners.

Chapter
seventeen

$\mathcal{M}$arc's face was stony – his jaw clenched so tight an angry pulse throbbed in his cheek.

'You mean you're seeing him again? *Tu le vois toujours en fait, still?*'

We had stopped at a set of traffic lights, but his eyes were fixed on the road ahead, his grip tight on the steering wheel. We were headed back to my place, up towards Place de la République – this old path that we had taken so often, before he started taking me back to his apartment. Before *she* had obviously left.

'*No*, Marc, I don't mean that at all.' I paused, considering his hands, his knuckles – bone-white under the skin. 'Like I said, I had a lesson with him this morning.'

The lights changed and we moved off, a little too fast for my liking. He was watching the road, but turning something over in his mind. His narrowed eyes flickered over towards my lap, to my hands resting there.

'What are you thinking?' I asked, though I was pretty sure

I knew. My hand moved over my wrist – too late.

'Your watch. Where did you say you found it?'

I didn't say.

This watch had been mine practically from the beginning, as old as our relationship, short of two days – even older than Charlie. It had been with me through his birth, from those very first contractions at midnight, to that moment when they told me, 'Annie, you have a lovely baby boy,' at eleven o'clock in the morning. So when Carlo handed it to me this morning I had taken it, accepting it graciously – it had, after all, been mine. Yet that first time round, it had stayed in its box, shoved into the back of my cupboard, like the dress, until one day I had simply taken it out, when it meant nothing to me any more, when the memories of Carlo had well and truly dimmed.

It had ticked on relentless over the years, even when I'd been given others; others that I'd lost or broken or that had simply given up the ghost. I would put it to one side, back in its box, favouring the others, until they failed me. But this one had ticked on. A paradox – this persistent unwelcome present that he had given me, his last.

So why ask me this now? I wondered. We didn't have time – we had to find a way through this mess. Back to Charlie.

We had pulled up at the great intersection in République. *'Il te l'a donné ce matin, c'est ça?'*

I nodded. 'Yes, he gave it to me this morning.'

His *'c'est ça?'* was making me nervous, the Spanish Inquisition, French-style. This was just too ridiculous! So he had worked it out, *finally* – something that had never crossed his mind, not back then, *never,* until now: Carlo had given me this watch. Something that meant nothing now – and that had meant nothing even back then. I had met Marc.

But now he was obviously really working it over in his mind. And he wouldn't look at me. 'So this morning, just after you left me, you had a lesson with him, *just* like you did that first time we met. And he gave you this watch, *c'est ça?'*

'No, Marc, it's not that simple,' I said, sensing that we had definitely slipped into cross-examination. 'He gave me the watch, but I didn't want it.'

He turned to look at me then. And I realised, no, this wasn't sounding too convincing.

'So you were *still* seeing him, Annie, when we started going out, *c'est ça?'*

And so we were back at the beginning. If we'd been in court, Your Honour would have told him as much. 'Well, what did you expect – that I should say, "Oh, *sorry,* Carlo, I've just met a man, my future husband, *actually,* so I can't teach you any more?" *C'est ça?'*

He slapped his hand against the steering wheel. *'Non, tu n'as toujours pas répondu à ma question!* I'm not talking about *teaching* him. I'm talking about *seeing* him – *seeing* him, Annie!'

But I knew that. The thing is, I *had* told Carlo that first Monday back when I'd refused that small gold package: 'I've met someone. It's over, Carlo.' But had Marc done as much? Had he told Frédérique when he went back to her, that first night?

'Oh, *right*! You mean like you and Frédérique?' I was ignoring the look in his eye, the clenched jaw. 'Like you were seeing her, *still*? Like you're *still* seeing her?'

'*Merde*, Annie!' His voice was raised as he pulled the car over with a sudden swerve to the side of the road and a brutal yank on the handbrake. 'What are you talking about? *C'est complètement différent, ça!*'

We had pulled in across a bus stop. An elderly couple was staring at us – the man shaking his head. So now we had an audience. And above, there she was again, the great bronze lady towering over us with her olive branch extended. No, it would take more than this to make peace between us.

'Oh yes, my mistake. That's completely different, isn't it?' I reached down for the handbag by my feet. 'Because you're just *living* with her. That's all!'

'*Annie*, I told you, she is going to move out. I've already explained this. There's nothing —'

But she was there in my head again, his Sleeping Beauty. And a bus had pulled in behind us, looming menacing in the rearview mirror, the driver letting us have it with his horn. Meanwhile the old man had moved in on us, and was muttering angrily through my closed window. The woman was looking on, anxious, wringing her hands. I reached for the door handle.

'Oh, Annie, *ne fais pas ça.*' Marc's hand was on my wrist now, backing down. 'This is silly. Come on. Let's go home.'

But a wave of panic had engulfed me. *Home?* 'Where's home, Marc?'

I needed to get some air. My eyes were stinging. I didn't want to start crying, not here with this lot looking on, hostile. I opened the door and got out as the old man retreated like a small dog behind a gate – all bark.

I leant back into the car. 'To *your* place, perhaps? So tell me, Marc, where would I sleep – on the couch?'

But his foot was already on the accelerator before I could slam the door shut properly, the wheels skidding and screeching as he sped off – the smell of burning rubber.

The old guy was barking again, his hands flying up in protest. '*Oh là là là! Regarde-moi ça, ces jeunes fous!*'

Those young fools. He was talking about us.

I remember our very first fight. I say *fight*, but when I think about it, it was hardly worth a leaf of that grand lady's olive branch. Not back in those days.

It was my birthday, my twenty-sixth, and our first anniversary, so we had arranged to meet after work, around the massive shopping complex at Les Halles, in the middle of Paris. Marc had discovered some new bar and declared it to be *the place* to go to on my birthday, with him, my lover.

That morning I was running late for work, still dressed in only my bra and underpants, sitting cross-legged in front of my bedroom mirror, lipstick poised, fire-engine red, to herald in my birthday, herald in my happiness... my new love. Those bright lipsticks I would gradually stop wearing in my thirties, the Femme Fatale blood-red crimsons fading like colours washed out by the sunlight, dimming gradually to a subdued Misty Rose as I matured into an older woman.

Dimming, as would this passion.

'Tell me where the bar is. I'll meet you there.'

'*Non.*' He leant down to kiss me on the back of my neck, on my ear, in a rush to get to work, his tie flapping over my forehead, tickling my nose. 'You'll get lost. And that would be very sad on your birthday. *Je te retrouve en haut de l'escalier, aux Halles, à la sortie*, at seven.'

Right, I'd thought as I pursed my painted lips like a geisha girl in the mirror – at the bottom of the escalators, near the exit. As he reached the doorway, he turned back to me, grinning, standing in his blue shirt, the colour of his eyes, the colour of a summer sky, the colour of my world. 'That lipstick won't go with your *foulard*!'

'*Scarf?*' I called after him. 'What scarf?'

But he had already slipped away. I caught a glimpse of it in the mirror, a flash of colour, like a ray of sunshine, burning bright in the corner of my eye. I turned and there it was, spread across our unmade bed, across the crumpled white sheets – this ripple of fabric, burnt orange, exquisite in its intensity, like a still life: Cézanne's *Apples and Oranges*.

Seven p.m., and I was on time for once. It was my birthday, after all. I had come straight out at the exit to the métro and was standing at the bottom of the escalators, like he told me. And so I had waited, keen for him to come, standing there in my little black dress and my glorious scarf – a birthday girl waiting for her lover. Beattie had picked out a vivid rust-red lipstick for me in our lunch hour, from Printemps. 'A birthday present to ya, honey,' she'd drawled. 'To match your cowgirl's shawl.'

But at seven-thirty I was still waiting, still keen but slightly disappointed that he had chosen this night of all nights to be late. I had looked around, anxious for him to arrive, pulling my scarf a little tighter around my arms, as a group of guys called to me, '*Viens avec nous, cherie! Il ne vient pas!*' Come with us, darling! He's not coming!

Not exactly the nicest of places for our rendezvous. Les Halles is an enormous underground labyrinth, a maze of shops, cinemas and bars accessible from the métro at its base. Long, steep escalators span several floors, leading up to the outside world from various angles of the complex like something out of *Brave New*

World – rows of faces gliding up and down, staring coolly at each other as they move in opposite directions. It was not the ideal meeting point, given its sheer size and orientation and that, back then, mobile phones weren't quite *à la mode* yet. So perhaps I had misunderstood Marc's instructions? But *no*, he told me to wait by the exit at the bottom of the escalators. And so I had, for an hour and a half. By 8.40 p.m. I had of course gone up and down the escalator a fair few times, and even tried the other exits. But there was no trace of him.

Finally, two hours later, when my lipstick had worn away with my fretting and when I'd had enough catcalls to make me want to get a gun out and shoot the blighters dead, I gave up. When I threw the front door open, letting it bang against the wall hard enough to leave a dent, the phone was ringing. I had heard it as I walked through the front courtyard and up the corridor when I reached the second floor. By this time, though, I was feeling so sorry for myself, I didn't feel like running for it.

Let him sweat. He had obviously completely forgotten about me.

But his voice on the other end, shouting into the phone over the raucous party-makers in the background, said it all. 'Where *were* you, Annie?'

'Waiting for you, like you told me to – at the bottom of the escalators, by the métro exit!'

'*Non!*' He had to holler over the crowd as they sang out '*Bon Anniversaire*, Annie!'. 'I said at the *top* of the escalators, *en haut*.

At the exit to Les Halles, Annie!'

· And so it dawned on me. I had confused the words *en haut* and *en bas*. At the top and the bottom, just like I always confused *à droite* and *à gauche*. To your right and to your left. Even in English I would confuse them – hence the reason I could never read maps. And the reason I missed my own surprise party at the new bar.

'You're a goose, Annie MacIntyre!' I heard Beattie call out from somewhere in the crowd.

So how could we stay angry with each other? Back then, they were merely lovers' tiffs, bridgeable with a kiss.

Chapter
eighteen

Back in Lherm I often used to stand by the window in Charlie's darkened room as he slept – a stolen moment when I could take a good, long look at our son without him protesting, without him pulling his face into that tough-boy scowl, the dreaded lead-in to adolescence. In sleep, his face was as beautifully perfect as when he was little.

I'd look up at the sky from his window, sprinkled with hundreds of stars. On a clear night in Lherm I could always see those stars, and sometimes the moon, looming large among them.

Back in Sydney when Charlie was still a baby, he would some-times wake in the middle of the night, his screams piercing the calm. And we'd find him standing in his cot in the dark, his face hot and sticky, stained by his tears, his hands clinging to the cot bars and his body shaking, wet with sweat.

'What is it, Charlie? Did you have a bad dream?'

But he couldn't tell us what fiendish beast had terrified him so. We could only see it in his eyes – wide open, glazed over – and hear it in his screams. So I would take him in my arms, this inconsolable little boy, his fears exposed like a raw wound and not yet hidden by a scowl. As I held him, felt the moist heat of his body, my lips caressing his hot cheeks, breathing in his sweet baby smell, I'd draw back the curtain of his bedroom window. Pointing up to the purple–grey sky, I would whisper in his ear, 'Charlie, can you see the moon? Can you see it there?'

He wouldn't hear me at first, through his cries, through the thick fog of his semi-consciousness, but then suddenly he would catch in his breath, a little shudder rolling through his shoulders as his eyes glanced up at the sky, his finger shooting up, following mine and pointing with me at that strange grey–white circle. His fears would instantly be forgotten, chased away by that magical ball in the sky.

But tonight, here in Paris, from my old bedroom window I could see nothing – no grey–white ball to calm my fears, to dry my tears. And no Charlie in the next bedroom.

Nothing.

Beattie was out. I had no idea where. But then I remembered... She'd had a lover.

It must have been going on around the time I was seeing Carlo, or Marc perhaps. I couldn't remember. Beattie and I had always been close, yet strangely she kept this one well hidden. We lived together in our small two-bedroom apartment, but I had never met him, not once. Unlike Marc, he never came back here. And so she would disappear, sometimes for an hour or so, sometimes for a few, but never for a whole night – stolen moments that she refused to talk to me about, despite my questions, despite my teasing: 'Tell me then, young lady, where were you last night? Out with *him* again?'

So I wondered, was she with her mystery man now? I wished that she was here with me, my old friend, the *older* Beattie – the woman I could confide in and laugh with about our boys, about our men. She would know what to make of all of this.

'Annie,' she'd say, 'it's a sign.'

For Beattie, everything was a sign. When Charlie was born, she called me. 'Annie, I've been thinking,' she said. 'That bump on his head, it's a sign of intelligence.' And I'd laughed. 'No, Beattie, it's just a sign that he got knocked around a bit when he tried to push past my cervix.' And later, when Marc lost his job, 'That's your sign, Annie. It's time to come back to France.'

There was a reason for everything. Her faith kept her sure of that. As far as friends went, Beattie and I were an odd pair. She'd grown up in Ireland with strict Catholic parents – schooled by the nuns, with mass every Sunday and hell to pay if she missed it. Her father would still ring her every Sunday at midday, straight after mass. I was raised in Sydney, a public-school girl with a staunchly atheist mother who forbade me to attend scripture classes, *on principle*. 'I won't have them filling your head with that religious crap,' she'd say. So every Tuesday morning while my friends went off to scripture – to their Anglican, Catholic, Greek Orthodox or Hebrew classes – I would sit in the school library alone, with the feeling that I was missing out on something.

Paradoxically then, Beattie's faith was like the forbidden fruit. It intrigued me, her stories about saints, about the nuns with their wicked punishments, confession and the eternal guilt – like something out of those old midday movies I'd watched during the school holidays: Audrey Hepburn in *The Nun's Story*.

So as I stood there in my old bedroom, looking up at the cloudy nothingness, wishing for Charlie, I wondered, if I told Beattie the truth, what would she say about all of this?

Chapter
nineteen

She was turning her teapot, three times in one direction, three times in the other – clockwise, then anti-clockwise.

For as long as I'd known her, Beattie had *always* performed this ritual every morning – just like my grandmother used to, except that Grandma had always done it the *other* way round first: anti-clockwise, then clockwise. I wondered fleetingly as I watched Beattie now, whether this was because Grandma had lived in Australia, in the southern hemisphere, so her actions were controlled subconsciously by the moon – like the tide, like water going down the plughole anticlockwise, in the opposite direction to water going down the plughole in France. Of course, Marc would say that this was me getting off the point *again*. But then, he wasn't with me that morning. And, to be honest, I was purposely trying *not* to think about him, about where he was at that very moment, where he was all last night. And with whom...

It was Tuesday – my third morning back in the crazy time warp, so I was simply trying to think about nothing much in particular except to stay sane, to let the tide pull me whichever way she wanted, to offer no resistance, nor even try to swim across her.

I was all out of puff, floating out to sea now without a paddle.

Beattie seemed to be in a particularly good mood. She was humming, even though it was 7.15 a.m. precisely according to my watch, *his* watch, and we had only another five minutes before having to head off together for work. Yet here she was, sitting across from me at our small kitchen table, in a black woollen skirt, tights and a polo-neck jumper, the colour of jade, the colour of her eyes, fully dressed, except that wrapped around her head was a white bath towel.

She had come in late last night, long after I had finally thrown myself into bed, desolate and lost in my big double bed, the smell of Marc's body on the sheets still, the smell of his skin, his hair on the pillow – making me want to cry out loud for him, for *us*, for Charlie.

So I was still wide awake when I heard her slip the key into the lock and as she crept around the apartment like a cat-burglar. I had wondered again, why the mystery? We used to tell each other everything. But her mystery lover had remained a mystery.

She was looking at me now, over the brim of her steaming teacup. 'So have you told him?'

'Told who what?'

'An-*nie*!' She had that look in her eyes – amused. 'You know *who*! Car-lo!'

I stared at her, blank, wondering what she meant; those green eyes, the arch of her auburn eyebrows in cross-examination mode.

'Well, you know…' She blew on her tea softly. 'You *did* have a lesson with him yesterday.'

'Yes.' I nodded. 'So?'

'Well?' She took a sip, slow and cautious. 'Didn't you tell him about your Marlboro Man?'

'If you mean Marc, Beattie, no, I didn't mention him to Carlo.'

I saw it then, a flicker, her surprise, as she placed her cup down – a delicate movement, like a cat placing its paw, its preening complete. 'You didn't tell him? But why not, Annie? Surely you —' Then she paused, her eyes drawn to my wrist. She had obviously noticed the time.

I pushed my chair back. 'Yeah, we should go.'

Why, I wondered as I moved towards the sink, was everyone on my back about this: first Marc and now Beattie?

But then I remembered, in the week leading up to the night I met Marc, I had moped around this apartment lamenting my decision not to go away with Carlo and driven Beattie mad with my foolish misery, until finally on Saturday she had ordered me to go shopping with her – for some serious therapy. So we had gone to Galeries Lafayette – and there they'd been. The stilettos. 'A sign,' she'd said. 'You'll meet Mr Right in those.'

Beattie hadn't moved from the table, so as I stood over the sink rinsing my plate, I wondered if she planned to take the métro with her white turban atop her head. The old rituals that I had performed in this apartment, day in, day out, some fifteen years back, felt stiff and unnatural now – the taps unfamiliar, the cupboard drawers, *and where on earth did we keep the washing-up liquid*? Below in the courtyard, our neighbours were talking: the elderly lady who lived above us with her small white terrier and the dark-haired, arty-looking man with horn-rimmed glasses who played the clarinet and lived up the hallway; his cool, sensual refrains floating through our open doorway every evening as Beattie and I prepared dinner. I had long forgotten about these people, this little world that I had once lived in.

'Annie?'

I turned. Beattie was sitting very still with her back to me. Yes, we were going to be late again. But this was typical of Beattie; time wasn't something she worried about. The world outside could wait, as far as she was concerned. 'I haven't seen that watch before. When did you get it?'

Like my mother said, there *really* was no free lunch. I was paying for it now, for this watch that I had clipped on to my wrist without thinking.

'Yesterday,' I murmured quickly. 'Shouldn't we get going, Beattie?'

She stood up then with a sigh, her hands moving up to her turban. Wet, her hair fell smooth and dark around her shoulders like burnt toffee. 'What's going on, Annie?'

I hadn't expected this – her gentle directness caught me off-guard. Beattie was a green-eyed nymph, a fairy elf from my past. I could see it in her eyes as she stood across from me in our small kitchen, blocking my path to the doorway. Beattie knew about the watch. I didn't have to tell her – she just knew. She had endured my tortured deliberations about whether I should tell Carlo we were through, my angry outpourings that I couldn't take it any more, waiting for him to call, but then seen me fly out the door after he'd rung to tell me where to meet him. He'd only have to click his fingers.

So suddenly I wanted to tell her, tell her about the predicament I was in now, just like I used to, about this crazy mess – that it was *me* but older, even though I mightn't look it. Even though I certainly wasn't acting it. To tell her *about Charlie*.

'Oh, Beattie —'

'It's *him* again, isn't it?' she said, cutting across me as she began twisting her hair up into a bun on top of her head. 'Oh, Annie, for goodness' *sake*, why didn't you just tell him it was over?'

I realised then, *no*, of course I couldn't tell her. This was the Beattie from my past – the Beattie that only knew about insignificant problems, problems that meant nothing now in the bigger scheme of things, in the life that I had lived since.

As a woman heading into my forties, I had moved on.

Chapter
twenty

$\mathcal{W}$e met for lunch at the Panis, on the Quai de Montebello, left bank, just across from Notre Dame. That's the thing about being together for so long: you fight, but you don't keep it going. You can't be bothered.

Marc was there ahead of me again, already seated with his back to the room, a bottle of white on the table, two glasses already poured. I wondered if he'd ordered our favourite, the one he used to make *me* order because I could never pronounce it properly.

'*Poo-il-lee Foom-eh, s'il vous plaît,*' I'd say to the waiter, who'd inevitably stare back at me, blank. It was only after I'd had a few goes at it and made a *complete* fool of myself that Marc would intervene.

'*Pouilly Fumé,*' he'd say smoothly, as only a French person can, with a wink to the waiter.

And the waiter would smile back. '*Ah oui, bien sûr!*'

Their little joke together.

But this time Marc had obviously gone ahead and ordered a

bottle without waiting for me. Funny, that. Once he had found me *so* enchanting. Now he just needed a drink.

As I came up behind him, I thought how weird it was not to see his bald patch. I realised then I actually missed it, that bare part of his head, that tiny vulnerability that he'd developed, even though it was no bigger than a twenty-cent coin. I reached out and tapped the top of his head lightly with the palm of my hand as I slid past him into my chair.

'Gone,' I said.

'*Quoi?*' He smiled at me, puzzled. 'What's gone?'

'Nothing.' He'd always been a little over-sensitive about it, so it was best not to push it. 'Nothing that we won't get back.'

'Ah, *oui*.' He was nodding, as if he'd understood. 'That's right, Annie.'

His eyes looked into mine, earnest, and his voice held such conviction that I realised he must have thought I was referring to something much more serious than his bald patch: to us, to Charlie. I recognised this post-fight look. He was making an effort. Like me, he didn't want to keep it going. There was too much at stake. So I leant over the table, kissed him, my lips on his, soft. I had forgotten just how soft they were. Marc reached his hand over to mine and just held it.

I smiled. 'You seem up.' Had he found the answer, I wondered? Would we be out of this mess by the end of the day? By the end of the week at the worst? I could bear it then, I could get through it if he could tell me he had; that we would be home with Charlie before we knew it, before we'd even ordered the main course!

He raised his glass and clinked it softly against mine. 'Well, I'm just happy to see you again. *C'est tout.*'

But there was something about the way he averted his eyes, distracted, something about him that I could only perceive having lived with him for so long, that made me wonder. Yes, I did wonder – about Frédérique. I pulled my hand away.

'No.' I took a sip of wine and watched him brush breadcrumbs off the tablecloth, nervous. 'Tell me what you're *really* thinking about.'

There was something on his mind, of course – but not Frédérique. His eyes met mine again. 'My father rang me at work this morning.'

It is rare that I am lost for words, but I was then. His leg was jiggling up and down under the table, making the wine in my glass vibrate, its surface forming perfect concentric waves. I reached across the table, my hand on his.

'Your father?' My heart was beating fast.

But he shook his head and smiled. 'We should eat something.' He raised his hand to signal the waiter. '*Tu as faim?* Christ, I could eat a duck!'

The 'duck' thing was an old one, a confusion of expressions about the horse and Marc's favourite dish, *Magret de Canard*. But I'd suddenly lost my appetite, thinking about his father. I had forgotten about him.

'Marc – please, don't do this!' The couple at the next table shot us a look. I tried to pitch my voice lower. 'Tell me, *please*. Tell me what you plan to —'

'*Non, mais alors,* Annie!' He had that defensive look in his eyes, pure innocence. 'I'm not *planning* anything. I just told you my father called me. *Et alors?*'

The waiter was standing over us suddenly, pad in hand, impatient. '*Et alors?*' Echoing Marc. Cheeky, I thought. '*Vous avez choisi M'sieur, 'Dame?*'

I decided I should ignore Monsieur Echo. '*Please,* Marc, we need to talk about this!'

But Marc's attention was on the waiter now, not me. '*Magret de Canard pour moi.*'

He knew I hated it when he ordered for himself first. According to my mother, my father would never have done that. But Marc always did it when he was pissed off with me.

The waiter had turned to me. '*Et Madame?*' I wondered suddenly if that's how waiters picked the rude ones – by the way they didn't order for their partners first.

'*Sandwich au fromage.*' I smiled up at him to let him know that it was okay, I was used to it.

'*Madame,* this is not a café.' His English was perfect; the tone as cold as fish. 'We don't serve sandwiches.'

Chapter
twenty-one

I'd met Marc's parents, Rosa and Maurice, very early in the piece. We drove out one weekend in April, leaving the capital behind, and headed south-east into the countryside, towards Marc's family home. Ozouer le Voulgis is a mere forty or so kilometres from Paris, yet once there it is as though you have stepped into the middle of nowhere. The land out there is flat, *dead* flat. You can walk along the road leading into Ozouer and see for miles — a clear view from the cemetery, through the fields of beetroot and corn to the church and out the other side to more fields of beetroot and corn. There's a post office, a café, one shop, one *boulangerie* and that's it. They took the train station away a long time ago. But there are *two* cemeteries — which says it all.

'This is where you grew up?' I teased that first time he took me out there, playing the city slicker too well. 'Where's the nightlife?'

'*Tu verras.*' He smiled. You'll see.

That evening, he took me down to the river just as the sun was going down and we lay in the long grass at the water's edge, hidden from the fishermen standing on the bridge, a rickety wooden arch spanning the river some two hundred metres further along.

I saw it then – Ozouer's nightlife.

'The sky,' he said after, as we lay on our backs in the damp grass, looking up, shivering but happy. 'You see now? This is the nightlife in Ozouer.'

It was true. The beauty of Ozouer is in its sky. No matter where you are, as you look out across all the flatness, the sky spreads around you like a giant Imax screen, an astronomer's paradise.

We were on our way home, walking past one of the cemeteries in the darkness, with just the light of the full moon to guide us, when he squeezed my hand. '*Mes grands-parents et mes arrières grands-parents* are in there. You want to meet them?'

'No!' I pulled away giggling, breaking into a run and screaming as he ran after me.

'*Tu en es sûre*, Annie? You really don't want to meet them? I'm sure they would *love* to meet you!'

Marc's parents lived in the centre of the village in an old stone farmhouse that his great-great-grandfather had built in the late 1700s. Years later, during our trips back to France from Australia, Charlie would disappear into the attic for hours, riffling through the ancient trunks, through the dusty boxes of old wooden toys, the stacks of cartoon magazines, cobwebs etched between the crumbling yellowed pages – a child's treasure chest.

I remember that first weekend together, waking up in Marc's

old bedroom, the sun streaming in through the French doors on to the garden. I had crept around his room before Marc had woken, exploring the books on his shelves, books from his childhood, a collection of model cars and fighter planes, plastic soldiers piled high in faded Poulaîn chocolate boxes. A pile of little boy drawings – cars and horses, and others of soldiers fighting gory battles with guns and canons. And the later drawings, obviously from Marc's more turbulent teenage years – pictures of young women, their giant breasts rising off the pages like swollen water-filled balloons, ready to burst.

Later that morning, we had wandered down with Maurice to the local *boulangerie*, a hundred metres or so down the road just opposite the village church, its bells ringing out Sunday morning's mass. The bells ring out a lot in Ozouer.

Maurice was a quiet man, like Marc, I suppose. He certainly didn't have a great deal to say to me. I was, after all, some strange creature from a faraway country who had wooed his son, who would eventually woo him to the other side of the world. He would watch us and shake his head.

But Rosa would sit with me in the garden, this petite woman with dark eyes and grey hair, once as black as Marc's, telling me stories – about Marc, about the world he had grown up in. She would bring out the stacks of dusty old albums, black-and-white photos, staged portraits of Marc's ancestors, his great-grandmother Morvan, standing straight-backed and solid, decked out in a long black dress – her grimace as stiff as her steel bodice. Someone had obviously died.

It was interesting to watch Marc and his father together – so complicit as they walked side by side in the garden, communicating without talking. There was an easy silence between them that I'd never had with my mother. Maurice was shorter and thicker set than his son, yet the likeness was in their faces – that same beautiful regularity in their features, a strength there that had originally attracted me to Marc: this beautiful, dark knight, his blue eyes piercing a hole in my heart through the visor of his silver armour.

So I wondered, was that what had attracted Rosa to Maurice? As a young woman, she had lived through the Second World War – another world, another time. But like me, she met Maurice in Paris. She'd been sitting on the 18.06 train at Gare de l'Est, waiting for it to pull out and take her home to Gretz, another village south-east of Paris. She was tired, having worked the double shift at the Hôpital Lariboisière. When Maurice got on and sat down beside her, he had smiled and said *Bonsoir*. But that was it. In those days, men were more polite. It was a given. But they didn't speak for the rest of the trip. *Not* that he didn't think about it, he would tell her later – this petite young woman who had smiled back at him with her big brown eyes.

When she got off the train, she didn't notice straight away, not until she had reached her bike by the side of the platform, that she had left her shopping bag behind on the luggage rack overhead. Times were tough back then – it was post-war France, when the population was still in the throes of going without. And so she had cursed her own foolishness out loud, cursing herself in no uncertain terms. It was only when she saw him just a few metres away from her, standing awkwardly with her shopping bag in tow, that she fell suddenly silent.

Years after, they would laugh about it, this funny first encounter. Because Maurice had simply handed over the bag, dipped his cap and then walked the rest of the way home – a very long way, as it turned out, having got off the train one stop too soon. And she hadn't even thanked him for his troubles. Not until the next evening, when he got on the train, on the exact same carriage and sat on the exact same seat… as had she.

It wasn't until many, many visits later that I noticed how old Maurice seemed, having aged almost overnight. He was ill, but we hadn't known it then. Rosa will tell you the story over and over again. He was only fifty-nine, just a year away from retirement. He'd been tired, *so tired*, but he wouldn't go to the doctor. 'He always hated doctors,' she said, until one day he just couldn't get out of bed.

He died not long after we left together for Australia.

I often wondered if Marc blamed me somehow… whether he thought, if he'd been around he could have done something; that he could have prevented it.

But then, wasn't it just fate? Whether Marc was in Australia or France was neither here nor there. His father was dying. Leukaemia, they said. 'If only we'd made him go to the doctor sooner,' Rosa had lamented. But I wondered, would it have helped?

He was dying.

'How *is* he, Marc?'

The question was absurd, grotesque in its simplicity, in its implications. But I didn't know how else to put it, wanting to go in gently. Yet in my panic I had donned leaden gloves. The thought of his father, the thought of this man who had meant so much to Marc, whose death had left a wide open wound in his heart, a wide open rift between us...

He was still alive.

We had left the Panis and crossed the Quai de Montebello to take the métro at Saint Michel and make our way back to work. But when we'd reached the top of the stairs leading down into the underground labyrinth of tunnels, lunchtime commuters pushing like frenzied ants behind us, I slipped my hand into his and pulled him aside. He hadn't answered my question.

'Marc?'

Nothing, except his sigh, like air released from a pressure cooker.

We were standing over by the wall bordering the River Seine, the blue–grey serpent moving beneath us. Beyond, in the eerie light of this blustery grey Tuesday, the Notre Dame rose like a great white castle on the Ile de la Cité opposite, a fairytale castle, like in the pictures I had pored over as a girl.

'What did he say, Marc? What did you talk about?'

He shoved his hands into his pockets and shrugged his shoulders against the cold. 'Stuff.'

His half smile, a boyish smile on his young face, made me want to cry. This was Charlie's face. This was even Charlie's *word* – the word that we had both adopted since, this great word that said it all: I don't want to talk about it. But I didn't want to play the game now. This was too important.

'That's all, Marc? *Stuff?*'

He pulled his hands from his pockets then turned, his back to the river, arms folded, defensive. '*Oui, c'est tout.*'

And again he reminded me of Charlie when he was three, when he refused point-blank to take off his Batman suit, insisting that he *could* wear it to bed, even though it was skin-tight neck-to-toe 100 per cent black nylon, two sizes too small for him and we were in the middle of a heatwave. He had folded his arms across his chest, determined, his face closed just like Marc now. I'd had to wait until he'd fallen asleep to slip it off him, to wrestle his little arms and legs out of that costume, his skin hot and sticky – breathing in that lovely sweet smell of him as he slept.

'Oh, Marc. . .' I reached my hand up to his shoulder and felt it tense under my touch. 'Can't we talk about this now?'

Chapter
twenty-two

The public parks in Paris are beautiful, like a child's drawing – pathways winding through perfect vivid-green grassy banks, clusters of flowers, neatly clipped trees dotted here and there, and a fountain in the middle where model sailing boats float, pulled along by string.

But you cannot walk on the grass.

When I first told Marc I wanted to return to Australia, that I missed the ease of walking up the street in shorts and a T-shirt, walking barefoot on the grass, in the sand, that I wanted him to see the country *I* had grown up in, he said, '*Eh bien, on y va!*' Fine, let's go!

By then, we'd been together for three years. In those early days in France, nothing was a problem. I was homesick, so he would take me home. But I don't think he had really contemplated the distance. It was only when we arrived, after we began to set up our new home in Australia and had found work, that it hit him, I think. Australia was a long way from France, and not merely in terms of kilometres.

Up until then, *I* had been the *étrangère* – the one with the accent, the funny person who made the French laugh when I tried to pronounce certain words, when I tried to roll my *rrrs* to no avail. But now *he* was the stranger. And I had no family to offer him. I was a rolling stone with no history. My grandmother had died some three years back, and I hadn't spoken to my mother since. I didn't even let her know I was back.

'Do you miss your family?' I would ask him in those early days.

'*Non.*' He'd smile. 'I have you!'

But I would wonder sometimes what he was thinking about on those evenings when he'd arrive home from work, the strain written across his young face and in his frown as he stared off into space at the dinner table: the strain of learning a new language, of coping with our Australian ways – the 'she'll be right, mate' ease of his new colleagues at work.

I fell pregnant in that first year we arrived in Sydney, within those first few months, as if my body had decided, I'm home now. And apart from the sheer thrill of that news, I had felt it then – a sense of relief. Now I could offer Marc something of *my* family, something of *me* – we could make our own family, starting with us. Starting from zero, with this baby.

'*Epouse-moi,* Annie,' Marry me, Annie, he said when I told him; the simplicity of his words making butterflies flutter around our unborn child, fluttering mad around my heart as we walked barefoot in the sand down at Tamarama beach. We stood together at the edge of the water and looked out to sea. I had swum out the back here as a girl, diving under the water with my girlfriends, holding on to the seaweed as the waves rolled over us.

'Marry me, Annie, *marry me, marry me!*'

So the next day we hopped on a bus, heading for the Rocks down past the Quay, running past the ferries and tourists, the smell of fish and chips and the harbour, heading for the Registry to book our wedding.

Births, Deaths and Marriages. Take a ticket, please!

Marc whispered in my ear as I pressed on the button, 'Don't take the wrong ticket, Annie!'

We had waited on blue plastic seats for our number to be called, sitting next to a couple holding their newborn baby, the simplicity of it all making us laugh, and laughing still when the woman behind the counter told us, 'You have to wait at least one month and one day to get married – it's the rule.'

It was only after, when we'd stepped back out into the harsh sunlight of that Sydney summer and were walking alongside the harbour, our reservation receipt folded neatly away in my purse, that he said it.

'*C'est tout?*' Is that all?

'Yep!' I smiled, slipping my hand into his, kissing him square and hard on the lips. 'It's as simple as that!'

'But don't you want to invite your family?'

I turned to him as a coach pulled in beside the kerb up ahead, a load of Japanese tourists clambering down in front of us, blocking our path and taking pictures of one another standing in front of Sydney Harbour, one by one lined up against the railing.

'*What* family, Marc?'

'*Ta mère, non?*'

'*My mother?*' His question seemed absurd.

We were married one month and one day later, in a civil ceremony down at the Registry – a happy heathen's wedding. Without my mother.

But one night, as we lay in bed together, his hand sliding over the curve of my stomach, he asked again. '*Mais* Annie, *tu ne veux pas lui dire?*' Don't you want to tell your mother about the baby?

'You don't understand,' I told him then, my hand firmly over his. 'It's not like your family. It's not like that between my mother and me.'

After that, he didn't mention her again – not during the pregnancy at least. And so I assumed then that he understood.

Chapter
twenty-three

*W*hen Marc's father died, I was a big, round seven months pregnant with Charlie, so I couldn't travel back to France with him for the funeral.

From that first call, when Rosa had told him that Maurice was dying, and in the weeks leading up to his father's death, Marc sank into a deep and silent state of immobility, grieving for his father before he had died.

His silence scared me – the stony, sullen stillness. He was morose, which was to be expected, of course. But there was such blackness in his grieving. It was *more* than sadness. He was angry. Never in the three years I had known him had I seen him like that. I wanted to reach out and take him in my arms, envelope him with my body, press against him, press *into* him, take his pain away. An open wound of hurt glistened in his eyes whenever he looked at me – those clear blue eyes, that mischievous glint, the mirror of my soul, my happiness, had become dark grey pools of sorrow and bitterness.

'I'm going to bed,' he'd say, getting up from the kitchen table without warning – without looking back.

And I would find him lying in the dark on his back staring up at the ceiling, his body like a cold, rigid corpse on top of the bed covers. That happy young man who had walked with me along the sand when I told him I was pregnant, who had cried out to sea, '*Epouse-moi*, Annie!', lay hidden, buried underneath a great mound of grief that I could not penetrate.

I soon became frustrated, frustrated with my big bloated body, bloated with endorphins, overflowing with hormone-induced happiness. I wanted to give them up to him and say, 'Here, take this, it will help you sleep. It will take the pain away!'

To take his pain away with a kiss.

But when I would lie down next to Marc, rolling my great tummy towards him, my arm across his chest and my hand sliding over his heart, feeling for its beat – a beat that was once in sync with mine – he would shrug me away with his elbow and turn over on to his side, his back to me. So I would lie there, in the shadow of his silence, telling myself, it will be all right – he is grieving.

I would sleep and dream of his hand on my swollen belly, where it had lingered throughout the earlier months of my pregnancy, his fingertips running over my skin stretched tight, searching for Charlie's already funny elongated feet kicking from below the surface. But I would wake, woken by the silence, still in the shadow of his back.

Déjà Vu

Sometimes Rosa would ring late at night and he would shut the door in the hallway behind him, speaking in hushed tones. But through the closed door I could hear the agony in his voice, the pain in his heart. And long after he had put down the phone, I could hear the fear in his silence, when he would stay in the hallway, sitting in the darkness, while I waited, anxious, hovering behind the door, wanting to go to him, to encircle him with my arms and tell him it was okay, I knew he was afraid.

His father was dying. But what scared me most of all was that a part of Marc was dying with him. His immobility terrified me. *Why wouldn't he go to him?* Those two men, their faces so alike, their movements, their silent complicity. I was afraid for him, afraid that one day, looking back, he would regret it and that his regret would consume him with guilt. And his guilt would make him bitter – that the bitterness in his voice, in his eyes when I caught him staring at me, would stay. I had lived with bitterness as a girl – I had seen it in my mother's eyes, heard it in her voice. 'She wasn't always this way, Annie!'

'Marc, why won't you go to him?' I asked one night.

But he wouldn't look at me.

'Are you afraid to leave? Are you afraid the baby will come when you're over there?'

'Is *that* what you think it is?' Such venom in his voice. I let it ride. He is grieving, I told myself.

But that last night, when Rosa's call had come finally, *inevitably,* as we lay in bed together in the dark, his bag packed in the corner, ready for his flight out in the morning, I tried to tell him, 'I understand, Marc – what you're feeling...'

Nothing.

It wasn't until I was just beginning to doze off that he said it. 'You understand *nothing*, Annie.'

His grief had become a venomous snake, *and oh, how it stung*, as I bit my lip and held my breath, trying not to cry.

'Stay as long as you need to,' I told him in the morning as we sat opposite each other in the airport café. 'Stay longer if you want. Don't worry about the baby. It won't be here for a while.'

And he nodded without saying anything. Silence.

Then he left.

Two weeks off from the due date, I became anxious. He had been gone a month. Despite what I'd said, I was hoping he *would* be back sooner, for I was afraid the baby would come early after all.

But then he rang, and I could hear it in his voice, still – the anger. So I lied, saying I was fine, *we* were fine, and that he should take his time. 'You understand *nothing*, Annie,' he'd said.

He came home eventually, of course, just before my nine months was up, the *decent* thing to do – yet not the most reassuring.

When I tried to get him to talk about his father, he would slip into his stony silences, sullen and unreachable, not the old Marc at all. And I fought back my rising panic that it was as I feared; that something in Marc had died when he buried his father back at Ozouer.

And I thought of the cemetery that we had walked past, that I had run from, giggling and screaming, its high stone wall bordering the road leading into the village, leading towards his home. 'Do you want to meet my great-grandparents, Annie?' He had buried his father there, as his father had buried his. That dour history was repeating itself – his ancestors' grim faces in those black-and-white portraits haunting our present, our future.

'He's angry with me, Beattie.'

'Give him time to grieve,' she told me over the phone.

'He blames me.'

'*No*, Annie, it's not that – you don't understand.'

There they were again – his words to me about his father. And I remembered then, they had been mine too – my words to him about my mother.

So I decided to let the wave crash over me, over my great big tummy, the promise of our rosy future, our happiness. After death comes birth, I told myself, like those buttons for the tickets at the Registry office. When he was ready, he would come back to me. Beattie was right. For now, he just needed time to grieve.

And then there was Charlie.

But once he'd pushed his way into the world, kicking and

screaming, hardly ever sleeping until he hit three, I'd barely time to brush my teeth, much less dwell on the meaning of life and death.

Chapter
twenty-four

*I*n those early days, those lazy Sundays when we drove out to his family home, I had envied Marc his childhood – this couple that had loved him, that had kept his room as it was from his beginnings to when he left home as a young man, and beyond.

But following his father's death, when we would return with Charlie as a baby and Charlie as a small boy, Marc's home, his old room, this *still life* like a shrine to his childhood, to his ancestors in those grim black-and-white photos, made me anxious. Rosa had kept his bedroom safe for him, even as a married man with his *own* son. But it wasn't just his room. The house had become a memorial to Maurice, to his ancestors: drawers and cupboards cluttered with documents, records and broken bits, piles and piles of things that served no purpose any more. The history that had once intrigued me, this house where Marc's father had grown up, and his father's father and *his* father before him...had become claustrophobic, strangely morbid. Like a map, yellowed at the edges, already charted for Charlie.

Those objects I had once picked up and treasured in my hands – worn wooden pipes, silver spoons and china plates – had become nothing more than dusty, chipped relics from another era, of other people's lives that were foreign to me.

And as I sat opposite Rosa at the kitchen table, I would listen to her stories over and over, until I couldn't listen to them any more. Long after Maurice was gone, the dour, tough lives of his forebears had become her ball and chain. And I didn't want them as mine, *as Charlie's*.

I had grown up in another country, another world, with a mother who had kept nothing – nothing but a photo of my father that was never intended for *my* eyes. My mother had denied the past. She had constructed her own truth: my father was a good man.

But he was gone from our lives without a trace, save for a stolen photo.

Chapter
twenty-five

'*You* make a wish first.'

My *you* echoed like the owls hooting in the forest beyond our bedroom window back in Lherm, bouncing off the massive marble pavement stones at our feet, off the walls, floating weightless up to the ceiling.

'Not a *wish*, Annie,' Beattie hissed. 'A *prayer*. You say a prayer.'

It wasn't the first time she had brought me here, to La Madeleine – this massive church hovering like a Greek temple at the end of rue Royale, so incongruous in the middle of Paris. Corinthian columns lined up like giant fat soldiers all around its façade. We would come here after work, on those evenings when we were headed for the station, when Beattie would pull up suddenly at the corner, her hand on my wrist.

'Wait now... let's go light a candle first.'

But this evening, by the time I reached the staffroom at the end of this Tuesday, this *interminable* Tuesday when I had wondered with a sinking heart if this was to be it, if this was to be the present from now on in, and Charlie just a memory – Beattie had already decided where we were headed.

'You look like crap,' she'd said as we grabbed our coats and handbags. 'Let's go light a candle.'

I needed more than a candle. I needed a miracle.

It had been a long time since I'd popped a coin into this old collection box. 'The more the better,' as Beattie always said. We'd take our pick from the boxed wooden shelves crammed with candles the smell of vanilla cream – boxes and boxes of tapered candles, meticulously stacked, according to length, according to price...

'Who's to know if I only pay twenty centimes and take a big one?' I'd joked the first time she brought me here.

'*He'll* know.' Her gaze had lifted to the giant frescoed arched ceiling, high above our heads. 'And worse, *I'll* know. So pay up.'

Here we were again, some fifteen years on, before the candelabra stand in La Madeleine. The last time I'd stood before one of these was on my wedding day in Sydney. After the ceremony, I had slipped off by myself. I had something I needed to do.

'Light a candle for me,' Beattie had said. 'Light a candle on your wedding day, to save your soul, in the biggest cathedral you can find in that God-forsaken country.' So I had gone to Saint Mary's alone, on my wedding day, to light a candle. For Beattie.

But now, in the flickering light, Beattie looked slightly diabolic, clutching her candle, dancing shadows deepening the crevices of her eyes – her wavy mass of hair like a fiery halo.

'Okay, Annie, what are you going to *wish* for then?'

'No,' I said, smiling as I held the candlewick to the flame of another already burning on the stand, watching as it caught alight. 'It won't come true if I tell you.'

Charlie.

His candle towered high above the others, hovering like a star on a Christmas tree. I had spent up big this time.

We were making our way back through the church when Beattie stopped short suddenly, her hand on my elbow. 'Wait now...'

He was there in the shadows of the enclave, smiling at us from his pedestal like an old friend, Saint Anthony of Padua, this massive man set in stone – Beattie's favourite, her patron saint for lost causes. '*He* can find anything for you,' she'd told me.

I knew the words off by heart: 'Saint Anthony, perfect imitator of Jesus, who received from God the special power of restoring lost things, grant that I may find...'

I could hear the words in my head, hear them bouncing off the walls as Beattie took my arm in hers. *Grant that I may find him...*

Over and over, *and over*. My wish for Charlie.

Chapter
twenty-six

Even after I'd returned to Australia with Marc, Beattie and I had remained close. We would write long handwritten letters, like journal notes, scribbled thoughts, intimately intricate, about life: life back home in Sydney, hers still in France, our husbands, their annoying habits (the endless list), the birth of Charlie, then a year on her Seamus, and how many stitches we'd each had. I'd had less, but then her stomach had *supposedly* gone down quicker than mine, which admittedly I would have preferred.

'I miss you, Annie,' she wrote. 'Come back. All is forgiven!'

Her jokes.

And when we brought Charlie back once, when he was still a baby, she christened him as we bathed him in her big old tub – 'To save his soul,' she said – while I held our wine glasses and laughed as he christened her too, like a fountain over the rim of the bath, right into her face.

'Forgot to warn you about that,' I said.

'Might have known. It's in his genes.'

We didn't see each other again for a long time after – an eternity, it seemed – not until Charlie was around five, when we came over for another holiday. Beattie organised a big party in our honour. She had invited everyone: all our old friends from work, even some ex-boyfriends, long forgotten and long since married with children. 'Come casual,' she said.

I remember driving to her new home out near Fontainebleau, about sixty kilometres south-east of Paris. We'd got lost trying to find it. Marc was driving while I was supposedly navigating. But I was too distracted, too excited to focus my attention on the map, which even at the best of times, I could never follow. So we pulled up in front of Beattie's an hour late, flustered and angry with each other.

'How do I look?' I asked, suddenly nervous as I flipped down the sunshade, glancing in the mirror to check my mascara wasn't running while Marc turned off the ignition. 'Tell me honestly. Have I changed?'

'*Ca va*. You look *fine*.'

But he'd barely glanced over at me, barely looked up from the Michelin map, all his efforts concentrated on folding it neatly away. This wasn't exactly reassuring. And as I watched him meticulously smooth each section down, layer over layer with the palm of his hand, I thought about the time we drove out to Belle Ile, that first time we went away together. I'd opened the map, opened it right out on my lap. And he'd laughed.

'What?' I'd asked, smiling at him, so happy, *so* deliriously in love – 'in love with love' as my mother would say. 'What's so funny?'

'*Mais*, Annie, *chérie*, you just have to unfold it at the spot we're at.' His hand reached over, his fingers running through my hair – a lover's caress. 'Not open up the whole of France!'

'Oh, right.' I'd held the whole page up then to see if I could find the spot, spreading it out over the dashboard, its edges flapping furiously in the wind through the open window.

'So where exactly *are* we then? Can you give me a clue – in this top section, here? Or over here somewhere?'

But he never got a chance to tell me. In the next instant the map was whisked out of my hands, caught up like a parachute by the wind through the window, up and away. I turned and there it was, sailing up into the sky behind us, billowed out like a sheet on a clothesline, in the opposite direction along the autoroute, teasing the other cars as they honked behind us, the map hovering menacing over their windscreens.

I will never forget the look on Marc's face as he glanced in the rearview mirror – the wide smile, his eyes sparkling in surprise, his delight at my folly.

Where was that look now? I wondered.

I watched, silent as he reached across me, flicked the glove box open and slipped the map in, his movements brisk.

'*Bon.*' He snapped the glove box shut with a sharp click. '*Allons-y.* Ready, Charlie?'

Where had it gone, that tenderness? 'Just paper tigers,' my mother would say.

Beattie was in the living room, in among a group of familiar faces. I recognised the song, an old Fleetwood Mac tune, those familiar words and Stevie Nick's nasal lament. We used to dance to it together, turning it up loud in our apartment, singing along with Stevie, over and over: sad words to lovers past about remembering what they'd had...

Beattie was dancing to it now in a long, willowy black dress that fell in layers, flowing like billowing silk around her hips, her ankles and her bare feet. She looked like a fairy princess with her mass of red hair. Like Stevie on the front cover of the record jacket.

'Come casual,' she'd said. I had. I'd worn jeans.

I waved at her, grinning, and she smiled wide, obviously excited as she pushed her way over to us. I had to scream over the music as I gave her a hug. 'You look *wonderful!*' I turned back to Marc. 'She hasn't changed, has she?'

It was nothing really, barely perceptible: just a flicker in his eyes. Nothing at all. But I saw it nonetheless.

Then he said it. '*Tu es magnifique*, Beattie.'

'You look *fine*,' he'd said to me in the car.

They didn't kiss.

Then suddenly Pierre, Beattie's husband, was standing among us and their two boys were jumping up and down around our legs, excited about seeing Charlie, and it was over.

The moment was forgotten...for the time being, at least.

Once as we were walking home from school, when we were still in Australia and Charlie was around seven, he asked me what the difference was between a secret and a lie.

'Well...' I wondered what he was hiding from me as we stood on the median strip on Oxford Street, and thought, not for the first time as the cars shot past us too close for comfort, we really shouldn't cross here any more.

'A secret is something that is true, that you can keep to yourself – something special you don't have to tell anyone.' But then I thought, *no*, correction – post addendum. 'Except, of course, your mother!'

He made a face at this, that 'Yeah, right' one he'd recently picked up from his schoolmates – the beginning of such faces.

'Now, a *lie*...' I was thinking hard, trying for succinct clarity, this kid being a harder cookie to convince than some of the judges I'd stood before. 'That's a *very* different thing.'

Yes, I thought, as he looked up at me – still so trusting despite the face – I think I'm on the right track here. But we were having to wait too long for a break in the traffic, so I decided it was now or never to make a dash for it.

'A lie —' I had stepped off the median strip, taking the plunge as I pulled Charlie along with me. 'A lie is sort of like a *bad* secret.' But I realised I'd confused the issue even before he opened his mouth to object and an oncoming car sped up, obviously to teach me a lesson by killing us.

'But you just said a lie was *different!*'

He was pulling on my hand just as the driver hollered through his car window, swerving to miss us only at the last minute. 'Get off the road, why don' ya, lady!'

'Ah, yes, let's see...' We had reached the other side, safe but a little out of breath. I was thinking I'd have to backtrack and that at least the guy had called me *lady* and not something else, something much worse, the meaning of which I would then have had to explain to Charlie and that would necessitate a giant cognitive leap from secrets and lies.

'The difference is...a lie is something that *isn't* true that you say to people.' I looked to see whether he was taking this in. 'And that is *wrong.*'

He seemed pretty happy with this, which worried me, because I don't think the *wrong* bit bothered him particularly, judging by the giant grin that had spread across his face. He was hiding something for sure.

'And...' I squeezed his hand to make sure he was still paying attention, 'that is something you should *definitely* tell your mother about!'

Yes, I'd got his attention all right, the mouth having taken a sudden downward turn at both ends.

'So what's the difference then,' he whined, disappointed, 'if I have to tell you both?'

But that was the thing with Charlie: I always knew when he was lying anyway, whether or not he told me. He was an open book.

It was just with others, others I thought I knew so well, that I had no idea.

Chapter
twenty-seven

We took another trip out to Belle Ile, not long after our first. I remember it was just after Beattie met Pierre. This time all four of us drove out together, Beattie and I and our new lovers, leaving Paris at midnight, taking the ferry at Quiberon at the crack of dawn – Pierre snoring in the back as Beattie's eyes met mine in the rearview mirror.

We camped in our favourite spot down by the beach, lone campers pitching our tents at a far enough distance from each other so that, as Pierre joked, we could all get some sleep. He was like that, Pierre: just a big friendly bear, a nice man with a booming laugh that could crack your eardrums if you got close enough, and a voice like Paul Robeson singing 'Ol' Man River' – thunderously deep, 'Loud enough to wake the dead,' as Beattie always said. He was the kind of bloke everyone liked to have around – a good laugh at parties, especially once he'd had a few – but not the type I had expected Beattie to end up with.

We hired bicycles and rode round the island, picnic baskets

strapped to the front, baguettes sticking out precariously as we tackled hills and whizzed down the other side, Beattie and I screaming wildly, our feet raised either side off the pedals, the rush of air blowing our hair up as we soared dangerously around bends. We'd ride home again just as the sun was setting behind the rocks, like four kids, sandy and sunburnt, while fat toads croaked at us on the hot bitumen road.

I remember one evening riding up ahead of the others, crickets singing in the tall grass as we passed whitewashed cottages with blue shutters; that eerie twilight hue making the colours incandescent. But I wasn't sure of the way back to our campsite. So every now and then I'd call to Marc, 'Which way now?'

'*Tout droit*, straight ahead,' he yelled. 'If you get lost, just keep pedalling and you'll end up back where you were. *Ne t'inquiète pas*. You can't get lost on an island.'

Beattie laughed. 'Annie could.'

And as the light was fading, shadows playing tricks on my vision, I heard Marc call to me, his voice soft from behind.

'*A droite*, Annie! Turn right!'

So I turned off without looking back, pedalling harder now, attacking the hill, thinking I would get home before them and have the first shower. Last person home always ended up standing under cold water in the ablution block, and that was usually me, having struggled up the final stretch of road, lucky last. 'But not tonight,' I panted out loud, forcing myself to go faster.

Déjà Vu

I had gone about a hundred metres to the top of the slope and was about to start the easy downhill run before I heard it. It made me stop, my hands gripping the brake levers so suddenly I nearly fell headfirst over the handlebars.

At first, I couldn't make it out. It sounded like owls hooting. Then I heard a ripple of laughter – Beattie. So I knew they were somewhere back there, in the dark, obviously still on the road I had turned off, but further on.

'Come back, Annie!' Beattie was calling, laughing. 'You're going the wrong way!'

I realised then *why* they were laughing – I was in for another cold shower. So easily fooled.

Chapter
twenty-eight

*I*t is Saturday – a week to the day since we drove to Toulouse, when we sat down by the River Garonne, a week from when we were sitting on the couch back home in Lherm, listening to Charlie playing upstairs. I can hear him now, hear his feet on the floorboards as he crashes to the floor, jumping off his bed, even though we have told him over and over not to do that, *please* Charlie.

'One day you will go right through the floor and end up sitting on the couch, Charlie MacIntyre-Morvan!'

I hear a dog barking, skittering across the floor. It's not Charlie. It's the neighbour's terrier.

So I know it now. We won't be out of here by the morning. I will wake up back here tomorrow morning as I did this morning, as I did all the other mornings this week. This is our reality from here on in – this is our present. I stand by my bedroom window, staring out into the empty courtyard, and wonder, why has this happened?

Beattie has gone out, disappearing mysteriously again. As I pace around the apartment, pulling on my hair, cursing out loud, moving from my room into the bathroom, then into the kitchen, pacing like a caged animal – a lonely lioness – I am struck by a yearning. I am overwhelmed by my desire to ring Marc, to be with him, to tell him how much I *miss* him! I don't want to wake up every morning without him. I have lost Charlie. I have lost both of them.

We were going to separate.

But I *have* to see him.

And then it hits me, like a fist to the stomach, taking my breath away, making me keel over in the living room, making me cry out. *What a fool I've been!* I have acted like a silly young thing, a *silly jealous fool!* Because I know now, Frédérique is nothing in the scheme of things – in what we had, the passion we lived back then. And this is what he has been trying to tell me, what he tried to tell me when we went back to his apartment, when he called to me down the stairwell, 'It's not what you think, Annie!'

My heart is beating fast as I reach for the phone. But it rings before my fingers touch the handpiece.

It is Marc. 'She's gone,' he says. 'Pack your things up. *Je viens te chercher.* I'm coming now.'

I sob into the phone like a fool. '*Good!*'

I throw some clothes into a bag. I write Beattie a note and leave it on the kitchen table. I will come back to pick up the rest later, along with a cheque from Marc for the rent. Back then, the cowboy used to earn more than Beattie and I combined.

I am out the front waiting for him within ten minutes. It has obviously taken Sleeping Beauty a whole week to pack up *her* stuff, but then first up she'd have had to find some clothes. But I don't care! None of that matters now. *We* matter – *Charlie* matters. And that is all. Frédérique is just a tiny blip, a *bleep*, as Charlie would say, in the past.

As we pull up outside his apartment and I reach for the door handle, I am thinking, it's going to be okay now. We can get on with it.

His hand reaches over to mine. '*On repart à zéro*, okay, Annie? *On fait comme ça?*' We start from zero, right, Annie?

'Yes.' I nod. 'From zero.' But this word in my mouth, this word so empty, so *final*, fills me with terror all over again, making my heart start up, beating too fast. I can't breathe, my hand waving in front of me. 'There's no air in here, Marc!'

I am remembering Charlie – Charlie at five – pulling on my sleeve when I'd called Marc at work, inconsolable, telling him what I'd done, that I'd taped over our only video of him on his second birthday – a silly, *stupid* accident. 'We have other videos of him, Annie!' Marc had said. But what about *this* one, Charlie at two? It was like a piece of our past had gone forever.

Charlie was screaming up at me, trying to get me to listen. 'It's okay, Mummy, I'm still here! Look!'

I am crying again, wailing out loud, trembling as we sit in the car together outside his apartment. '*No*, I can't do this, Marc! I *can't* wipe the slate clean!' Because now there is no Charlie *at all*.

Déjà Vu

Through my tears, I see him – Marc running around the front of the car, opening the door. He is crouched down beside me now, his arms wrapped around my waist. '*Viens*, Annie. It's going to be all right. *Tu verras!*' You will see!

I am standing under the shower, hot water pummelling my face, soothing my swollen, stinging skin, washing away my tears, running over my hair, down my back. He is kneeling before me, his soft lips, his tongue sliding warm between my legs, his hands clutching my hips, pulling me to him as my fingers slide through his hair, fingertips pressing into his scalp.

And I cry out loud, clutching him, pressing into his scalp, for the agony of our loss, for this release – this bittersweet pleasure.

We move around his kitchen preparing our first meal together. Bryan Ferry is singing to us, crooning in the background – *Avalon*, that old record I used to put on all the time. '*Pas encore*, Annie, not again!' But tonight he doesn't seem to mind. I am all washed out, my skin stretched tight across my face, scrubbed clean, my hair dripping wet on my T-shirt. But I am relaxed for the first time in what seems like an eternity, when really it has only been a week.

'It's weird, us being here together alone. It feels like Charlie is just away on camp.'

'*Oui*.' He takes a sip of his beer and looks over at me. A sly grin has crept across his face. 'We should use the time *constructively*.'

I smile back. It is the expression we always used, our running joke, when Charlie took his afternoon nap as a baby. I turn the stove off. Dinner can wait.

We lie in bed together, intertwined, content, our clothes strewn across the bed and floor, smiling dumbly up at the ceiling. It has been nice, I think, like it used to be.

'*Dix sur dix.*' He holds the old pretend card up – ten out of ten.

'Nah, more a nine.' He turns to me, feigning shock. 'But if it's perfection you're aiming for, I'm willing to give it another go.'

He laughs, then stares back up at the ceiling, thinking about something – about *someone*? Was *she* perfect, I wonder?

'Do you ever think, Annie...' He pauses. 'That apart from Charlie, this might be our chance to change things, our chance to get it right this time around?'

'Get it right?'

'*Tu sais ce que je veux dire.*' You know what I mean.

And I think about it. Yes, I do – somewhere along the way we had drifted apart.

'Yeah, maybe...' But I wonder suddenly which bit he wants to change, to *get right*. 'You mean moving to Lherm?' I am fishing.

'*Non*, before that.'

My heart beats faster. '*When* before that?' But I think I already know the answer, even if I don't know *what* actually went on at the time.

172

'Je n'sais pas.' He shrugs, evasive. 'There's no specific time that I mean.'

But I *know* now that there is – that *something* went on back when his father died.

'Viens.' He is leaning over me, his lips on my neck, on my lips, kissing me, so tender that tears well up in my eyes. 'Let's make dinner.' His face is over mine. And I see it then, see it in his eyes – something I haven't seen in so long.

Chapter
twenty-nine

*I*t is late. But I don't want to go to bed. I need to get out, to feel cold air on my face, to breathe it in in great gulps, to disperse the thoughts menacing my calm: that we will be going to bed together soon, without Charlie in the next room. So we leave our dirty dinner plates on the table, the red wine in the bottom of our glasses, and step out on to rue de Championnet, headed towards the main square.

The boulevard is alive with restaurants, the smell of couscous and spicy lamb; groups of men out on the pavement in pristine white fezzes, talking loud, their voices pitched high and sharp as if they're arguing. But they nod and smile as we walk past.

And I remember how we used to wander down here every Sunday morning when the whole street was alive with market stalls – rows and rows of fruit and vegetables, orange and yellow powdered spices piled high in deep punnets, roasting golden chickens rotating on skewers in glass ovens; halvah and sweet syrupy pastries, dripping with honey and layered with crushed green pistachio nuts and buttery almonds – the colours, the scents of Morocco, Turkey and Algeria, all here in this street.

He tells me now – about his father. That he will drive out there tomorrow, just like he used to, like *we* used to, for Sunday lunch. He doesn't want me to come. They haven't met me yet, not *this* time round. 'And I need to do this alone, Annie.' I nod. But as we step off the pavement heading over towards the park, I take his hand, uneasy. I don't like this.

The road is busy – young men cruising past, their cars throbbing out rap music turned up a million decibels, so loud it doesn't sound like music any more as it pulsates in contra-rhythm to my heart, beating too fast now. Because I know what this means to him. I know what it has meant, how it was for him.

And all the while, I am uneasy. I squeeze his hand. 'What will you say, Marc?'

He breathes out, hard. 'Ah... *Je ne sais pas*, Annie! I just want to talk to him about it – *c'est tout*.'

The park is closed, locked for the night. I watch as Marc straddles the waist-high metal gate in one leap, the agility of his movement making me smile. He grins back at me. My turn. I slip one leg over the top of the gate, aware he is watching. Yet even as a girl, I was never too good at this stuff. High jumping over that bar at school freaked me out – *what if I missed?* But then he slips his hands round my waist, firm, holding me steady as he eases me over gently. His lips are on mine, biting, his tongue sliding over my lips.

We head up the pathway in the dark. It is quiet here – a quiet, stagnant calm radiating from this dark, leafy haven. I look out across the grass flat and see a shadow, a tiny form, over by the base of the great, thick-trunked fig tree in the middle of the flat – a squirrel. He has spied me too, frozen still, the silhouette of his bushy upright tail, his big round eyes glistening at me in the dark.

I speak softly. 'You mean you'll tell him that he's sick? Or — '

'I want him to see a doctor, Annie. I don't want him to —' He stops suddenly, breathing out hard as he stands still, as still as the squirrel, in the middle of the pathway. 'Ah, *Annie!*'

I reach my hand out to his cheek and feel the heat of his flushed skin, the heat of his exhilaration, his certainty that he must do this. 'I know, Marc.'

I have lived with his pain, his frustration, for so long. So I know he must do this, because I remember how it was back then, how he changed – his anger that changed our relationship so brutally and lingered on like a third presence between us, uninvited. Until now, it seems – now that we are back here, and his father is alive.

Yet I am torn. Because in my heart of hearts, I don't want him to do this. If he does, he will change how the past went. One tiny change, and it could set the chain in motion – like meddling with the train signals at a fork in the tracks... our lives might take a different direction.

Then what? *What of Charlie?*

'*Non*, Annie. . .' He is shaking my hand, shaking me out of my thoughts. 'It changes nothing. It's just my father, *d'accord*? It won't change anything else.'

It is early – the sun barely up. I take Marc's car keys from off the buffet in the hallway, creep to the front door in my socks, carrying my shoes, and let myself out of his apartment – trying not to wake him. I want it to be a surprise.

I will take his van, drive to Beattie's and pick up the rest of my stuff. I should be back with croissants before he even knows I'm gone. I want to get *all* of my things – the rest of my clothes, my scattered paraphernalia – so that I am not hovering between two places, between two worlds, so that I can get on with the next stage of our lives.

It is Sunday morning and I drive through Paris, smiling as I head up the main street of Place de la République, that lady with her olive branch waving it at me.

It is strange. I feel like I have been pulled through a washing wringer, that this week has flattened me like a steamroller, knocking me senseless. Yet, despite it all, despite my deep unfathomable fear that I will never see Charlie again – this fear that makes my heart beat out of control without warning, makes me want to cry out loud, '*Help me, please, someone! I've lost my baby!*' – there is something else lurking in the undercurrent of my emotions, an irrational contradiction stirring in my heart. It is something new, something that I woke with this morning, like a ray of sunshine on my pillow – like waking when I was a girl, knowing that I was happy about something, but forgetting what it was. Was it Christmas, was it my birthday?

And I realise I am happy, simply happy – about last night. Something happened, I saw it in his eyes. I felt it in his touch. I won't go on about it, that 'yucky mushy stuff' as Charlie would say. But it is as my mother always said, 'Annie MacIntyre, you are such a hopeless romantic.'

And other than that, I just *feel* happy for no particular reason – the chemistry of my body is singing, defying my brain, defying logic.

As I turn into rue des Lyanes, our street, I remember another time when I felt this exhilarating buzz, the feeling that the world is just a sparkling oasis of pleasure waiting to be discovered. I don't want to think about that now, but I do in spite of myself. It was back when I went to see Doctor Hardy, when I thought I'd contracted some sort of stomach bug. I hadn't, of course. I was just pregnant. I remember the drive home, smiling dumb at anyone who had the misfortune to drive up level with me. I grip the steering wheel now, determined not to think about Charlie for the moment.

This morning I *will* be happy, just happy.

I turn down a side lane and grab a park out the back of our

apartment building. I don't want Beattie to see me behind the wheel of a car. She'll think I've *really* lost it. I can see her bedroom window from the front entrance. Her shutters are closed, a good sign. I glance at my watch – still only 6.30 a.m. Beattie was never an early riser, and certainly not on a Sunday morning. I take the lift up to the second floor and let myself in softly, slipping my shoes off again.

I am like a shadow, sliding in and out like the Sandman, as the world sleeps.

I move around our apartment, a cat-burglar, picking up stray objects – my tarnished brass jewellery box, hairclips, lipstick, a note from Carlo, letters from Australia, photos – and cram them all into my sports bag. I start with my room, then work my way around the living room. I am just about to stake out the bathroom when I hear her door open. I hang back, ducking behind the living-room wall. I don't want to have to see her like this, not now. I want to be out, and then just explain it to her calmly over coffee. Someone is padding out into the hallway, heading for the bathroom. It's not her. It's a man – I can tell by his deep throaty cough. And I smile, thinking it's *him*, her Mystery Man. So this time she has brought him back with her, when she thought I wouldn't be here. She read my note.

I peep out. His back is turned to me as he opens the bathroom door. He is stark naked. I stare, my eyes frozen on his bare back, his bum, the silhouette of his balls, the swing of his penis as he reaches round to flick on the light, his body framed by the doorway. I watch open-mouthed. And my heart sinks. This body is familiar, *very* familiar. His majestic grace, the imposing stature like a Greek god.

He closes the door. I have only glimpsed him from behind, but I know. I have recognised him.

It is Carlo.

Chapter *thirty*

I drive through Paris, a woman possessed, seething, my foot pressed too hard on the accelerator as the lights flick to green, *finally* – my hand slamming down hard on the horn, thumping at the wheel, cursing out loud. That feeling of serenity has left me as quickly as it raised its stupid, *gullible* head! I picture him, picture *them* together in the apartment – making love, taking a shower, washing their intimacy away. Does he use *my things:* my shampoo, my hair comb? Does he rub himself dry with my towel?

Do they laugh about me together?

I feel betrayed. I feel stupid, *so bloody naïve!* This girl, this *woman* that I have known for so long, that I have trusted – *my best friend!* My mind is racing, trying to put the pieces of this grotesque puzzle together.

I think of him – that time he rang me from Italy. 'Come to Florence, *Anna!*' And Beattie, standing in my bedroom doorway, arms crossed, exasperated, watching me pack. 'What about work,

Annie?' The voice of reason. *My conscience!* I thought she was genuinely worried about *me*!

And silly me, caught up in the flurry of his whims, his promises, his smile, that look of delight in his eyes. I was beyond reason, beyond Beattie's warnings, intoxicated by the thrill of his unpredictability. 'Bugger work!' I'd said, laughing.

'Tell that to Ice Maiden. I'm sure she'll be thrilled.'

'I'll tell her I've a heavy cold.'

'Hmm... from your sick bed in Italy?'

And the next morning, a brisk cloudy grey day in December, he was there on the platform, at the Stazione Centrale, waiting for me as I stepped off the train. We drove round and round, up one-way streets that seemed to take us back the way we'd just come. But no, for then we were there, outside his apartment off the Piazza del Duomo.

Carlo in Italy was like Charlie when he was little, wanting to show everyone, in fact *anyone* who just happened to drop by, his toys. Italy was Carlo's playground – the Galleria degli Uffizi, the Statue of David in the Piazza della Signoria, the Ponte Vecchio, the endless cafés. He wanted to show it all off to me – *his* Italy. '*Stay!*' So I did, staying longer than I'd planned – not that I was planning anything at all. 'Forget your job, Anna. I'll give you one!' His promises – promising me the world. So my fictitious heavy cold turned into the flu, then into pneumonia.

'Mmm,' said Ice Maiden, hanging up cold.

Beattie's warnings to me over the phone: 'You'll lose your job, Annie!'

Now, waiting at the traffic lights, stuck in the middle of Paris, I'm thinking back still, but this time I'm not moonwalking. I'm going *right* back to the beginning, a whole seventeen years back to the very first time I met her, that first day when Ice Maiden was showing me round the school, when she was racing from one room into another like White Rabbit – 'I've so much to do. I'll explain later' – showing me nothing at all. I was following her along the corridor, trying to keep up. And that's when Beattie appeared, heading towards us.

She was carrying a stack of books, piled up high, steadying them with her chin, her red hair twisted up, loose and messy, on top of her head. Ice Maiden was telling me I could start Monday over her shoulder, her blonde hair flying out behind her, her long legs moving fast – efficiency in motion. So she didn't notice Beattie until it was too late, until they collided head-on, and the books lay scattered at her feet.

'Oh, *Beattie*! You really should watch where you're going!'

Beattie's green eyes taking me in as we knelt together on the floor, gathering up her books; Ice Maiden hovering over us, impatient to get on, her long steely legs in motion still, moving from one foot to the other like a colt keen to take flight, off down the hallway. '*Actually*, Beattie, you're *just* the girl I was looking for...'

Beattie's grin as she looked straight at me. 'Let me guess, Murielle, you'll be wanting me to show the new *girl* around?'

I had smiled at her then.

'Wonderful!' Ice Maiden called back to her, already off and away, Beattie's humour obviously lost on her. 'I'll leave you to it, then.'

Beattie had called after her, 'Tell me, does the new *girl* have a name?'

But Ice Maiden had already turned the corner, faster than the speed of light – leaving us still crouched opposite one another in the corridor.

So I'd held my hand out. 'Annie – I'm Australian.'

Her grip was firm. 'Pleased to meet you, *Annie. Australian,* you say? Well now, I'd never have guessed!'

I liked her then and there. She had a certain spark, a wicked sense of humour that could make you laugh or cry, depending on her mood.

I am crying *now*, as I pull up outside Marc's place. He is awake by the time I let myself back into his apartment. I can hear him in the kitchen. I drop his keys on to the buffet, my sports bag to the floor in the hallway and pause there, listening to water gurgle through the machine – the smell of coffee as it filters through. I have forgotten all about the croissants. I want to crawl back into bed and pull the covers over my head.

'Where have you been?' Marc smiles over at me as I walk into the kitchen.

But my head is hurting as I wave my hand in front of my face, gesturing *No*. I need a coffee. *I need to think about this!* I grab a cup off the shelf. He takes it from me and serves me without saying anything, and I take it without thanking him. I need to sit down, to think about *him*, Mr Mystery *Bastard*, and Beattie.

Beattie!

I am sitting at the kitchen table, staring out at the street. I feel Marc's hand on my shoulder, lifting my hair, his lips on the back of my neck as he takes a seat beside me, his knee pressing into my thigh. I am trying to work out when it started, when Beattie began her disappearing acts. I can't remember. Yet I am sure of one thing – I know that it was going on at the same time, the same time as *I* was seeing him. And in all the years I've known her since, in all those letters she wrote me from France, she never once told me, not even so much as a hint, not a shadow of guilt.

But then, confession is good like that.

I am stunned by this deception, struck dumb by this secret she has kept from me. I want to get them out now, those letters, and pore over them; search for a hint of her betrayal – to read between the lines of her handwritten thoughts. To see what I have not seen all these years. But of course, I can't do that. That great pile of letters, birthday cards and postcards I have kept safe in a shoe box on the top shelf of my wardrobe back in Lherm as a tribute to our friendship – like the candle on my wedding day – they've not yet been written.

I break the silence, finally. 'I've worked it out.' But I am talking more to myself than to Marc – my voice hoarse and flat.

Marc is rubbing my thigh. '*Quoi?* Worked *what* out?'

But I don't answer. I can't. I am remembering things she has said to me over the years. Why, *even* the other day: 'Why didn't you just tell Carlo it was over?'

'Worked *what* out, Annie?'

I thought she was worried about me! Stupid, *stupid* me! I thought she cared – when she took me shopping, when she pushed me into buying those ridiculous stilettos, when she asked me why I hadn't told him about Marc. But, *no*, it wasn't about that at all! She just wanted me off the scene.

'Annie?'

I turn to him. He is watching me over his coffee. She saw the watch. What *was* she thinking when she saw it on my wrist? Was she jealous, or did he give her one too? And I had wanted to tell her everything, to confide in her just as I had always done – wanting to tell her then and there about *Charlie*!

'Oh God, what a *fool* I've been!' I moan.

Marc's hand reaches over to my shoulder. '*Mais*, Annie, *qu'est-ce que tu as? Dis-moi!*'

So I tell him, 'I know who it is now.'

He obviously has no idea what I'm on about as he stares back at me, one eyebrow raised, waiting. And I wonder, what was she praying for in La Madeleine? Did she pray that I would just take up with Marc and leave Carlo to her? When she found my note that I left her yesterday, she must have thought all her Christmases had come at once!

His hand squeezes my shoulder. '*Mais, qui...quoi?*'

'I know who Beattie's *Mystery Man* is.'

It is as if I have hit him, as if I have struck him across his face, hard. He reels back suddenly, spilling coffee over his grey T-shirt, his tracksuit pants, his hand. He is on his feet, jumping up so quickly that his chair falls back, clattering noisily on to the tiles.

'*Merde*, Annie, I'm sorry. *Vraiment. Sheeet*, I'm *so* sorry!'

He has burnt his hand, but I think he might be overreacting. 'It's okay... But you should run your hand under cold water, maybe get some ice.'

He's not listening as he stands over me, gesticulating with his hands in that maddening, theatrical French way of his, going on about how sorry he is. I am not really concentrating on what he is saying, because now I think he really *is* making a mountain out of a molehill over such a little spill. I am only half-listening...

Until I hear him say something quite odd.

'*Je n'ai jamais voulu te faire du mal.*' He is mumbling, rambling. '*Je n'en ai jamais eu la moindre intention.*'

He never wanted to hurt me? *What is he on about?*

'Listen, Marc —' I try to talk over him, wishing he would calm down. 'It's *fine*. Look – nothing has spilt on me.'

But then I stop short and look up at him. There's something

else he has just said, something stranger still. So it hits me that he's not talking about the coffee. And as this thought occurs to me, he stops too. We have both fallen silent and very, *very* still. Our eyes meet. He has obviously realised as well, that we are each on about different things, two *entirely* different things.

My heart is beating fast, thudding against my throat. 'What did you say, just then?' I'm having trouble breathing.

He steps back and looks down at his hand, rubbing it with his thumb as if he really has burnt it. But I know now the problem isn't there, not with his hand at least. I wait. He looks like Charlie – Charlie when he is guilty about something, when he wants to tell me, wants to confess but doesn't know where to start. So I help him, help Marc now, like I would our eleven-year-old, by giving him a little prompt.

'You said something —' I need to take a breath before I pronounce the words. 'Something about Beattie.'

But I know it before he even says it. I know it.

Chapter
thirty-one

We used to go to the Tango, Marc and I. As far as nightclubs went, it was *the* place to be in Paris on a late Saturday night. It was a funny place; like a cave, a dark windowless hole tucked in behind the Pompidou Centre. There was no sign on the battered metal door, but the graffiti said it all. We'd buzz and the bouncer, his face battered and worn like an old bulldog's, would squint at us through the trapdoor, blinking as he checked us out, breathing heavy as he slid the lock back and let us in.

I love to dance. And the Tango was great for that – music thumping, loud and rhythmic, pulsating in my ears, bodies hot and sticky with sweat, writhing round on the dance floor like seaweed, all of us swaying on the seabed to the same rhythm.

We'd dance all night. I used to love dancing with Marc: the way he moved, the way he'd look at me, moving in close, the heat of his body pressing into mine, his lips on my neck, intimate, like sex.

Finally, come morning, we'd slide into his van, exhausted, our pores and clothes oozing with the smell of cigarette smoke, eyes squinting at the sun just rising, eardrums still pumping, deafened by the music, our voices cracked and slurred with alcohol.

We didn't dance together at Beattie's party, even though I wanted to, especially when Billy Idol came on pumping out 'White Wedding' and Pierre turned up the volume. We'd listened to him full blare driving up the highway, heading west on the A10 on our way to Belle Ile. It was our favourite.

But that night at Beattie's Marc sort of shrugged me off, told me I was slurring and that maybe I should go easy on the wine – right in front of everyone.

And Beattie had laughed and said, 'Well, *you* certainly haven't changed either, Annie – not in *that* way at least.'

I had turned away, stung, and watched Pierre as he danced round the living room, dancing solo, lumbering like a giant grizzly bear, sloshed, as the kids giggled at him.

Chapter
thirty-two

*I*f I could laugh about it, I would. For here's the rub – what happened between them, between Marc and Beattie, hasn't happened. Not *yet* at least.

Only Marc forgot that bit.

So, in a twisted sort of way, I realise the joke is on him. He put his foot in it. He need never have confessed. But then, to be fair on him, I guess, being a *man* the thought never entered his head that the mystery lover wasn't him. And Marc being Marc simply assumed he was the only stud to have had it off with my best friend.

He tells me.

I am sitting still, *very* still at the kitchen table. His words roll out fast, as if the guilt of this sordid secret he has kept hidden from me for so long is a weight, a great heavy burden that he is lifting from his shoulders – *at last*.

And I am his confessor. Nothing can hurt me – I am beyond that now.

It is a story about another world, another time – a legend, for after all it has never taken place. What he is telling me is simply the missing link to the story that I have already heard. Those pages that were ripped out have been found. I know all the words, like Charlie when he was little, reciting his favourite story, *Bananas in Pyjamas*. I know all the lead-in and the follow-up bits. I remember how it went – how Marc was back then, how he sank into a sullen, silent depression in Sydney... when he changed from that happy young man into someone else. 'He is grieving,' Beattie told me at the time. And so I'd told myself, yes, he is grieving.

She was there, at his father's funeral.

I am stunned – I recall their awkward silences over the years, their strained smiles whenever they were together. 'Why would she go to the funeral, Marc?' I say flat. '*Why?* You didn't even like each other that much.'

He looks at me. And then I realise, of course, she is Catholic. They are *both* Catholic. Beattie's faith overrode everything. She went as a friend, I think. She went to the funeral of her best friend's father-in-law – the right thing, the *decent* thing to do.

'You weren't there. She wanted to be there for —'

I hold up my hands, speaking softly. But my heart thuds loud against my chest. '*Spare* me.'

She rang and told him she would come. He picked her up

from the station. She went to the church in Ozouer, stood opposite him at the cemetery, came back with his family and friends to his home. And after, when all the guests had left finally, he dropped her back to the station.

But she missed her train.

They'd got caught up at the level crossing, watched the lights flash red as the barrier slid down – watched her train fly past on its way to Paris. They sat there in the carpark together as the sun went down over Gretz – that station, I remember, where Maurice handed the shopping over to Rosa; their awkward first exchange in the lead-up to their courtship.

He had cried then, *there* in the driver's seat of the stationary car, *finally*. And I think about him, the man who lay next to me in our bed, who turned from me when I was pregnant as I reached for him – when I tried to tell him that I understood. This man who I had loved. 'You understand nothing.' Those were his words back then. But I realise now, of course, *Beattie* understood. She understood what I could not. I had no family. That's what I had told him.

She missed the next train, and the next and the next...

'You wouldn't talk to me, Marc.' I am calm. It is so long ago now. But *still*, I have to know. 'Where did you go?'

'*Je suis désolé, Annie!* I'm so sorry.'

But my hands fly up again, trembling in front of my face. '*Spare me, spare me, pleeease, spare me!* Just *tell* me where you took her!'

I am crying, the tears streaming down my face as I rock back and forth. Because I am remembering now, that first time he took me to Ozouer, when I asked him, 'So where's the nightlife?'

'*Tu verras!*' he'd said. You'll see. Did she see it too? Did she lie in the grass with him? Did they look up at the sky together after? Back in that world that no longer exists…

'*Non*, Annie,' he says. 'I didn't take her *there*.'

He has read my mind again, this man who has taken my heart and left a great gaping gash in its place. But I cannot let it go now – I have to know. I have to let him turn the knife.

'So where *did* you take her, then?' I am rocking still, my arms crossed tight across my chest.

'It doesn't matter —'

But the pain is unbearable. '*Tell me!*' I scream.

His voice is a whisper, but I hear him – his words resounding in my ears like the bells in Ozouer, ringing out over and over, tolling their sin, 'To a hotel, Annie.'

He has confessed at last. But I do not forgive him. I will never forgive him. He has betrayed me. He has betrayed Charlie. *Both* of them have betrayed us.

As a girl, I would sometimes look at my mother and wonder what she was like before my father died.

Déjà Vu

If I squinted my eyes tight and cupped my hands around them like binoculars, when she wasn't looking my way, I could see it. I could see how beautiful she was, how beautiful she must have been. She was like a dark-haired version of Marilyn Monroe. I know the whole point of Monroe's beauty, her *raison d'être*, was that she was a flaxen blonde – but my mother was like her nonetheless. She was the Norma Jean side, those photos of her without make-up, without the hard black lines drawn along her eyelids, the garish red lipsticks. She was Norma Jean strolling barefoot along the beach in a white shirt, Norma Jean coming out of hospital after her miscarriage with that sad, vulnerable, soft look in her eyes.

So I used to tell myself that behind my mother's anger, behind that tough exterior, that hard-edged mask like a movie star's, she was just like Marilyn Monroe without make-up – her big brown eyes, her dark wavy hair cut around her face, her small, white shoulders in that sleeveless white cotton dress she used to wear, my favourite, cut simply with the yoke neck, accentuating the softness of her arms, the curve of her breasts.

So when Grandma told me the truth about my father, I used to wonder how he did it, how my father could have sat in that café and pressed his knees into another woman's. *Couldn't he see how beautiful Mum was?* Didn't he know how lucky he was to have her? Didn't he ever think about how it would destroy her?

Chapter
thirty-three

'It's over,' I tell him simply.

So strange, these words, words that we merely talked around just a week ago in Toulouse, that we didn't dare pronounce. It has taken all this, all this crazy tangled mess, to say it finally.

'Can't we start again, Annie?'

His voice is hoarse. We are tired, drained. It is late. We are sitting, hunched over his kitchen table, the coffee cold and murky at the bottom of our cups. It is the afternoon already, yet we still haven't moved. The sun has slid away from the kitchen window – now just a tiny ray peeping through in the corner in the living room beyond.

'And what do we start with, Marc? We have *nothing* now – no Charlie, no trust, *nothing*. Even my friend —' My voice wavers, dangerously on the brink again, my nose is running and I have no tissue. I swipe at it with the back of my hand. 'Blow your nose,' I would tell Charlie.

'We have each other, *quand même*, Annie.' His voice is soft, pleading. 'We can start with that, *non?*'

'*No!*' I shake my head. But it's no use – I cannot control them, these tears, this bottomless well. 'No, we can't go back, can't turn back the clock.'

His fist comes down hard on the table, making the coffee cups ring on the marble surface and my heart thud harder. '*Mais, t'es sérieuse*, Annie? We *have* gone back! That's exactly it. We *can* start again!'

I want to crawl into bed, cover myself over with the blankets. I am cold, shivering as I stare at him. 'Start *what* again exactly, Marc?'

He reaches out, his hands rubbing my forearms. '*Mais toi et moi*...You and me, of course!'

'You and me? *You and me?*' I am struggling to get up, but his grip tightens around my arms. 'What about *Beattie*, Marc? And what about Carlo, and —'

'*Sheet*, Annie! *Non*, just you, me...*et* Charlie.' He is looking into my eyes, holding me still but I struggle against him.

'No, *no*, Marc!'

His chair screeches on the tiles as he pushes it back, releasing me. 'What do you mean, "no"?'

I pull myself up from the table, weary. 'I mean, *no*, I don't believe you!' I feel much, *much* older than the girl who crept out of here this morning, older than I have ever felt before – this young body just a shell as I move out towards the hallway. 'I don't *trust* you any more, Marc.'

He calls after me. 'What are you doing? *Tu vas où?*'

I have to get some things together, I tell myself. I have to leave. And I realise it's what I should have done a long time ago.

My sports bag is where I left it this morning, full of junk that I don't want to take with me. But I am *so* tired and I can barely see in front of me for the tears. I ease myself down on to the floor, sitting cross-legged next to it. I have no idea where to start.

'You have to let me prove it to you – that it will be different this time.' He has followed me into the hallway. 'We have to give it a *try*, Annie!'

I don't look up at him.

'Annie, *please?*' His voice wavers. '*On ne peut pas faire une omelette sans casser des oeufs.*'

You can't make an omelette without cracking eggs? Funny that he should say that now. It is what my grandmother used to say, but in a very different context. 'You have to take risks, Annie. You have to crack some eggs... No regrets, no backward glances.'

'True,' I say. 'But there is no point in making an omelette if the eggs are rotten.'

'Rotten?'

'*Pourri*, Marc.' I translate, frustrated that I have to spell it out for him. '*Des oeufs pourris!*'

'Why do you twist what I say?'

My hands are trembling as I fumble through my stuff – things to take, to leave, to toss. I have nothing now – my life, my past and future reduced to this messy bag. Carlo's note falls into my lap, that first note he wrote – *Meet me*. My mother was right, I think, as I rip it into tiny pieces, my romantic souvenirs – all false – falling and flittering like confetti to the floor. I was such a young, foolish thing. After all, it is as she always said, 'all such romantic nonsense, signifying nothing'. I will take only the bare essentials with me. I will start from zero.

'*Tu te rends compte alors?* You realise what this means, then, Annie?'

I look up. He can't hurt me now – I have lost everything. But I'm wrong.

'It means *no Charlie*.'

I feel the blood rising up my neck, my face, throbbing against my temples, stinging my lips. 'Is that some sort of threat, Marc?' I can only whisper these words – my heart pounding so hard I am sure he can hear it too.

'*Non,* Annie.' He slouches back against the wall. 'I am just telling you how it will go. Now *you* are the one who is changing fate.'

Chapter
thirty-four

$\mathcal{M}$y grandmother taught me to play cards. On those rainy grey days in my school holidays while Mum was at work, we'd spend hours together over the table, dividing the matches, dealing cards, playing poker, gin rummy and twenty-one. 'Snap is for the amateurs,' she'd say. She taught me all the tricks: how to shuffle, how to deal, how to bluff and how to bet. By the time I hit around seven or eight, I was a pretty cool card shark.

We'd play cards and she'd talk. She'd tell me about the past, about when she was a girl, when she was a young woman during the war, and the men she'd married. She knew a lot about men. Sometimes she'd forget and tell me the same thing over again. But I didn't mind. I loved her stories.

But if my mother was home, she'd shake her head and say through gritted teeth, '*Mum*, you've already told us that one.'

So I preferred it when she wasn't around, when it was just the two of us playing cards and talking. Sometimes she'd tell me about my grandfather, my mother's father and Grandma's first husband.

I had no memory of him other than her stories, for he'd died when I was a baby. And of course my mother never talked about the past. 'I've no time for nostalgia,' she'd say.

'Did you love him, Grandma?' I asked once.

'Oh yes!' She was fanning herself with her cards. 'I loved him the *best!*'

I noticed her neck had flushed red and as she waved her cards back and forth, I spied a King of Hearts and an Ace of Spades. I had two Queens.

'So why did you leave him, then?' I was surprised. Grandma had walked out on him when my mother was a baby.

She didn't answer me straight away. She was taking her time, concentrating on her hand, deciding which cards to keep, which cards to discard. She threw down two, so I dealt her two more. I watched her pick up, then smile as she rearranged her hand, holding it close to her chest. I wondered if she was bluffing again. She was a good bluffer, my grandmother.

'*Because*...' She was concentrating on her hand, still smiling smugly without looking over at me. 'Your grandfather didn't know what he had.'

Yes, she was *definitely* bluffing, I thought. But then I couldn't be a hundred per cent sure. I was watching her face carefully, the flicker in her eyes, the turn of her mouth as she smiled at her cards. My grandmother must have been around eighty then. I'd seen photos of her when she was young. My favourite was the one where she was sitting on the edge of a car fender laughing, with a soldier by her side, his arm around her waist. She was beautiful in her silk dress, cut on the bias, nineteen-forties style like the car, with her long wavy hair red like Rita Hayworth's, like a movie star. Even now, with her hair as white as snow, she was *still* a beautiful woman.

She was watching me over her cards. 'Never let them take you for granted, Annie. *Never.*' And then with a wink, she threw in three matches.

Of course, back then her advice about life, and particularly about men, was like water off a duck's back. At that age, I was well into fairytales – beautiful princesses carried off by handsome princes, happy-ever-after stories. The prince loved the princess and so that was all that mattered. End of story. They would live happily ever after.

My mother always said that was my problem, *even* as a young woman heading into my twenties – 'You leave yourself wide open, Annie MacIntyre!' – and that life out there was tough, and I had better wake up to it fast or I was in for a big disappointment. When Grandma died, my mother's only words to me were, 'Now perhaps you might come back down to earth.' But I didn't.

I bought a one-way ticket to Paris. To 'crack some eggs' – no regrets, no backward glances.

Chapter
thirty-five

I have found it.

It is in a small street, running parallel behind the rue de Rivoli, one further back again from the Seine – the hotel where I stayed when I came to Paris for the very first time. I had driven from Grandma's funeral straight on to Kingsford Smith airport and ended up here. I was twenty-three. It was before I met Marc, before I met Beattie, well before I met *any* of them.

Now I stand at the entrance to this funny little hotel again, with no stars, without even a bathroom in my room, as I recall – just a toilet and sink behind a torn partition, imitation Japanese.

The old woman behind the desk remembers me. I am surprised, for I *barely* remember her. I have just a blurred recollection of her face: her eyes overdone and outlined with heavy black kohl, her fine-pencilled eyebrows made into perfect arches, and her dyed blonde hair.

'*Mademoiselle Muucinntiire, ma belle petite australienne!*'

She clasps her hands together, smiling as she comes around

to greet me, to take my hand in hers. Her hands are small, like a child's. She is like a doll, a French Baby Jane. I smile, overcome by her warmth, so touched she has remembered me after all these years. But then, of course, it comes to me: it has only been a couple of years for *her* since I was last here. There will be many more surprises from here on in, I'm sure. This is the part I am changing. From now on, it will go a different way, my future.

She insists I take the same room, *Chambre* 402, even though I would have preferred a different one this time around, with a shower at least. For despite appearances, I am not the young girl I was, not so easily enchanted by the little quirks of Paris life. Still, I don't want to offend, so I take the giant iron key she pushes into my hand with a smile, nodding and thanking her profusely.

'Merci beaucoup, Madame,' I say over and over. I guess I haven't changed in that way.

My room is on the fourth floor, up a narrow, winding stairway, polished wood that creaks under my step so that when I get to the top, I am out of breath. My bag is heavy. I have lugged it on to the métro, across Paris, through the streets looking for this hotel. It has been a tough day – a tough *week*. I have left him. Marc has no idea where I have gone. I have no phone on me. Mobiles are not in fashion yet.

Anyway, like I said, *it is over*.

I open the door and flick on the brass light switch to the

left of the doorway. It is as it was. The three-quarter size bumpy bed that the French class as double, its thinning yellow–white bed cover, the pink and blue floral wallpaper coming away from the wall at its edges, the worn dark blue carpet and the window overlooking the street.

I sigh. At *least* it is familiar.

I throw my bag to the floor and collapse on to the bed. Yes, it is *very* bumpy. It is late, around 7 p.m. I should splash my face, ease my swollen, stinging skin and go out for some dinner, having eaten neither breakfast nor lunch. But I am too tired. I feel queasy. It is obviously the stress. I will just lie here for now and try to sleep, to slip under the covers, to at least close my eyes.

'You made your bed,' my mother would say. 'Now sleep in it.'

But I didn't make theirs, I think. And I can't sleep, remembering things Beattie said, things we did together, trying to find a reason that will somehow make it easier, that will make the pain subside – this dull ache in my heart.

I lie still, under the covers, and the tears slide slippery and sticky down my face like there is no tomorrow – because there *is* no tomorrow now. Was she out to prove something, I wonder, first with Carlo, then finally with my husband? Like when we weighed ourselves on that big old machine outside the pharmacy? Was *that* it – the competitive streak in her, turned cruel?

They are here with me in this hotel room. I can see her as she unclips her hair, his fingers sliding through those fiery waves, glowing red like a beacon in his hour of darkness. His hand on her neck, his fingers stealing beneath her shirt, beneath the delicate black lace of her bra as his pelvis presses into her – hard. And I hear him, his pained cry, '*Oh God, Beattie!*'; his hot breath in her ear, his arm around her waist as he pulls her towards the bed. But she pushes him back. 'Gently, cowboy.' So he watches her then, sitting beside me on the bed, *just here*, as she stands before us. She unbuttons her shirt, grinning as his eyes take her in – her bare, swollen breasts and her white skin, like in his teenage drawings. She is beautiful, a green-eyed goddess, truly *magnifique*. She can take his pain away. *She* understands. His hands reach out, sliding frenzied, clutching her breasts, her hips, as her skirt slips to the floor. 'Oh God, Beattie! *Tu es si belle…*'

His lips, his hot breath, his tongue, seeking the warmth, the softness between her legs… as my hand slides down to mine.

'*Tu es si belle,* Beattie.'

And I moan out loud, for their treachery.

'She's in trouble,' says Marc.

'Who?'

We are sitting on the edge of the old stone *lavoir*, in Lherm. It's where we used to always end up on our twilight walks in the warmer months. The *lavoir* is just a shallow muddy pool, no more than eight metres square and paved with great blocks of white stone brought in from the local quarry. Once upon a time the local women came here, crouched along its edge in their toil-stained aprons, with their sheets and their husbands' dirty linen. And they'd scrub. For us, though, it's just a good place to sit and think, as we dip our toes into the cool water.

'Who?' I try again.

He doesn't answer me as he rolls up his jeans, folding them back, layer over layer, in that meticulous French way of his. He's on his feet, a twig in hand, wading in knee-high, on a mission. He crouches over and squints at the water as he skims its surface with the stick.

'Ah!' His eyes are focused on the end of the stick. 'Got you.'

And I realise – he is talking to a bug, just a bug, so small I have to squint to make out its tiny stick-form perched on the twig's tip. And I think how funny it is that Marc has called it a 'she' and not an 'it'.

'What is it, Marc?'

'*Une petite sauterelle.*' He is whispering, as if the bug has ears.

'A grasshopper?' I'm disappointed. 'Well, don't you think a grass-hopper can swim? *She* might even like the water.'

He places her down gently, by the edge of the pool. '*Non.*'

Then he waits, crouched very still over his catch. I wonder if he's waiting for her to thank him. She doesn't. A 'thank you' is obviously the last thing on her tiny stick mind as she takes a flying hop straight back into the water.

'*Merde!*'

I laugh. 'You see? She *can* swim!'

'*Non.*' He stares after her, shaking his head. 'She's drowning.'

I am laughing still as I open my eyes, as I take in the torn Japanese screen, laughing softly at Marc and his kamikaze grasshopper, until I realise where I am – alone in my bed, back at the hotel.

I miss him. I want him here with me in this strange bumpy bed, his body against my back, wrapped around me, firm.

Rescue *me*, I think.

'That's your trouble,' my mother would say. 'You're still waiting for some knight in shining armour to ride by.' True, I think. I remember sitting with Grandma in the Randwick Ritz, sucking on Minties as Snow White chortled in her brittle, high-pitched voice, 'Some day my prince will come.' It was my very first time at the cinema. I must have been no more than four years old. But I will never forget that song.

Grandma used to say, 'There's a knight on every corner. You just have to learn how to recognise him.' I used to think Carlo was one – the way he'd just ride by when the whim took him and whisk me off, somewhere exciting, away from the humdrum. No strings attached, or so I thought back then.

I am tortured by thoughts of Charlie, calling for me to come and get him. But I can't.

I remember taking him down to Bondi for a swim after dinner one hot summer's evening. Marc was working late. Charlie was eight. We were mucking around at the water's edge, playing tag down at the southern end, away from the flag area – away from the crowds. Charlie had tipped me last, so it was my turn to chase him. He was pretty swift at that age, so I had to run hard. I'd nearly caught up to him when he swerved and headed into the water. I stopped, leaning over to catch my breath, holding my side to ease away a stomach cramp.

It hadn't occurred to me that he'd go in deep. I thought he was just going to run in the shallows. But by the time I'd straightened up again and looked over, he was already in waist-high.

'Charlie!' I held my hand up. 'Don't go out – come back in!'

He must have thought I was trying to trick him, trying to get him to come in closer so that I could tip him, because he just laughed, then turned away and went in further. The more I tried to get closer, the further in he went.

'Charlie!' I had broken into a swim. 'Come back. There's a rip!'

But it was too late. He was in over his head.

By eight, Charlie was a pretty good swimmer. He had a good strong style. He just had to work on his kick. But eight is a cocky age. You think you can do *anything*, until you're out of your depth.

And he was out of his depth now.

I'd say it didn't hit him until after the first wave crashed over his head, when the fear began to creep across his face. By the second, he was looking plain scared. There was a quite a swell. They were coming in one after the other, real dumpers. And the rip was pulling him out fast.

'Charlie!' I screamed, useless, my eyes fixed on his face as I swam out after him.

I have always liked to think I'm a strong swimmer, having grown up in Sydney's east. As a teenager, I'd swim out the back down at Tamarama with my friends, fearing nothing except my bikini top riding up. From a very early age, Mum had pushed me into the swimming squad, insisting that a bit of competition would do me good. 'It'll give you some backbone,' she said. It didn't. It just gave me the shits.

But that day, it was as if I was swimming in slow motion, as if the water was pulling me in one direction and Charlie in the other. I couldn't get out to him fast enough. And we were outside the flag area, a whole length of the beach outside. There wasn't another soul around. The lifeguards were all up the other end.

I didn't notice him at first: a man swimming alongside me, then right on past. He was taking long slow strokes, steady and rhythmic, as if he really wasn't in a hurry. But then suddenly he had reached Charlie, and Charlie was climbing on to his back. And they were riding a wave, sailing on past me into shore.

By the time I'd caught the next wave back in, the man had already turned to go, heading back along the beach towards the northern end.

'Thanks!' I called after him. 'Thank you so much!' But he didn't turn around. So I didn't even get to see his face.

Déjà Vu

I think he might have been one of those knights Grandma was talking about. Where is he now? I wonder, as I lie alone in my hotel bed.

Chapter
thirty-six

$\mathcal{D}$aylight falls across my window, a blue–grey veil floating stealthily over the flowers on the wall towards me. It is Monday morning.

My heart weighs heavily in my chest. But I rise. There are some things in this world, Annie MacIntyre, that you just have to face up to. So I take the stairs down to the ground floor and lift the key to the common bathroom off the board behind the reception desk. I smell coffee. My stomach growls. I am weak with hunger, with fatigue. I have to go back up to the first floor to take my shower. I have forgotten to ask for a towel, so I rub myself dry with my nightie. I am out of practice, I think. I will have to take the key back down again to reception before climbing the stairs up to my room to get dressed properly. This is all too hard, going *this* far back in time. I am at rock bottom, and plunging deeper still.

By seven o'clock I am sitting by the window in the breakfast room, keen for Madame's coffee and croissants. I just want to eat and not think. She emerges from the kitchen with a full tray, smiling wide at me. I like Madame, I decide, despite the make-up. She pours steaming hot coffee into my bowl, then frothy milk. She has remembered how I like it. I recognise her perfume: Arpège, I am sure of it. It reminds me of my grandmother. I want to hug her. I don't, though. Instead I just smile back, thanking her profusely again. She has given me two croissants, 'An extra one,' she says, pinching my cheek, because I am looking skinny and pale, '*trop pâle, ma cherie.*'

There is rhubarb jam, *faite maison*, home-made, she tells me, served in a small white dish with a lid. I slather it on to my croissant and take a bite as she bustles back into the kitchen with her empty tray. A man sits over in the corner opposite, decked out in suit and tie, looking stiff and uncomfortable as he smooths down his overwaxed hair. He is obviously here on business. He watches me through eyes slightly crossed and set close over a very long nose as I wipe jam from the edges of my mouth with my serviette. He doesn't smile. I wonder if he is jealous because she has served him only *one* croissant. I take another bite, then another. He turns away.

My blood sugar shoots up like a bell bar at the fair. And I think of Charlie in the morning when he rises cranky and objectionable until he hits the Weet-Bix; Mr Grumpy until he's into his fifth mouthful. The transformation is always spectacular – like Dr Jekyll and Mr Hyde.

But my hand moves over my mouth now. I am overcome by a

wave of nausea, thinking of him. *Charlie!* What I would give for that grumpy little morning face now! I am trying desperately not to cry again, holding my breath, stifling the moan inside me that threatens to surface. The businessman's crossed eyes flicker my way. He is pretending not to notice.

I cannot go to work. I cannot face the thought of seeing Carlo first thing. The image of his body framed in the bathroom doorway troubles me. And of course, there will be Beattie.

I ring from the hotel. Madame has given me a line out as I stand in the small telephone cabin at the base of the stairs and she smiles over at me from her desk. Ice Maiden picks up. I tell her I can't come in. This time I don't give her an excuse – I simply can't come in. She is silent for a moment at the other end as my grip tightens around the handpiece.

'And what am I supposed to do with Mr Vitali?' There is definitely an ice-cold wind blowing in along the telephone line.

But Madame's jam and croissants have given me courage. 'Get Beattie to fill in.' And then I hang up. I have *really* done it this time – I have quit.

Chapter
thirty-seven

I wait in the reception area. The girl at the desk tells me to take a seat. I prefer to stand. The phone rings. She picks up, listens, nods, then puts the receiver down.

'*Monsieur Vitali vous attend, Mademoiselle.*' She is smiling politely as she swivels round in her chair, indicating the lift to her right, her face as blank as an air hostess going through the security drill, pointing to the exits in the event of a plane crash. '*C'est au quatrième étage.*'

I press the button for the fourth floor. The lift doors slide shut and I am alone. I check my reflection in the mirror behind me. I see Grandma's face. 'You are just like her,' my mother would say ruefully. I am beautiful, I tell myself, smiling encouragement. I can carry this off. Like poker. I just have to play my cards right.

The lift opens on to a magnificent high-ceilinged room, windows from ceiling to floor. The view on to rue Royale takes my breath away. Crystal candelabras hang from the ceiling, extravagantly elegant. It is like stepping into La Galerie des Glaces, Louis' ballroom at his Palais de Versailles, not an office. But then, as Ice Maiden would say, 'Mr Vitali is no ordinary client', so this is no ordinary office. And Moratel is, after all, one of France's most prestigious and powerful telecommunications companies.

A woman rushes over to me, the light tap of her pumps on the seventeenth-century polished floorboards like the echo of Irish dancers. She is impeccably dressed in a beautifully cut skirt and jacket that hug her figure: a perfect cut, just like her. Her hair, ash blonde against a perfectly fake-tanned face (it is, after all, only April in Europe), is slicked back into a *chignon*, not a strand out of place. This must be his personal assistant.

'*Mademoiselle* MacIntyre.' She smiles as though she knows me well, as if I am an old friend. '*Monsieur Vitali vous attend.*'

He is waiting for me. This is what the girl at reception told me as well. So as I am ushered through the room, then into another and finally another, both as majestic as the first, I imagine Carlo waiting for me. I picture him sitting behind his desk, tapping his pen on its smooth polished edge, stark naked. And the thought gives me strength, the courage of my conviction, that I am doing the right thing.

As it happens, he is fully dressed today. And as his PA ushers me in and then discreetly clicks the door shut behind me, I have the feeling we will not be disturbed, that he doesn't even have to ask. He gets up, moves round his desk and steps towards me, his arms outstretched as if he is about to ask me to dance. His smile is dazzling, devastatingly dazzling. He has *no* idea, I realise.

Déjà Vu

'Anna!'

'Carlo.' I smile back at him.

My knees weaken slightly, but I am okay. I take his outstretched hand and he pulls me to him, his lips pressing hard on mine, passionate, his hand firm on my back as if I am his, and he is *all* mine. And I am less okay than I was a second ago, especially when his tongue slides into my mouth for a brief moment. But I should be fine...

'Anna!' His hands are on my waist now, tightly possessive, holding me away from him, just far enough to run his eyes over my face, my body. 'Anna, I've been so worried about you. You weren't there this morning. Are you ill?'

'I am better.'

He looks into my eyes, his hand on my cheek, a brief gesture without speaking as if he is deeply moved – a skilled player. He takes my arm in his and leads me over to a corner of his office that is set up rather like an exclusive showroom: a Brunati couch, Tolomeo lamps on either side and opposite, two club armchairs, nineteen-thirties style. Set down in the middle, there's an extravagant arrangement of flowers atop a coffee table, clear glass, like something out of *Elle Décor*. I take an armchair, even though I have the feeling he was steering me more towards the Brunati. And as I sink into its soft leather, he pulls the other armchair over, bringing it in closer.

He sits, but is leaning towards me, so close his knee presses into mine. 'So, Anna... What a wonderful surprise!'

I wait for him to ask me. And he does.

'But tell me, what brings you *here* to me?' He gestures with a wave around the room. 'To my office? I've *never* had this pleasure!'

I wonder then if it *is* a pleasure, for it is true that up until now I have never ventured here. We would meet where he said we should meet, see each other when *he* decided, at his whim but *never* in his office. It was implicit, our understanding, the affair strictly on *his* terms. I was the perfect mistress.

'Never let them take you for granted,' said Grandma. Well, I had – but not any more. It's time to play cards.

I reach into my bag. 'I've come to ask you for a job. And I've come to give this back to you, Carlo.'

He is watching me, unsure at first. But as I slide the gold box across the coffee table towards him, he shakes his head. 'No, Anna, I want you to have it – as a gift.'

'I'm sorry, Carlo.' My voice is firm. 'But I don't want it.'

He smiles – that old *silly, funny Anna* smile. 'Oh, Anna! Why not?'

There it is again – his seductive, beautiful smile that lights up his whole face and makes me want to *be* that old, silly funny Anna once more; makes me want to say something, *do* something to delight him, intrigue him again, if only to hear him say, 'Really, Anna?'

But I shake my head. 'You should give it to Beattie, Carlo.'

I see it then, a flicker in his eyes. *'Beattie?'*

I nod. 'Beattie.'

'Ah...' And his beautiful smile vanishes.

This is not what he was anticipating at all. This is not how the game goes. And it is as if a mask has dropped away. The playfulness in his dark eyes has disappeared. He leans back, his hands coming down on either side of the armchair, fingers tapping the soft leather.

'I wondered – when you didn't come today... Anna, I'm so sorry. I have caused you pain, I think.'

I am surprised, overwhelmed by his honesty. I wasn't expecting this – his easy admission, this apology. His sincerity has caught me off guard, as I have him.

He leans forward suddenly, his hand moving up to my face – a caress. 'I am a silly old fool, Anna.'

His hand is warm on my cheek, his voice soft. I feel the undercurrent of my emotions rise again, that treacherous swell of tears. He is not the *only* old fool here, I think. Because I understand now – *yes*, I finally understand as I look into his eyes, as I search his face, what it is that first seduced me, what I fell for so long ago – that indefinable *something*, the indefinable magic of this man. It wasn't the devil streak in him; it wasn't that at all. I can see it now. I see it in his dark hair, in his eyes, and in his gentle smile.

I had run away to the other side of the world, run from my mother, from my grandmother's death, seeking all those things my mother had warned me against. And I had fallen for this older man, this man so like the one in the photo, the only photo I have – of my father.

'Tell me, Anna. How can I help? How can I make it up to you?'

I smile as I pull myself up. I am older now. I am starting to wise up, *finally*. 'Just a job, Carlo.' I figure he owes me that much. 'No more gifts.'

And he nods. 'No, no more gifts.'

This time around, we have a deal – no free lunch, no strings attached.

When I get back, there's a message waiting for me at the hotel. Madame hands me the pink slip of paper. Carlo has obviously not lost any time.

It's from Beattie.

She has tried me three times already. I smile. It's only been an hour since I walked out of his office. Her message is simple.

Call me.

I don't.

The phone rings just as I am making my way downstairs for breakfast.

Déjà Vu

'*Oui, un moment s'il vous plaît,*' I hear Madame say.

I realise it's for me because she has fallen silent, perhaps listening for my footsteps on the stairs. It must be Beattie. I don't want to talk to her. I hesitate on the third last step, about to do an about-turn and creep back up. But it's too late.

'*Mademoiselle Muucinntiire!*'

Madame nods at me as I peep my head around the corner, waving her cigarette and gesturing towards the phone cabin, her poodle barking at the ash falling on to the reception desk. The businessman is watching me from his corner in the breakfast hall, tapping impatiently on the table. He wants his croissant. So I have no choice but to take the call.

'Mademoiselle MacIntyre?'

I recognise the voice straight away. It's not Beattie. I sigh, relieved. It's Carlo's assistant.

I've landed myself a job. I start tomorrow, as the company's liaison officer. As Grandma always said, 'It's not what you know but *who* you know.'

Chapter *thirty-eight*

I am standing in the middle of the exposition hall at the Pompidou, Paris' Cultural Centre. This massive glass building, built back in the nineteen-seventies, is like a giant Meccano gadget, a child's toy, with boldly coloured bits and pieces: red, blue and green tubes, rotating wheels and great vents rising up out of the ground like Dali's swaying tubular eyes. Its skeletal underbelly is exposed in brazen defiance to the world, as a celebration to the seventies, as a celebration of modern architecture. The modern world, back then.

It is the annual International Trade Fair, and I am here as Moratel's representative, talking and smiling to the Japanese businessmen. As the company's newest recruit, this is what I must do – talk and smile as they crowd me into the corner of the display stand. I have learnt the spiel off by heart. But beyond that, I basically don't have a clue what I'm talking about.

I can do this, I tell myself. *I can do this standing on my head,* just like I can teach. The hard part is smiling. I consider standing on my head. Maybe that'll get a laugh. But as Charlie would say, 'You're a dag, Mum.' When he was little, his face used to light up when I acted the clown, those blue eyes wide with delight like Carlo's when he'd say 'Really, *Anna*?'; but the closer Charlie got to adolescence, the more his delight turned into sheer embarrassment, and I was just a *dag*.

The exposition hall echoes with announcements over the PA, recorded voices accompanied by hypnotic jingles promising over and over the dawn of wonderful new advances in telecommunications, up-to-the-minute technological marvels that will revolutionise *the way we do business*, taking us with a flying leap into the twenty-first century. I smile. Mobile telephones aren't quite there yet – they are still these big, unwieldy lead bricks, like kids' walkie-talkies, not yet the sleek, miniature, million-and-one-functioned gadgets of 2006. It is, after all, only 1991.

The stand opposite is marked Google. They will go far, I think. Knowing what I know, I really ought to buy some shares. But my heart's not in it. Money can't buy what I want.

Around mid-morning there's a break in the crowd. My stand is temporarily quiet. I grab the opportunity to take a look around. All the big international companies are here. I hear the other representatives speaking in their faltering English, their potential clients barking back at them with American, German and Japanese accents.

I don't see the stand until I reach the far end of the hall. It's over in the corner. Alsttel. I should have known. They were, after all, right at the hub of it during the booming nineties, when the Internet really started to take off.

It occurs to me suddenly, Marc might be here. I haven't seen him, haven't spoken to him since that Sunday. A whole month has elapsed since then – a whole lifetime during which I have woken each morning in my hotel room and thought, *here I am again, and here I will stay* – acceptance weighing on my heart like a prison sentence. And I got life. So I have lumbered around in this strange new existence, doing what I must do to survive. But that is all I can do. I have no energy to find a permanent place to live. Permanence in this strange new world scares me. While I stay in the hotel, nothing is set in stone, not yet. I wake, I work and at night I dream – of Charlie.

Of Marc.

I take refuge behind a column, peeping out to check if he is there. A crowd swarms around their advertising screens with a few representatives hovering, smiling, keen to sell, keen for their commission. I can't see him, but I wait just in case, still watching cautiously.

'*Tu cherches quelqu'un?*' Are you looking for someone?

He has come up behind me, taken me by surprise, so I reel around too quickly, knocking his paper cup to the ground, black coffee splashing over our shoes. *Marc!*

He grins. '*Je te fais autant peur que* ça?' Am I *that* scary?

I smile back, embarrassed. My heart pounds, and it is not

entirely due to the shock. His smile still does it for me – and not merely because it's Charlie's.

'*Alors*, what are you doing here?' I notice his voice is a little breathless, that way it fluctuates when he's nervous, as he leans over to recover the cup.

'I'm here *on business*. My stand's over there.' I point off into the crowd, vague. He whistles. 'Impressed?'

'*Very!*' He laughs.

I've always liked the way his laughter comes from deep within his throat – a movement, a tiny tremor right in the hollow of his neck, above his collarbone, making me want to reach out and touch it with my finger, to feel his soft skin – even softer as he aged. That tiny vibrant tremor, his vulnerability. I am *hopeless*, I think.

'Meet me for lunch, Annie,' he says quickly.

'No.' I shake my head, looking over in the direction of my stand. 'I should get back.'

'Christ, Annie, *just* lunch. *C'est tout!*'

I turn back to him, startled by the urgency in his voice, this plea. His eyes meet mine. And I see it then, his pain. He is suffering too. I want to place my hand on his neck, to pull him to me, press into him and whisper in his ear, 'Come on, let's go home now!' I can see right into the pupils of his blue eyes, right into that blackness where I used to look and see into his soul, see *myself* in his soul.

But I don't see me there any more. I see *her* – Beattie, standing before him, his green-eyed goddess.

'*S'il te plaît*, Annie, can't we get past this? Can't you forgive me?'

Yes, I want to say. *Oh God, yes!* But she is there, standing between us, my old friend – grinning. 'So you're *Australian*? Well now, I'd never have guessed!' And I can't see past her.

'I should get back...'

'*Après alors*...After work, tonight.'

I shake my head. If I start crying now I am doomed.

'Don't say no, Annie, don't even say yes. Just —'

Something on my chest has caught his eye. I look down. I had forgotten – the ID card pinned to my jacket. 'Annie MacIntyre,' he reads. 'Liaison officer, Moratel...*Moratel?*' I see the flicker of recognition in his eyes as his mind ticks over, putting two and two together. 'Isn't that Vitali's company?'

'Yes, I —'

'Ah...*je vois*...' I see, he cuts across me, wincing as if stung, a shadow sliding across his features, a mask.

No, you don't see! I'm thinking. Because I can tell what *he's* thinking from that look. And I am struck dumb by his foolishness. Doesn't he know me better than that?

'Marc?'

But it's too late. I watch, staring open-mouthed, as he turns and heads back to his stand.

Chapter
thirty-nine

*I*t is Sunday morning, 10.58 a.m., two months to the day since I left Marc. But who's counting? I am, as I stand in the middle of Gare de l'Est, staring up at the giant blackboard, watching the train times tick over, times and destinations click-clacking over as speedily as fortunes at the stock exchange.

There's a train headed for Gretz-Armainvilliers, due to pull out from platform fourteen in just two minutes. Do I take it or not? I hear the muted sing-song drone over the PA, a woman's voice. No one can make out what she's saying – except me.

'Take it, Annie,' she says.

So I make a run for it. The platform is empty except for a couple of guards standing around, caps pushed back, pulling on their cigarettes. But the train is still there, only just though, as the big hand on the grimy old clock above the platform slides on to the twelve – 11 a.m. It's due to depart. I jump aboard as the whistle sounds and the train starts to move off.

I am headed for Ozouer le Voulgis, Marc's home town.

I don't know exactly *why* I'm headed out to that tiny village: whether it's just to see the house in rue de la République, up the road from the square; to see his parents moving beyond the window; or perhaps Marc's van parked out front, just like old times when we used to come for Sunday lunch. And maybe, *maybe* if I look hard enough, up at the small attic windows in that old house, I might glimpse Charlie burrowing around in the old trunks. Though I know what my eleven-year-old would say if he looked out and saw me, standing forlorn across the road, looking up at him. 'You've lost it, Mum.'

Yes, I think I might have.

I stare out the train window, watching Paris' ugly sprawling suburbia, the boxed-concrete supermarket complexes, transform into flat open countryside, so sparse and monotonous compared to the rolling green hills enveloping Lherm.

A man sits opposite, three rows along. He looks up from his paper and smiles. I turn and stare out the window again. I will have to take the bus from the station. I am not invited for lunch this time. So why *am* I doing this?

I think I know why. I've lain in my hotel bed at night and cursed him, *hating* him – my rage fuelled by an uncontrollable wave of despair. *How could you do it, Marc?* How could you do this to me? To Charlie? With my best friend? Yet, despite it all... I have missed him. I have woken in the night and felt the weight of his body on the mattress, the pull of the sheet as he turns over, my hand sliding, reaching for him in the dark, sure that I can see the silhouette of his body, sure that I can hear him breathing. And when I wake in the morning my head turns, seeking his face, his eyes, the crinkles when he smiles on the pillow next to mine. '*Marc?*' But he's not there.

'We were going to separate, Annie,' I hear him say. I know, I think, shaking my head, wishing the man opposite would stop staring at me and just read his paper. *I know!*

The bus pulls into the square as the church bells ring in midday – this quiet village square that I know well, its imposing, stern grey church and bell tower casting a shadow over the poplar trees at its base; the café tabac, *Le Carmiya*, where the locals come for their caffeine and tobacco hits. Opposite, the *boulangerie* is set in among the shuttered, cream-stone houses leading up towards Marc's family home. And it hits me as I stand in the middle of the square: she stood with him *here*.

There's a queue at the *boulangerie* overflowing into the street, the pre-lunch rush come to fetch their baguettes before closing time. I glance quickly up and down the line, looking out for Maurice, for his grey hair and familiar face, so like Marc's. Perhaps they are here together. But the coast is clear, except for old Madame Murat, their neighbour with her cane and purse and tight-lipped stare, waiting among them. I smile and nod, but she turns away. And I realise, *of course* she doesn't know me. So even if I was to walk straight into Marc's parents, they wouldn't give me a second glance either. They haven't met me yet! I take a seat on the stone bench under the poplar tree.

I am invisible, a shadow, just a cloud passing overhead.

A group of five men are playing boules on the dirt flat a few metres away. Marc's not here either, though he would know most of these men, I am sure. He'd often stop here for a moment on our way down to the river, out for a late Sunday afternoon stroll.

I watch them now, their arms folded, contemplating the game, kicking at the ground, murmuring together, laughing and occasionally throwing their arms up. And then I notice a large man among them, a brown straggly dog with a red scarf tied around its neck hovering at his feet. My heart beats faster. I recognise him. It is Serge, Marc's old friend, the one that drowned.

A shiver runs through me.

They are bowling in my direction. A boule has rolled in close, by my feet. I consider getting up to move off, out of the way. But then suddenly the game is over and Serge is walking towards me, coming my way to collect his boule. I hold my breath, wondering if he has noticed, if he has recognised me. Marc introduced me years ago, before we left for Australia, before he... Then I realise, in 1991 I am just a stranger to him as well.

'*Bonjour!*' He smiles as he kneels down to recover the ball, his shadow falling over me as his dog sniffs around at my feet, its wet nose tickling my ankles.

'*Bonjour.*' I nod back and reach a hand out to pat the mutt's head, the hairs on my arms rising. I am ill at ease with this great big man standing before me, so vibrant, so *alive*. I have seen into the crystal ball – I know what he doesn't know.

He pauses. He has heard my accent and is curious as he tosses the boule, silver and battered, up into the air, up and down, up and down, without moving off. He has a good face. There's a softness in his brown eyes and dark curly hair, even though he is built like a fighter, square and solid – a packet of muscles. *Une force de la nature.* I smile back at him. 'A smile costs nothing,' I used to tell Charlie. But I want to give him more, *much* more than this.

He looks as if he wants to ask me something. Ask me and I will tell you, I think. Please, just ask me!

'Serge!' one of his mates calls over, impatient, as they move off, heading towards the café. It's time for an apéritif. *'Tu viens ou pas?'*

My leg jiggles up and down as he waves them on. I don't know what to say. How do you tell a man, a stranger, to watch out, to be very, *very* careful when he goes down to the river – that he will drown if he jumps in after his dog? How do you tell someone on their way to work that they shouldn't go in *at all* that day, because a plane will crash into the office; that they mustn't go down to the beach because there will be a tidal wave, or an earthquake? They will smile perhaps, even *laugh* at you, and then they will do it all the same. I am just a strange woman sitting on a park bench.

I cannot change fate.

But he has such a nice face, I have to tell him *something*. I open my mouth to speak, but the words won't come. I could talk about the weather, what a beautiful day it is. It's true, the sun is shining, casting a dappled light through the poplars here in the square, like a Renoir painting – far too beautiful a day to bestow such dark tidings. And I wonder suddenly if April was Renoir's favourite month to paint, with this crisp dry air accentuating the colours in the leaves, raising his spirits as he dabbed his paintbrush lightly on to the canvas. But I doubt if he ever came to Ozouer. Then I think, no, perhaps Serge's dog would be a better place to start. Yes, the French *love* to talk about their dogs, more so than their children. So I consider leading in with 'Hey, nice dog... But watch out – he'll be the death of you one day.'

Charlie is right, I *have* definitely lost the plot. Serge is smiling at me still, probably amused more than anything else by the way my mouth keeps opening and then shutting like a fish, an indecisive fish.

'*Eh*, Serge!' Someone else is calling to him now.

My heart thuds hard against my rib cage. Serge's massive body blocks my view. But I know the voice.

He doesn't see me at first, not until he comes up level.

'*Salut*, Serge!' he says as he reaches over to place a hand on his friend's back. He smiles down at me, obviously expecting to see someone else, *anyone* else but me, sitting here on a bench in the middle of Ozouer.

He steps back, startled, truly startled. 'Annie.'

Marc's young face takes me by surprise all over again. My breathing has quickened. It seems I am still governed by my heart — my silly, *silly* heart. I nod up at him, for the moment reluctant to say anything. I am feeling strangely guilty.

'*Mais, vous vous connaissez?*' Serge is obviously surprised that his friend should know this strange woman.

'*Eh...oui.*' Marc reaches a hand up, rubbing his forehead.

And I remember that first time he introduced me to Serge all those years back, that look in his eye, his pride, his hand resting on the small of my back. Was it the same with Beattie that day she came out here? Did his hand linger there softly, barely touching but feeling the heat of her body rising from underneath her dress?

He looks from me to Serge and back again. We are silent, awkwardly silent. Marc's eyes are searching mine, an eyebrow raised. And I realise he is wondering if I have said something, something about the river, about Serge's dog.

I shake my head, no.

'*Bon.*' Serge claps his giant hands together. '*Je vous laisse. Je vais au café.*'

He is off to the café. Marc nods and Serge slaps a hand against his back. They are old friends. Then he turns, whistling to his dog, his *best* friend.

'*Au revoir, Mademoiselle!*'

I watch as he pulls open the café door and disappears inside.

He is gone. We've let him go without saying anything, without warning him.

'We could kidnap the dog,' I venture.

'*Non.*' Marc shakes his head. 'He'll just get another one. He's always had a dog, ever since he was little. He likes them.'

'Obviously.'

The square is empty now. The *boulangerie* has shut up shop for lunch. We sit in silence, the two of us on the bench. I remember Charlie playing here when he was five, when we came out from Australia to visit Marc's mother. He liked drawing shapes with a stick in the dirt, at our feet, just here. I remember wiping his small soft hands, sticky and grubby, as his face and lips screwed up in protest. 'No, Mummy!' I look down. But of course the shapes are not here now. They will *never* be here.

I glance up at the church tower as the bells ring out one o'clock. 'Let's make a wish.'

'A wish?'

'Yes,' I nod, getting up. 'Come on.'

It is my first time inside. I know though that Marc has come here many, *many* times. His mother has shown me photos from when he was just a newborn, his face contorted, crying as the priest dripped cool water on to his forehead; then as a gangly pointy-elbowed adolescent, hair slicked back, face scrubbed for first Communion. The thought of Marc walking up the aisle, his hands clasped together in prayer in a starched white frock, makes me smile, bitter – the good little Catholic boy. The good son, the good man, sitting in the front pew with his wife's best friend – in memory of his father.

We stand at the entrance. Its interior is bigger than I had antici-pated, much more spectacular. I look up at the Gothic arches and the saints perched above, decked out in their standard drab brown smocks tied with rope and their bowl hairdos, each with a babe in his arms, looking down at us benevolently from each column.

There are wooden confession boxes over in the corner. Marc told me once how as a child he'd have to line up with his school-mates and confess, even when he had *nothing* to confess. So they'd wait their turn and make things up – white lies – just to get it over with and please the priest. Jean-Claude would say he'd hit his baby brother; Philippe, that he'd cursed his father; and Marc – what did Marc invent? Did he come here to own up about *her*? I stare at the little wooden boxes, wondering how a man could ever fit inside, *two* men – a man and a priest. It's like Charlie's first joke: how many elephants can you fit into a mini? Like Marc's joke on me.

Forgive me father, for I have sinned. I cheated on my wife. With her best friend. When she was seven months pregnant.

How many sins can you fit into one? I wonder. And what did

he have to do as penance? Five Hail Marys? Maybe he and Beattie even said them together.

How quaint.

A woman arranges flowers at the alter. As we walk through the body of the church, she smiles over at us. Long-stemmed blooms lie fanned out across the pavement stone, a bed of colours at her feet – purple, orange and crimson. She takes each flower up, one by one, cutting the stems, arranging them in her vase like a sculpture, with such care, such *devotion*.

I am looking for the candles. There's a small candelabra stand over to the left. It is not as big as in the Madeleine, but it should do the job anyway. I veer towards it. Marc follows. There's a box marked *Cierges*, filled with long tapered candles. There's not a lot of choice here, so I take one.

'Have you got any change on you?' I want *him* to pay for this one. I figure it's the least he can do. He reaches into his jeans pocket and pulls out a franc, just a franc. 'Is that all?'

He smiles at me and shrugs. 'It's just a candle, Annie.'

'*Is* it, Marc? And you call yourself a Catholic.'

'*Mais tu sais bien*, Annie, I don't go in for all that stuff any more.'

As my mother would say, though, 'Once a Catholic, always a Catholic.' I take the franc and let it drop into the collection box. It drops to the bottom with a dull thud – metal on wood. There is only one other candle burning on the stand. Obviously not a lot happens here in Ozouer.

Déjà Vu

Marc is standing behind me as I place my candle beside the other. 'You know what I wish, Annie?' I wait, watching the flame tapering thin and narrow, too weak to make my wish come true. I don't turn around. But I feel his breath, hot on my neck, then his jaw, bristly against my skin. 'I wish it never happened.'

'Wish *what* never happened, Marc?' I have turned on him, so suddenly he stumbles back. 'Which part?'

I want to hear him say it here in the church, *his* church. But it's barely a whisper.

'Between Beattie and me.'

'Between Beattie and you? You already got that wish, Marc.'

He steps towards me, reaching for my hand. '*Annie* —'

I step back. I don't want to dance. 'You know what *I* think, Marc?' I hear the flower lady's heels tapping quickly on the church tiles, heading towards us. 'You just wish you never told me!'

'*Shhhht.*' She has lost her smile.

Marc's hand has moved up and through his hair, embarrassed. '*Pardon, Madame.*'

I look up to stop the tears swelling, threatening my pride. There's a saint hovering just beyond Marc's head. Is this him again, I wonder – Beattie's Saint Anthony? Well then, why doesn't he help me out here? I try to focus my blurred vision on him instead of Marc – on his benign smile, not the baby in his arms. But it's no use – the tears brim over.

'*Why*, Marc? *Why did you do it?*' The flower lady hovers,

murmuring, gesturing with her hands for me to quieten down. But I *cannot* quieten my anger, my frustration, this ghastly pain.

Marc stands before me like a little boy, *our* little boy, his face full of despair. '*Je n'etais pas bien*, Annie! I felt so alone! *Je ne savais pas comment te dire*. I couldn't —'

'Oh, Marc!' I am struggling to say the words without screaming, without crying out loud for the pain of hearing this now. 'You *weren't* alone! You couldn't explain what you felt *to me*?'

He shakes his head, a sad half smile breaking across his face. '*Non*, Annie, I couldn't talk to you.'

And I am crying – crying as I remember lying next to him, turning to him, wanting to envelope him with my big, unwieldy body, and how he would always turn from me. 'I would have understood. You could have told me! You were grieving, Marc. I knew what you —'

'*Non*, Annie!'

I am startled by his cry, its booming resonance echoing through the body of the church, reverberating against my eardrums, in my heart – silencing the flower lady, stilling her hands. '*Tu ne comprends pas*, Annie! I *couldn't* tell you. You kept telling me that you understood, but I kept thinking how *could* you?'

I am breathing hard, because I know – I know what is coming.

'You didn't have a family. You wouldn't even talk to your own mother!'

I watch as the flower lady turns, leaving us finally. I cannot look at him – the pain, the hurt, is unbearable.

'When I heard about my father, I felt so alone. I felt so *angry*. I was scared, Annie.'

'And you thought I didn't know that?' I whisper.

'You were pregnant, Annie. You were so happy. You were so . . . *complète*.'

'Complete?'

'You didn't need family —'

'I needed *you*, Marc!'

'You didn't need *me*. You've never needed anyone, Annie!'

I feel it then – as though I am very, *very* far away, as though I am somewhere high up, floating with Saint Anthony. 'Hey!' I'm calling to the young man down below. 'Can you get me down from here, please?' But he's not listening. So I'm stuck up here. All I can do is watch as the woman turns from him, runs down the body of the church and out through the door.

And so I can't tell him how *much* I do need him – really, *really* need him – stuck all the way up here, so far away.

Chapter *forty*

*I*n the evening following Charlie's birth, after the nurses had bathed him, I remember stroking his soft, downy head as he lay in the glass crib beside my bed, his tiny form wrapped in a hospital swaddling blanket. That moment of subdued calm, of pure serenity – the sheer exhaustion! They had dimmed the lights along the hospital ward. 'Time to go, boys!' the hospital sister called. Marc was gathering his things together, preparing to leave. And that is when the dreaded question came again.

'What about your mother?'

So the moment of calm passed. Why did he have to mention her now? I could hear the women in the next room laughing – the gay couple. Sister had forgotten about them.

'What about her, Marc?'

'*Eh bien*... aren't you going to ring your mother to tell her you have had a baby?'

I stared at him. I thought that when he asked me this the last time, in the early months of my pregnancy, he had understood. The baby made a funny scratchy bleating sound like a kitten. I turned, my hand reaching down to feel for him breathing – those tiny hot puffs on the back of my hand making me smile in spite of Marc.

'Why would I ring her after all these years? Why *should* I?'

He shrugged and walked towards the door. He was going to leave, like *this*? 'Marc?'

I saw it then, when he turned back to me – the dour, dark anger in his eyes. 'You should ring her, Annie. *Je ne te comprends pas!* One day she will die and —'

So this was what it was about – his father. 'Marc, *stop!*'

His shoulders were set firm; a warrior framed in the doorway. How could he be like this, tonight of *all* nights! I had wanted, *wished* for him to be happy, for this to be the happiest day of his life – for the pain of his father's death to be forgotten, for now at least. Because I had been telling myself that once the baby was born, he would feel it – the infusion of happiness I had felt, the endorphin rush. That once he saw our baby in the flesh, once he could take him in his arms, he would feel it too – and he would start to see beyond his father's death. That the healing process would begin with our baby, with us *as a family*.

'Listen to me, Marc, the relationship I had with my mother —' Just those words in my mouth – *my mother* – made it difficult to breathe. I tried again. 'The relationship I had with *her* was not like what you had with your father —'

He cut me off. '*Ah oui, ça je sais*, Annie! That's the problem, isn't it? You *don't* know what it's like! You don't know what it's *been* like. You don't understand *anything*!'

I could hear voices, a flurry of nurses out in the ward, padding towards the room. 'So tell me, Marc, *tell* me *please* what I don't understand!'

'All this, Annie! *Us*, the baby! *Je ne peux pas*, Annie! I *can't* do it!'

And I wanted to tell him then, right then and there, but Sister's ruddy-cheeked face had appeared over his shoulder, wedged between Marc and the doorway. '*Whoa* there, you two! We can't have this now, can we?'

So I *couldn't*. I couldn't tell him that I knew he was scared, that I knew he was confused – that we would get through this together because I understood what he was going through, I *really* did, and that I loved him... *God, how I loved him!* I couldn't say any of it because Sister had well and truly muscled her way in, placing her broad, bosomy body between Marc and me, hands extended either side as if to hold us off each other.

'I think we might all be just a *wee* bit overtired here tonight after such a big day, don't you think?'

And I wanted to say it was okay, we would be fine, that I could deal with this if she could just give us a minute alone, *please*, before she sent him away. But another nurse had appeared in the doorway as Marc edged his way into the corner of the room, silent and tense like a boxer – so far from me, *so* unreachable. And my chin was wobbling weirdly, like they'd warned me – that the hormones turn you into a blubbering mess. So I couldn't tell anyone anything then.

All I could do was watch as they ushered him away in their true flat-shoed-no-nonsense-nurse mode: 'How about we call it a day, and come morning we'll both be feeling a lot better, eh? How does that sound?'

I had wanted to shout out, 'No, please let him stay!' Because I knew it then – come morning he *wouldn't* be feeling a lot better. And the moment would be lost, that moment when I had seen into his eyes, seen the fear lurking behind his anger. Because what I feared *most* of all was that the scared little boy behind this angry young man face would hide himself away from me forever, hiding under a panoply of bitterness.

Chapter
forty-one

*I*n the early days, I remember playing that silly game with Marc – the one where I would tell him three things I loved about him, and he would tell me three things about me; that silly, self-indulgent game that always deteriorated into jokes about what we really, really *hated* about each other. Back then, those 'hate' confessions were always the funniest, the most ridiculous things we could invent.

Just a funny lovers' game.

It was late in the afternoon. We were lying on the sand at Belle Ile on that sparse open beach of fine, white sand, set down low in between massive boulders; not another living soul around for miles except a raucous flock of seagulls soaring in and out between the rocks, hovering low over the water as it lapped back and forth.

I was lying across Marc's back, face up to the sky, mesmerised by the brilliant red glow beneath my closed eyelids, the warmth of his skin seeping into the back of my shoulders, into *my* skin. The ecstasy of his body beneath mine.

He wriggled his shoulderblades. '*Trois choses? Voyons...*

Three is a lot, *non?*'

But I waited, knowing he would do this, that he would tease me when his turn came. 'The way your hair tickles my back right now. *J'adore ça.*'

'That doesn't count,' I said. 'Think of something less ephemeral.'

'Less ephemeral?'

'Yes.'

'*Ton amour.*'

'My love?'

'*Oui,*' he said, but this time without moving his shoulders, without moving anything; his body still, like a rock under mine. 'Your love for me.'

And I had smiled up at the sky, without saying anything.

'*Alors, la deuxième*... the second is always very hard to find.'

A seagull cawed in protest as I waited patiently, basking in the heat of the sun, in the warmth of his words.

'*J'aime ton courage. J'aime ton courage de rester seule.*'

'My courage in being alone?'

'*Oui.*' I felt his shoulders wriggle underneath me as he searched for the words. 'You have no family, but you don't mind. You are, *comment dire? Comme une pierre qui roule.*'

'A rolling stone?'

'*Oui,* you are like a rolling stone. I love that too.'

So I wonder now, when did this turn into a thing he hated – that he *really* hated about me?

245

Chapter
forty-two

I wake with a headache to end all headaches, threatening to crack my skull open. The pain makes my skin creep, my stomach churn over. I lie flat on my back in a cold sweat on my bed, unable to lift a finger. To try to open my eyes again would be sheer folly.

It is Monday morning. I know this because the colour behind my eyelids has turned from black to red as the daylight creeps through the window across the carpet, finally reaching my bed. But that's all I know.

I hear footsteps on the stairs, and a dog barking. It must be very late. I have missed breakfast. I should be at work.

'*Mademoiselle Muucinntiire?*' Madame calls softly, knocking cautiously on my door. But her poodle couldn't give a damn. Its yapping, high-pitched and merciless, makes me groan. '*Shhht,*' she hisses. But the dog *really* couldn't give a damn.

I can't answer. It would involve having to move my tongue. All I can do is groan. I hear the key rattling in the old lock, then the door creaking open. She is standing over me. Her shadow moves across my closed eyelids. I feel her hand, small and cold on my forehead.

'*Oh làaa,*' she coos. '*Ma pauvre petite chérie!*'

I hear her running back down the stairs, the dog scampering after her. She has forgotten to close the door. It makes me anxious.

A woman's voice wakes me. I must have slept, though I don't know how. My head is still pounding, but less intense. I lift my eyelids, slow and cautious. I don't know this face hovering over me.

'*Bonjour.*' The face beams. 'I'm Doctor *Wade.*'

The accent is unmistakably American, as is the smile – a flash of teeth, dazzling white. I try one back, but can only manage a grimace. It's probably for the best, as I suspect my teeth are not up for comparison, especially not this morning. She takes a seat beside me on the bed.

'The concierge tells me you were running a fever.' Her hand is on my shoulder. 'Would you mind if I check you over just quickly?'

'Okay,' I croak, though I sense I have no say in this as I pull myself up into a sitting position. 'But I think I'm fine now.'

She smiles. 'Great, that's great.' Her hand squeezes my shoulder. 'But we'll just check you over anyway.'

She reaches for her case, flipping it open on the bed. 'It's *Annie*, right?' She's obviously trying to distract me as she pulls out her paraphernalia. 'You're Austraalian?'

'Ye—' In goes the thermometer. My teeth bite down hard on the glass, trying to hold the damn thing in place as she whisks a pressure belt around my upper arm and starts pumping. 'You know, I really think I'm fine now,' I mumble.

'Sure you are!' She's still pumping away, though.

'I don't think this is necess—'

Her hand shoots up for me to be quiet while she concentrates on taking my pressure.

'Right.' Her manner is brisk as she pulls on the velcro and whisks it off and away. I'm hoping that's it. 'Mind if I ask how old you are, Annie?'

'Thirty-nine,' I say.

She whistles. 'Well, honey, I'd sure as hell like some of whatever it is that *you're* on!'

I stare at her, wondering where Madame has dragged her up from. Then I realise. 'Just kidding,' I say quickly, forcing a smile. 'I'm twenty-five.'

'Oh, you Austraalians! I've heard about your sense of humour.'

Yes, I think, *Crocodile Dundee* really put us on the map.

'You know, Annie. . .' She pats my knee through the bedcovers. 'I need you to do just one more thing for me.'

I stare at her, hoping it's not what I think it is. She reaches into her bag again and pulls out an empty plastic container. Shit, it is. Not here in this room behind the screen – surely not?

'If you'd just like to pop up and do a little pee for me, that'd be great.'

God, how I hate the word 'pee', I'm thinking as I try to relax enough to do it, balanced precariously over the toilet, aiming for the container at the same time. My head is pounding and I know she can hear everything: the sound of me *peeing* behind the paper-thin screen.

'*Alrighty*,' she drawls when I hand my sample over to her. 'Just one more little test and that should just about wrap it up.'

She has pulled out a litmus paper. I wonder what the point is – all these silly tests that have nothing to do with my head. I let her go through the motions anyway, to get it over with.

'Annie.' She is smiling, flashing those pearly whites at me again. 'You'll be happy to know what you have is not catching. So there's nothing stopping you from returning to work tomorrow.'

I stare at her. Well, I already knew *that*. It was just a headache, a very bad headache. I am wondering if I should have asked her for some ID. She could, after all, be anyone – a tourist staying at the hotel perhaps, who just happened to wander past my open door. Though I don't recall seeing her in the breakfast room...

I don't see it coming.

'Honey, what you have is just a very severe case of morning sickness.'

It has happened when I least suspect it, just as it did that first time – the miracle. Only last time the miracle was Charlie, *my*

Charlie. I'm not interested in this one. She can take it away with her, along with her bag of tricks.

It is two months since we made love at his apartment – just the once. Weird how we'd tried and tried for Charlie, and yet this time...

This time around, I feel no joy. I just feel sick.

Chapter
forty-three

'*A*nnie?' The voice is eerily like mine – an echo. *So* like mine, yet I cannot think what to say to her. I'm trembling as I grip the phone; trembling like a little girl again, even now, for it has been so long since I have heard this voice… Since I've heard my name on my mother's lips.

'Annie, *where* are you?'

Where to begin? I think. So I take a breath and tell her. 'I'm in France, Mum.'

'You're in *France*? For goodness' *sake*, Annie, what have you done?'

If I wasn't so tense, I would find this funny – *very* funny – to have reached this age, for so much water to have passed under the bridge, and now, having finally made the call from Madame's telephone cabin at the base of the stairs, to be asked this! As if I am a child, no older than Charlie. But whether I am twenty-five or thirty-nine is neither here nor there. I am still a silly, flighty thing to my mother, who has done something silly *again*.

It has been a very long time since I took that plane, since I left without saying goodbye after Grandma's funeral. But for my mother, of course, it is only two years.

'Go somewhere nice, Annie,' Grandma had said. 'Somewhere special with your mother. Then make a wish and throw them to the wind. Make a wish together.'

But we didn't.

We hadn't spoken in five years, since I'd left home at eighteen, slamming the door shut behind me. But at the funeral she had turned to me *finally* and said, 'Now you might come back down to earth.' And I knew as I looked into her face, looked into those dark eyes, their black centres, that *blackness*, I couldn't ask her.

I just couldn't ask her to do it with me. My promise to Grandma.

We were like two women standing on opposite sides of a highway, neither of us able to cross over to the other's side. And Grandma was gone now. Her mother, my grandmother. We had no common ground any more, no common lifeboat to cling to – we were swirling down the plughole in opposite directions because we inhabited two different hemispheres. Two different planets.

So I had walked away, crying into the wind, 'Let her keep the ashes!'

And as the plane gathered speed along the runway, its great mass creaking in protest, lifting finally like a pregnant pterodac-tyl, I said it again, my head pressed hard into the headrest as the plane moved up and up. But the tears seeped treacherously down-wards, diagonally across my hot, bloated cheeks, cold puddles of disappointment in my ears. Because the romantic side of me had believed it would go differently this time, that annoyingly persist-ent inner affirmation from deep within my heart, that fairytales and happy-ever-after endings really do exist. I had thought that over time, and with the death of her mother, her soft side – Norma Jean – would surface again, *finally*; that she would turn to me at Grandma's funeral and say, 'Annie, I've missed you.' I thought I would look into her face and see it there – her fear. Her fear, like mine, that with Grandma gone we could lose each other forever if we didn't try to make peace. Because I *really* believed she wasn't always this cold and impenetrable. So I had planned to tell her then and there that I missed her too. But she'd missed her cue, and so had I.

Yet it was only after I climbed four flights up the hotel stairs, when I first arrived in Paris, that the full force of what I'd done *really* hit home – some 17 000 kilometres later.

I had deprived Grandma of her final wish.

I remember my mother once asked me, 'What do you want from me, Annie – a *National Velvet* mum?' I used to watch that old black-and-white series every day after school, at 4 p.m. on the dot, watching Velvet come home from school too, milk and cookies waiting for her on the kitchen table and her ever patient, softly spoken doe-eyed mum always, *always* there for her. Martha

Brown – she was really something as far as mothers went. Yes, that was exactly what I wanted. Even now. 'Well, Velvet dear…'

My grip tightens over the handpiece as I stand in Madame's cabin. I can feel the tiny holes, imprints in my flesh, as my palm presses hard against the plastic. I could just put the phone down, I think, and leave things as they were.

'You wouldn't even talk to your own mother,' he said.

True. I didn't ring to tell her about Marc, about Charlie; that I was married, that I was pregnant… that I'd had a baby boy.

'You didn't need family, Annie. You were so complete.'

Was I? So what is this great gaping hole of emptiness inside me now? Why am I crying into the phone, weeping like a lost child as my mother listens, silent at the other end of the line?

And then, before I even know I am going to, before I even draw another breath, I say it.

'I'm pregnant, Mum.'

So it's out there in the dark stillness of the telephone cabin. Gone – like an email sent too hastily that I cannot bring back. There's no recalling this one. She has it – she knows now. I'm pregnant. *Voilà!*

And *tell* me – why do I feel this incredible sense of relief? Like coming up for air, breathing in great gulps of it, surfacing *at last* from this tidal wave of emotions…

'So why are you crying, Annie?' she replies.

But she already has the answer to that one, because she knows the story well – her story. *Our* story. It's about a girl, a silly young thing, who believed in love, romance and Mr Right. But like she always told me, there are no such things as fairytales.

And therein lies the problem.

I have a vague memory, *so* vague I used to wonder whether it was just a dream because my mother told me long ago, no, it never happened.

I am standing on a stool in the bathroom, leaning over the sink, leaning in close to the mirror, poised there in my mother's black pointy high-heels that I have retrieved from the back of her wardrobe – princess shoes I have never seen her wear. I am applying lipstick – crimson red – smoothing it thick and luscious over my lips like a professional. My tiny fingers sink into a pot of rich, vanilla liquid, oily and dense like clotted cream. I smooth it over my face, applying it generously, meticulously to my forehead, to my cheeks, my chin, *everywhere* – turning my face into a magnificent ivory mask. My eyelids are a rich plum–brown; my cheeks perfect circles of rose; and my eyelashes are thick and blacker than black. I am delighted as I smile at my four-year-old face in the mirror. I am beautiful – I am my mother.

But then I hear noises, the click of heels in the hallway – too fast to be Grandma, who I have left sleeping on the couch. Mum is home early from work. My heart races as I hasten to climb down, my hands brushing against the open jars and powders. The stool topples from underneath me and I fall in a heap, a dull thud resounding in my ears as my head hits the tiles, then the crunch of broken glass.

Blackness.

I am aware of her shoes first, glass splintering under the soles as her hands reach under my armpits, gathering me up, holding me close to her body. The touch of her hand on the back of my head – the sticky wetness there. Her scream. But I can't open my eyes to tell her to take a look – to ask her if she likes my face. Her murmurings into my ear as I am rocked back and forth: 'My silly little Annie, my silly, silly little Annie.' Her wet cheek on mine. I want to tell her to be careful not to smudge the make-up.

I can hear Grandma's voice. 'She is you all over again, Elsie.'

'No, Mum. I won't let her be.'

I think of it sometimes, when I find myself rubbing that funny line of raised skin on the back of my head – the place where the stitches went in, which she said never happened. And I think of it when she tells me now: 'Don't make the mistake I made, Annie! I should have listened to him. I should have let him tell me what happened. I should have forgiven him.'

Déjà Vu

But I am disappointed – disappointed that she is still living the lie that my father was a good man: this man who caused her so much pain, whose loss made her toughen her heart to life, to me.

Chapter *forty-four*

Si vous marchez dans les pas de votre mère, attention...

If you follow in your mother's footsteps, beware...

They haunt me now, those words.

I search my room, my bag, turning my wallet inside out. Where could it have got to, that slip of paper? I had kept it, a funny souvenir of our friendship – for always. We'd been so close, Beattie and I, even in weight, give or take point three of a kilo. I'd slipped it underneath my credit cards, safe in my wallet, and left it there for years and years as it frayed and softened beneath the leather.

But it just isn't there any more. It doesn't make sense.

I say the words out loud now, over and over, as if that will help me find their meaning, find the ending to the sentence, just *find* the bloody thing. But it doesn't. I go to bed, finally. But I can't sleep. By 4 a.m. an idea comes to me: I will go there in the morning, before work – back to the pharmacy.

I need to know.

I take the métro, changing trains at Châtelet, headed towards Gare Saint Lazare, looking around the crowded carriage, anxious that I might see her – her red hair clipped up loose, those green eyes watching me, suspicious.

It's still only early – 7.50 on Friday, a particularly cold morning for April. I should be able to do this and make it into work before nine, even though Moratel is back the other way. I pray Beattie doesn't have an eight o'clock start.

I descend into the Cour de Rome, walking quickly, on past the giant sculpture *L'heure de tous*, a pile of black-framed clocks forming one great column like rubber tyres stacked haphazardly in the middle of the square. I reach the café, looking in furtively like a rabbit as I dart past the doorway. The familiar faces are over by the bar, but I don't see hers among them. Good. But the barman has spotted me. He waves. I pretend I don't see him and keep going.

It's on the corner, just up ahead – the pharmacy.

But then I remember, that first Monday morning back, when I made my re-entry into this past world, the weighing machine wasn't there... and on reaching the entrance I see it's not here even now. It doesn't make sense. Even after hours, the machine was kept outside with a massive chain and padlock wrapped around it. I take a look inside, wondering if they're still closed. The lights are on and the cross is flashing but the grill door is halfway down. So he's about to open. I will wait and see if it's inside.

I am anxious, my coat pulled tight around me, wondering what I should do and praying I won't run into Beattie, when suddenly a truck pulls up. The driver hops down, winking at me as he strides round to the back. I smile politely, watching as he swings the doors open, leaping in one swift movement, a would-be athlete, up and on to the back of his truck – obviously for my benefit. He leans against the side, arms folded, chewing gum, his eyes darting over to see if I am still watching. I am, unfortunately. A metal platform slides down. Great trick, I think. What's he going to do next – bang his chest?

I see it then, sitting in the truck, just as the grill door slides up behind me and the pharmacist hurries out to greet him – and his new set of scales.

So this is why I couldn't find the slip of paper. It hasn't happened yet!

This must be it then – the day we stood out here in the cold and weighed ourselves. Has fate brought me here? I wonder. Or is it me changing fate, like Marc said? I glance up at the Gare Saint Lazare clock, this ancient white timepiece with its faded Roman numerals set up high above the station's grand entrance in intricate stone framework – this clock that I have glanced up at so many times in the past, as have others from another era, from another century. It is 7.58. I look back towards the café. No sign of her. We were running late that day. My breathing quickens. She could turn up any minute.

Déjà Vu

The machine is set up and in place. This is where we came in, Beattie and I.

I look around for her, then back up at the clock – 8.01. I can do it quickly, I think, if I jump on now.

I slip a franc into the slot and wait, glancing up at the clock again. The machine lets out a high-pitched bleep and out rolls the slip of paper, just as the big hand shudders over the third minute past the hour mark.

'Annie?'

My heart does a somersault, but I don't turn around as I reach for the message, easing it out carefully so as not to tear it this time.

'What are you doing here?'

I have it in my hand, safe, as I hop off the scales, feeling slightly ludicrous. 'Weighing myself,' I say cold.

I don't want to look at her, but I do. She is clapping her hands together, trying to get the blood back into her fingers, her head cocked to the side, a half smile, obviously bemused to find me here like this.

'You've come a long way just to do that.'

'You're right.' I glance up at the clock again – a nervous tic. 'I should get going.'

But as I turn to go, back towards the station, she reaches out and grasps my elbow. 'Don't go.' She speaks softly. 'We need to talk.'

'I don't.'

'*I do.*' Her hand grips my arm, firm.

But I *really* don't want to look at her – to look into her face, my old friend, especially now that my eyes are starting to sting. And it's not because of the cold. So I wrench my arm free, to start back.

'Annie, *please* – it's not what you think!'

I turn to her then, seething, my cheeks burning in the bitter cold air. Here it is *again*, this familiar expression, this great blanket phrase they have *all* fallen back on – my father, Marc and now her.

I am shaking as I look straight at her. 'So tell me then, Beattie, what *am* I meant to think?'

She is calm as she stares back at me, as if I am the difficult one here. 'You don't understand.'

'What's there to understand, Beattie?' I throw my hands up, exasperated. 'You slept with him. You can't get clearer than that.'

'Yes, you're right, I did.' She nods, and her red waves bounce soft around her face, her white skin, her fine features. She is like an angel. 'But I've been sleeping with him from the beginning.'

I am stunned by this bald-faced admission. *Have I ever really known this woman?*

'*What?* And that's supposed to make me feel better?'

'You're not *listening* to me, Annie.' She moves towards me, fixing me with her green eyes. 'He was coming out of your class, your first lesson with him. We bumped into each other in the hallway. He asked me out...'

I hadn't seen it coming – like a blow to the stomach when you're anticipating a slap across the face. I reel back, remembering how *I* met her – in the hallway, with her books stacked all the way up to her chin. So I picture it – the two of them crouched opposite one another, so close their knees touch, gathering up her books, his hand brushing against hers as they reach for the same one, eyes meeting. 'Ah!' he exclaims, enchanted. She extends her hand to him, her grip firm. 'I'm Beattie.'

'I'm sorry, Annie, I —' Her voice falters as she steps closer, reaching for my hand. 'I *truly* am.'

Seething still, I step back. 'You couldn't tell me this, Beattie? We were supposed to be friends – *remember!*'

But then I notice her face change; she averts her gaze and stares at the ground. I am taken aback. I have never seen her do this, in all the years I have known her. She is crying, tears streaming down her face.

'When I started going out with him, I *couldn't* tell you – I didn't want anyone to know. Because I knew he was married. *God*, Annie, if my family knew, my father would *kill* me! Their daughter going out with a married man! But I couldn't stop seeing him. You *know* what it's like, Annie, what it's like to be with him!'

And it hits me as I hear these words, as I look at her now – how young she is. She's just a girl, just a young, silly thing. As I was. Yes, I know, I think. I know what it's like. But I am thinking of Marc – not of Carlo.

'I kept thinking I would tell him it was over, but then when he'd call me, when I'd see him. . . I couldn't, Annie! I just couldn't. And when *you* started going out with him too, I was so desperate, so *unhappy*! I just kept praying you would see reason – that you would realise —'

'Realise *what*, Beattie?'

'That he wasn't good enough for you, Annie! That he was married! That —'

'Oh, *Beattie*,' I sigh. 'That's funny coming from you!'

But as she looks back at me, I see it: the illogical, unreasonable madness governing her thoughts, her heart. The passion. There is nothing I can say to her now. She's in too deep. So I turn away, heading back to the station, walking fast.

'Annie!'

But I don't turn around. Because my mind is racing forward, tortured, on to something that troubles me much, *much* more than any of this. Because I want to scream at her, 'So is that what you felt about Marc? Is that your excuse?'

And that's not something she can tell me.

Chapter
forty-five

The first thing I notice, after I've wrestled the slip of paper from my coat pocket, is that I've put on weight. 53.2 *kilos*, I read.

Well, I'd have given anything to be this weight at thirty-nine. Besides, I'm pregnant.

I stand in a crowded train carriage, headed back in the right direction, towards Moratel. The heat and smell, sweat off the commuters, all of us packed in like swaying sardines, is stifling. It's peak hour. As we pull into each station, I pray the mass of bodies pressed against me will surge forward, back through the doors, out on to the platform. But they don't. The doors whoosh open, and they just keep coming, pushing and shoving, elbowing their way in. Parisians are a tough lot.

So I don't take it in at first – what's written underneath:

Tu prendras le chemin du haut,
Moi, je prendrai celui du bas.
Mais attention,

Ce chemin ne te ramènera pas chez toi.
Change de route.

These words are different. *Where's the bit about my mother?* I turn the slip of paper over as though I might find them there, the words I'd expected to see, but draw a blank. There's no logic in my madness as I reach back into my pocket, wondering if I've somehow pulled out the wrong thing, searching for that fragile, torn bit of paper smelling of leather, frayed at the edges, so incomplete. My elbow brushes against a businessman to my left. He gives me a look to kill. '*Pardon, Monsieur.*' But he turns away, cold. Now more than ever I want it back, the way it was – the prophecy!

But all I manage to dig up is my métro pass.

So I take another look.

Tu prendras le chemin du haut

I turn the words over in my head, unable to read past the first line until I can make some sense of it.

You will take the high way.

What the hell is that supposed to mean? I wonder, frustrated and angry now. The heat is starting to get to me. And I'm aware of someone very tall, a man standing to my right, looking over my shoulder at my slip of paper. I jerk my face round to give him a look.

The first thing that grabs me about this man is his smile, the way it stretches across his face so easily. So I forget all about fixing him with a glare.

'What are you planning to do about it, then?' he says, with a Scottish accent so broad it's ridiculous, his eyes meeting mine. 'Go on a diet?'

I'm confused. It's not the fact that he has picked me as an English speaker – my freckles are a dead giveaway in this city of perfect solarium-induced tans, like his smile on this carriage full of cranky Gallic faces. It's the way he has spoken to me that has taken me by surprise – just launched in, as if we were right in the middle of a conversation about the weather, about my life.

'What?' I ask.

'Well, you're obviously *veery* disappointed with your result here!'

He has really quite a lovely smile – a lovely *face*, in fact, and his hair is messy like Charlie's at the beach, blown in every direction by the wind, as if he's just stepped off the Isle of Skye. All that's missing is the kilt – *shame*, that.

'So I wondered what you planned to do about it?'

I realise then, what he's referring to. 'Oh, *this*!' I flap the bit of paper about, embarrassed. The businessman to my left gives me another look. 'Nothing – it's not important.'

I am aware of others around us listening in, looking from me to the Scot, drawn in by the English, by this man's rich booming voice, the seductive lilt of his words – as am I.

'Hmm.' He's obviously not convinced.

Am I that transparent? I wonder. Perhaps it's *not* the freckles. Maybe it is as my mother always said, 'Annie, you're an open book.' And it was never meant as a compliment.

'What about the rest of it, then?' he asks.

'What do you mean?'

'*Weell*...' He points to my bit of paper. 'You *do* know what it is, don't you?'

But I have no idea what he's on about.

'Those first two lines.' He reads over my shoulder. '*Tu prendras le chemin du haut. Et moi, je prendrai celui du bas.*'

I stare back at him, blank.

He smiles. 'They're the words from the song. *Dooon't* tell me you don't recognise it?'

'Sorry.' I am shaking my head, feeling slightly guilty, though I'm not sure why.

'*Weell* then.' He shrugs. 'You leave me no choice.'

'How's that?' I laugh, nervous.

'Oh, ye'll tak' the high road...' The words come softly over the whirr of the train, its wheels screeching against the tracks. 'And I'll tak' the low.'

It's not *any* man who will sing to you on a crowded carriage with nothing but the ice-cold stare of an anonymous captive audience to stir you on, and no bagpipes.

'*Loch Lomond!*' My cheeks are burning, flushed red.

'Very good.' He smiles encouragement as he gathers up his coat and briefcase.

We have just pulled into Châtelet – the stop where most commuters have to change trains. He's obviously one of them, but not me. *Pity*, I think, as he steps off the train.

As the doors whoosh shut and the train pulls out, I catch a glimpse of the Scot, striding in his crumpled suit, cutting a path through the surging mass of commuters, towering above them as he disappears from view. And I haven't even thanked him for his song.

There's a free seat now, so I grab it, clutching my slip of paper, keen to crack the rest of the message.

Mais attention, I read. *Ce chemin ne te ramènera pas chez toi. Change de route.*

Beware... This way won't take you home.

Take me home, I think. Take me home...

And then it occurs to me: that road we were on when we were driving home from Toulouse – we were travelling along the autoroute, along the *highway*, on our way home to Charlie. That's when it happened. If I take *the high way*...

True – we never got there, never got back to Charlie.

My heart is racing as I read on to the end, as I turn the meaning over in my mind, as I realise its significance.

Change de route.

Of course! The answers are all here in this final sentence.

Change paths. That's it. To find my way back home, I *have* to change direction. We *have* to change our fate. We've no choice.

But where's home now?

Chapter
forty-six

*H*e rings me at work. Yet another month has passed since we have spoken, since the day at Ozouer. I don't recognise the voice at first, its deep, rich timbre making my breathing quicken and my stomach flutter. His voice enters the strange, lonely world in which I now move, like a familiar song, one that makes me stop and smile. The familiar lilt. He is the last person I was expecting to hear from. I have expected no one. I am a lonely traveller now with no direction.

'Come home, Annie,' my mother tells me when we speak on the phone. 'There is nothing for you over there now.'

But I know in my heart I cannot leave this country, I cannot take that plane without him – without Charlie. Without Marc.

He needs to see me. I hear the urgency in his voice, in his breathing, as I feel it in my own. I don't trust myself to speak. He tells me to meet him after work, under the glass pyramid at the Louvre – at 6 p.m. 'Okay,' I mumble, hanging up.

Then I smile. He remembers – it was once my favourite place in all the world.

At 6.40 I am running through the Passage Richelieu, this sombre, vaulted passageway off rue de Rivoli that cuts a path under the left wing of the Musée du Louvre, leading through to the Cour Napoléon. I'm very late – waylaid at work by yet *another* attack of nausea, standing in the office toilets, crouched in the cubicle, simply waiting for the wave to pass over me. Morning sickness has become *any time* sickness. It should have passed by now, but it hasn't.

Cool drops fall on my face as I come out on to the square, as I emerge from the dark into this vast open space of light. The glass pyramid sits seemingly weightless in the centre of the Cour, a modern counterbalance to the majestic pomp of the grand old buildings at its edges. By the time I cross over to the entrance, the rain is splattering hard on to the pyramid's clear glass panes.

Inside, I look up. The last time we were here, Charlie was with us – Charlie still five, when he planted himself under the pyramid, smack in the centre. It was raining then too. He'd stared up, his blue eyes wide, pointing up at the glass to the water rippling over its surface.

'We're fish!' he'd cried out. 'We're fish in a bowl!'

The pure innocence of his voice echoed around the massive open space, like a choirboy's.

I stand at the top of the wide spiral staircase looking down into the foyer entrance. He's not there. I glance at my watch. It's 6.45. So I'm late, but not *that* late. The circular descent makes me woozy again, so I pause halfway, breathing in deep, hoping it will pass. But I'm not feeling too hot. I cling to the steel railing. Tourists push past, bumping against my shoulder, staring back up at me.

Below, the crowd moves like trails of busy ants in all directions across the smooth honey tiles. I glimpse a lone figure over by the wall – a child. He looks to be around three or four, just a small thing, standing with his hand to his mouth, looking round anxiously, obviously lost. It could be Charlie. He looks just like him at that age with his sandy hair, his round face, the chunky little body. I scan the floor for his parents, even though I've no idea who they might be, but no one appears to be looking for him. The child stands still, his face as white as the wall behind. He starts to cry.

It makes me anxious. I scan the floor again, but still no one appears to be searching for him. So I start moving quickly down the stairs, keeping him within my view. I don't want to lose him.

I reach the bottom, level with the crowd, but lose sight of him. *Shit!* I am darting in and out, frantic, trying to catch a glimpse of him again. 'Excuse me. Excuse me,' I say, pushing past, losing patience as a large woman in a floral dress steps across my path, fixed to the spot like a Buddha. *Move, lady!* But she can't read my thoughts so she doesn't budge. I dart around her. There's a break in the crowd suddenly. I see him. He's still there. Good boy, I think.

I've always told him, 'If you get lost, don't move. Stay right where you are. Mummy and Daddy will find you.'

'It's okay,' I call. 'I'm coming!'

I am starting to attract attention. Some people have stepped aside to let me through.

'Thank you,' I say. 'Thank you so much. *Merci, Monsieur!*'

'I think she's lost her child,' I hear a woman say behind me; an Australian voice.

And then I remember, one really hot steamy day back in Sydney, taking Charlie down to Bondi for a swim. We'd waited till it was late in the afternoon to avoid the crowds, but the beach was still packed anyway. We were sitting on the wet sand at the water's edge, watching Charlie play as the waves lapped over our feet, soft sand oozing between our toes. He was running back and forth, playing chasing games with the waves, squealing as the frothy water splashed up around his thighs, clapping his hands, delighted.

He was *so* beautiful.

I remember it was only a brief moment, no more than a few seconds, that we'd turned away – distracted by a plane flying over, marking its message in the sky with white smoke streaming behind.

'I think it's an "O".'

'*Non*, it's a "C" – C *pour* Coca Cola.'

'Nah,' I replied. 'C for Charlie.'

And then I'd turned back and he was gone – just disappeared into thin air. We jumped up, searching frantically, first in the water, wading out, calling for him. 'Have you seen a little boy?' People stared after us, shaking their heads. 'He was playing in the water just here. Right here! Did you see him?' The look on their faces: how could they be so careless?

But it was *only* a moment.

I was splashing through the water, looking out to sea, diving under waves, taking in salt water through my nose, down into my throat, spluttering as I cried out for him. '*Charlie!*'

How could we be so careless?

I remember turning round, glimpsing Marc as he ran up and down the beach, stopping people, waving his arms around, calling for Charlie. I will never forget the look on his face – the fear.

I was stumbling out of the water when I noticed her – a girl, no more than eight or nine, walking along the beach, holding on to a little boy's hand. *Charlie!* She was talking to him, stopping as she approached couples, pointing to them as Charlie shook his head, his finger in his mouth, smiling. She was looking for his parents. He thought it was a great game.

'Charlie!'

'He came over to play in our sand castle.' The girl pointed up the beach towards her family. 'Dad said I should bring him back.'

He'd only been some ten metres away. Yet we thought we'd lost him, forever.

I have reached the wall. He is there, crying still, his little body shaking. I crouch down, reach my hand out to touch his cheek, hot and sticky with tears.

'It's okay.' I speak softly, to soothe away the tears. 'I'm here now.'

Someone touches me on the shoulder. 'Annie?'

I look up. Marc is staring down at me, a look on his face, the one that Charlie gets when he's not sure what planet I'm from.

I pull myself up. 'Marc!'

'What are you doing? *C'est qui?*'

'Matthew!' A woman's voice calls from behind. 'Oh, Matthew, you *naughty* boy! Where have you been?'

The accent is definitely English, very *la-di-da* English. She pushes past me, reaches down and takes the boy's hand, yanking him along behind her.

'He was lost!' I step after her. 'He didn't move from this spot. He was just waiting for you!'

Marc's hand is on my elbow, pulling me back. '*Annie!*'

The woman looks back at me, cold. *What is her problem?* I watch bewildered as she hurries off without even a backward glance.

'He was lost!' I turn back to Marc. 'She should be more careful. You should be more careful, *lady!*' I call after her.

People are looking over at me.

'Annie!' Marc's hands are on my shoulders, gripping them tight. '*Please,* Annie, *stop!*'

I stare at him. What's he so worked up about? 'Honestly, Marc, I was watching from up on the stairs over there. He was all by himself. *No one* came for him. Can you imagine? *Anything* could have happened to him!'

Marc is listening to me now, his eyes looking into mine, nodding as he strokes my face.

It hits me then. 'Oh, shit, Marc! Charlie's right. I've *really* lost it, haven't I?'

He smiles. 'Charlie?'

'Yeah —' I stop then, realising what I'm saying.

'It's okay, Annie.' He reaches over and pulls me to him. 'I hear him too.'

Chapter
forty-seven

$\mathcal{W}$e go away. He picks me up Friday evening after work, and we drive out to Quiberon in the rusty old panel van, arriving at midnight, sleeping in the back until dawn. Cold air on my face and the creak of the van doors swinging back wide wake me. Marc's already up and dressed, standing outside in his old sloppy joe, faded blue, his jeans worn to white at the knees. I smell croissants.

'*Reveille-toi,* sl*ur*py head!' He stamps his feet on the ground outside, his cold hand slipping under the duvet, gripping my bare ankle, kneading the sole of my foot.

I groan, pulling the duvet up around my ears, thinking of Charlie, always cranky in the morning and growling from under the covers, 'I'm not sl*ur*py, I'm sleepy. Get it right, Papa!'

And I remember that first time we took him camping when he was four – an Easter weekend in Australia when it pelted with rain, a solid downpour that promised to break the drought and fill Warragamba Dam as we drove south along the coast. We were travelling with cheap rubber roof-racks that could only be attached securely with the windows partly down – towels wedged through the gaps, water seeping on to our laps, our bottoms sliding forward on the wet seats every time Mark braked too suddenly. And he had to brake a lot that trip. We eventually had to pull over and grab the plastic groundsheet from the boot to protect Charlie from the flood in the back, pegging the corners to strategic points in the car, covering him from head to toe. So I can't put it out of my mind now, his small face beaming at us through the plastic – 'I like camping!' – until finally he dozed off, snug in his little plastic paradise.

As I reach for my jeans, I wonder if it will hit me when I sit up – the nausea. I haven't told him yet. I'm not ready.

We grab our backpacks and tent and head off for the ferry. The weight pulling my shoulders back feels good as we walk down to the pier, wind blowing my hair up and off my face; the smell of the sea and the caw of seagulls welcoming us back. I am feeling fine. The Atlantic is a grey–blue. There's no horizon as I look out to sea – no beginning or end between water and sky.

The wind drives sea spray up against the ferry windows as we sit snug inside, sipping steaming hot coffee out of polystyrene cups – our croissants still warm in the white paper bag, stained with butter. I am hungry, not sick. Not even the waves rocking us menacingly back and forth put me off as we sit perched forward on the plastic orange seats. So maybe it is passing – at last – as I move into the fourth month. Marc is opposite, smiling like a kid.

I smile back, hoping he will leave me the third croissant. But then he turns from me, looking out at the ocean, troubled.

'*J'étais fâché. J'étais bête*, Annie.'

I'm not sure what he's talking about. He was angry, he tells me – stupid.

He shakes his head. 'I didn't say goodbye to him.'

'To Charlie?'

'*Non.*' He speaks softly. '*Mon père.* I didn't say goodbye to Maurice.'

The coffee burns my throat as it tightens too suddenly, my heart pounding fast as I wave my hand in front of my mouth to ease the burning.

'I was *so* angry.' He reaches over, stopping my hand, gripping it tight. 'I blamed you.'

I turn to look at the sea, at the water swirling white, stirred by the ferry. 'I *know*, Marc. You don't have to tell me.'

He leans forward. '*Mais si*, Annie, I do. . . *Je veux que tu sâches.* I was angry, angry with *myself*. . . because I knew, Annie – I knew it already.' He breathes out hard through his teeth, swiping at his forehead with the palm of his hand.

I reach over, my fingers brushing his cheek. 'You knew *what* already?'

His eyes meet mine. 'I knew he was sick. I knew before we even left. I could see it, *tu sais*? I could see how tired he was. . .'

I smile, shaking my head. Because I remember that call, Rosa's first call with the news – his shock, the pain in his eyes. '*No*, Marc, you didn't know. We didn't —'

'*Si*, Annie, I knew! With my father, there were things we didn't even need to talk about.'

And I realise, *yes, he's right*: when I think about them together, their quiet conversations, their easy silences. . . how I had envied them, their intimate companionship – this mutual affection.

'*En plus*. . . he even tried to talk to me about it, Annie.' He winces, his guilt still red raw. 'One day when we were down by the river.'

My hand grips his knee. 'He *knew*?'

'*Oui*.' His hand moves over his forehead, fingers pressing into his temples as he breathes out hard. 'And I wouldn't let him talk to me about it. I could see he was worried. I could *see* it in his eyes. But I wouldn't let him tell me. I didn't want to hear it! *Merde*, Annie! *Quand j'y pense!*'

I see it now in his eyes – the shame, his guilt as he looks over at me. '*Oui, je sais*. . . I was in denial, Annie.' Charlie's words, Charlie's face.

'*Why*, Marc?'

'You wanted to go home. So I wanted to take you. I thought you needed to go – I thought you were ready to see your mother.'

'*Oh, Marc!*'

'*Je sais*.' A sad half smile. 'I got it wrong. I got it *all* wrong.'

No, I'm thinking, not *all* of it. He knew something about me that I wouldn't even admit to myself. . . something I had pushed into the back of my heart like a pair of old shoes. He wasn't the only one in denial.

'*Et puis*... when my mother rang, I got scared, Annie – and guilty, *so* guilty. I panicked. I thought, how can I be a father, a husband? I was just a kid – a stupid kid.'

I sigh. 'We both were.'

I remember taking him out to Australia – that sensation, a flutter in my heart as the plane rolled over like an eagle homing in on its prey, hovering low over the coast of Sydney. And when at last she came to rest on the tarmac of Kingsford Smith, I had looked out the window at the waves of heat rising from the bitumen, my hand in Marc's, and thought, I am home.

I had such plans! I would take him down to Bondi; for a picnic in Centennial Park; we'd have a beer at the Two in Hand down in Paddington; fish and chips on Manly wharf. We could drive up and down the coast... I was so excited, so keen to show him where I had grown up, to show this Frenchman from Ozouer *my* world.

But as we came out at the arrival gates, pushing our trolley of luggage down the ramp, following in the trail of other weary travellers, I had looked out at the sea of eager faces: relatives and friends standing behind the barrier. And that is when I felt it, when a niggling ache surfaced – from the depths of my heart.

Emptiness.

I had wished then for her face – *wished* for Norma Jean to be standing in among that crowd. 'This is Marc, Mum!' To have laughed when he kissed her on both cheeks – smiling proudly at their funny, awkward first exchange.

But then, how could she be there? *How* could she, when I hadn't even called her, when I hadn't even picked up the phone to tell my mother that I was coming home?

When I hadn't made that first step.

We sit still together, watching the seagulls hovering, guiding us into the bay. But as the passengers around us begin to gather up their things, moving into the aisles, he turns to me. *'Je veux que tu sâches…C'était un désastre.'* It was a disaster. You should know that.

I stare at him – my heart races, my fingers tingle, numb, gripping the edge of the seat too hard because I know what he is talking about.

'J'étais tellement perdu. I was so full of anger, full of rage. We spent the night together. But that was all, Annie.'

I sit frozen, afraid to move, afraid to think – to *feel*.

'We didn't —' But I hold my hand up. 'She said it was a sign —'

It's no use, I feel it now – my own rage stirring again. '*What?*'

'She said it was a sign that it was wrong, that it was never meant to happen – that you were too good for us both.'

I wave my hand in front of my face. I don't want to go there. '*Please*, Marc, not that...'

But he reaches for my hand, his eyes looking into mine, intense. 'It's true, Annie. *Je ne me suis pas rendu compte de ce que j'avais. She* tried to tell me that. I was a fool.'

But he has said something just now: it's familiar, this expression '*Je ne me suis pas rendu compte de ce que j'avais*'...so familiar, it makes me stop short. *Where have I heard it?*

I didn't know what I had...

Yes – it's what Grandma told me about Grandpa.

'Why did you leave him, Grandma?' I'd asked her.

'Because he didn't know what he had.'

As the ferry brings us into shore, I feel my heart rise, watching the seagulls take off from the old stone pier, taking in the white-wash of houses along the shoreline, boats bobbing in the bay with the lighthouse at its edge. A spectrum of colours, of memories.

I tell him, as we step from the rocky ferry boat on to the pier. 'I'm pregnant.'

His hand slips around my neck, his lips on my cheek, his

whisper in my ear. *'Tu vois*, Annie! This *is* our second chance!'

But as I watch the water rise, slapping up against the stone, its fine spray kissing my face, I tell him, 'No, Marc.'

Since we've come back, it is different. It *has* to be.

Chapter
forty-eight

*I*t's hard to forgive – harder still to admit there might be nothing to forgive. Nothing worth dwelling on, in any case.

My mother has told me her story – the rest, *at last*.

When my father told her 'It's not what you think, Elsie', he was right. It wasn't.

It was a business lunch, he explained, arranged by his boss for a new client – the woman in the café. But when his boss didn't show, she came on to him – pressed her knees into his, told him she fancied him, that they should skip coffee.

'I don't want to hear it!' my mother had cried.

'*Please*, Else, you have to listen to me...'

He told the woman, *no*, that he was married, that his wife was pregnant.

'I don't want to hear it! Your lame excuses!'

That he loved his wife.

'Please just *go*!'

She was at the funeral – the other woman. My mother turned

away when she tried to approach her. 'Please leave me alone,' she said. But the woman insisted, following her to the car.

'I'm sorry!' she cried to her through the car window. 'He told me he was married, that you were pregnant and that he loved you. I just wanted you to know —'

She could see the imprint of the woman's hand on the glass as she drove home, tears blurring her vision all the way.

The last time I saw Grandma she was sitting at her kitchen table, sorting through a dusty old suitcase full of photos, taking them out one by one, sorting them into piles, writing on the back of each in her beautiful old-fashioned script, meticulously looping, dotting or crossing each letter – intricate descriptions, who was who. It was the week before she died. I guess she knew.

'Your mother should have these. But she won't take them, *not yet*. So I'm giving them to you for now, Annie.'

'Why don't you just keep them for her?'

'She's not ready. You know how she is about photos – about *sentimental stuff*. We have to give her time.'

'How much time does she need?'

Her eyes fixed on mine. She'd heard it – the bitterness. 'More time than *I* have left. In any case, that's up to you, Annie.'

I wondered what she meant.

'Here's a photo of your grandfather.'

She was changing the subject. I could see him, upside down, this man with dark hair, solemn in his white shirt and tie. I reached over. But she held it still – her finger tracing a circle over his face, lost in the memory of him. 'Grandma?'

'He came to see me, not long after I'd upped and left with the baby – with Elsie.'

I didn't know. She'd never got this far into her story. 'He wanted you to come back?'

She nodded, looking up, staring out the kitchen window. 'He came to tell me he was sorry. "I'm so sorry, Nelly, so sorry... Won't you come home?"' She stopped then, shaking her head, obviously going over the words, those exact words. 'And I —'

I saw the pain in her eyes then, as if it was only yesterday. A shock. I had always pictured Grandma just moving on to the next husband, to her second, her third... the fourth – onwards and upwards, no regrets, no backward glances.

'So what did you say?'

She leant back in her chair. 'I told him to go.'

I glanced over at this lone upside-down photo of a man I'd never known.

'Go home, Nathan. We don't need you!'

Something in these words made me uneasy, something in her tone. And it was there in her eyes, in her *face* – a flicker, the first time *ever*... and I'd never noticed it, until then.

My mother.

'That's when he told me... but I was too proud. I was *Nelly Rae Beveridge*... I wouldn't listen to him. I wouldn't even let him in past the front door.'

Yes. I shifted in my chair. 'What did he tell you?'

She looked over at me and smiled, her eyes glassy, her finger still tracing a circle. 'It was the nicest thing any man has said to me – *ever*. I was shutting the door —'

I nodded.

'I remember he reached his hand up to stop me. His hand was on the door and that's when he said it. "Nelly, forgive me. I didn't know what I had."'

Now if my mother had been around, she'd have said, 'Mum, you've already told us this one.' But she'd have been wrong. *This* story was different. It wasn't how she told it the first time, when I was a girl sitting across the table from her, playing cards. Back then, she'd told me it was the reason she left him, that *he didn't know what he had*. So I'd always believed they'd been *her* words, *her* reason for leaving him – her *raison d'être*, the very essence of her strength.

But it wasn't that at all. It was more that *she* couldn't forgive.

He'd told her he was sorry, that he didn't know what he had. He had changed. But she just wouldn't let it go.

Yet she'd loved him, *best of all*, all those years.

It was only as I was leaving, when I'd got up from the table, the case of photos under my arm, that she said it.

'Go somewhere nice, Annie, somewhere *special* with your mother...'

So I understand now, after all these years, what she'd meant. She'd entrusted me with the photos, with the task of making the first steps towards my mother. The photos, her ashes – all just excuses...

She wanted us to be friends. *That's all* – her last wish. And it was up to me.

Chapter *forty-nine*

I keep the prophecy in my wallet, underneath the credit-card section as before, for always – a souvenir to our friendship, still. To Beattie.

'Don't cut off your nose to spite your face,' I used to tell Charlie. 'Forgive and forget.'

She was my best friend.

But it's hard. Of course, Carlo is just a memory now, a beautiful man who swept me off my feet, who whisked me off to Italy… But as a lover, he means nothing to me now. In any case, he was hers to start with. She fell for him first.

The problem is what happened between her and Marc. But then, how can I stay angry with her for something that hasn't happened yet? And it will go differently now.

It will take time, but I will ring her one day – perhaps when she is older, when she is wiser…

Regret is just a waste of time. But sometimes, at the supermarket, *particularly* the supermarket when I reach the aisle where they stock the Weet-Bix – Charlie's favourite – with my big round melon of a belly pushing up against the trolley handle, I can't help thinking, *if only*...

I remember now. It has come back to me, as I stand over the washing machine, pulling on one of Marc's old hankies, tangled up in the washing.

The crash.

I was talking to Charlie on the mobile when I noticed something, *someone*, on the road. A man was waving at us, just standing out there in the middle lane on the opposite side... He was built like a front-row forward, squinting at the rain as it pelted his scalp, flattening long strands of hair to his forehead. He was waving at us with a piece of red cloth.

'Hey!' I had held the phone away, distracted. 'What's *he* doing?'

'*Qui?*'

'That guy!' I was looking back over my shoulder as we continued on past, tyres swishing on the wet road, zooming up the autoroute. 'Didn't you see him?'

'What guy?' Marc had flicked on the indicator to overtake the truck ahead, his body tensed forward, squinting at the windscreen, seeing nothing.

He once told me when I first took the wheel on a French autoroute, 'To overtake, you just have to concentrate on looking forward, not sideways at the thing beside you. *C'est simple.'*

Sure, I was thinking, my hand tense on the dashboard, sucking my breath in. *You* can look forward, but I'll keep my eye on the truck.

I remember the sound – brakes screeching, rubber squealing, metal screaming against metal – my foot to the floor, slamming on a brake that wasn't there. The mobile bouncing off the windscreen.

Oh God, Marc! Oh God!

So I never got a chance to explain about the man on the road.

Marc reckons I imagined him, that I've reconstructed the accident. *Post-mortem déformation des faits.*

'No one was standing out there,' he says. 'It just happened. *C'est tout.'*

But I know what I saw. He was trying to warn us, trying to get us to slow down. So I regret that moment just before Marc flicked on the indicator, before we moved into the fast lane, when I could have said, 'Pull over, Marc!'

'Oh Annie, stop,' he tells me.

And I regret not saying goodbye. *Goodbye, Charlie.*

Regret nothing, said Grandma. But I do. I can't help it.

Marc reckons there was a truck lying on its side, great hunks of shiny metal strewn across the road, glistening in the rain, just up ahead. I didn't see it because I was too busy telling Charlie to get off the computer and looking sideways at the monster of a truck we were overtaking, praying we wouldn't skim against its giant tyres looming too close.

'It makes no difference anyway,' Marc tells me. 'We never had a chance, Annie.'

But I know what I saw – that man with his red rag, trying to wave us down. It was Serge.

'*Mais il est mort*, Annie. He drowned in the river.'

'Dead like us, Marc – like when we crashed?'

He was trying to wave us down – with his dog's scarf.

We take a drive out to Ozouer to meet Marc's parents, *supposedly* for the first time. They greet me, as before. They are charming.

Until they notice the melon.

I am six months pregnant. The alarm on Rosa's face is undisguised – red creeping up her neck as her hand moves to her mouth.

'It's okay,' I want to tell her as we sit across the table from one another, smiling politely. 'Marc and I have known each other for years.'

But then I realise, no, we haven't. That's the thing. In all the years we were together, we'd barely scratched the surface. So perhaps she's right to worry. We are, after all, just starting out, barely taking off. But it will never be the same.

Not without Charlie.

'Let's walk,' Marc says softly after lunch, afraid to wake his father – asleep in the garden.

Rosa smiles as she pushes us out the door. '*Ne vous inquiétez pas!* Don't mind him. He's just been working too hard,' she assures us. 'Just a few more years before he retires!'

Marc winces.

'Come on.' I squeeze his hand. 'Let's go down to the river.'

The L'Yerres gushes fast and strong underneath the bridge. I throw a stick into the water just like Charlie used to, and we watch as it hurtles on down, underneath the bridge, between the rocks and out the other side.

'You have to talk to him, Marc.'

'I already have... *Ca ne sert à rien*. It's no use. He won't see a doctor.'

'That's not what I *mean*, Marc.' My hand is on his arm, pulling him around to face me as we pause on the bridge. 'You should just talk to him, not about seeing a doctor – just *talk*, before he —'

'Before he dies?'

'*Yes*, Marc, before he dies.' He stares back at me. 'You said you wouldn't let him tell you, that you could see that he was afraid. So now let him tell you. Now's your chance.'

He nods, taking my hand as we head over to the other side, to walk along the river's edge. 'To get it right this time?'

It was what he was trying to tell me that day when we lay in bed together in his apartment, when we conceived this baby.

'No, we won't ever be able to get it *truly* right, not without Charlie. But at least we can try to make *some* things better.'

He squeezes my hand. 'With your mother?'

I nod. He knows me well.

He looks out across the field and points to the spot over by the river where the grass grows wild and long. 'Would you like to see the nightlife again?'

I smile. 'I'm all done with village nightlife.'

'*Alors.*' He slips an arm around my shoulder. 'So you don't ever want to go back to Lherm?'

A shiver runs over me. 'No! *Wild horses* couldn't drag me back to that place.'

'You don't miss the hunters?' he teases.

'I miss Charlie.'

Marc squeezes my shoulder and breathes out. '*Moi aussi.*' Me too.

We are heading back across the bridge, back towards home, when we hear it – a dog barking, a man's whistle.

It is Serge. He is heading across the grass, waving over at us, as he was on the road that night.

We wait on the bridge. His dog bounds over, barking excited as it scampers back and forth, its tail whipping the air like a crazed metronome. Serge whistles, but the dog ignores him. There's a splash, and it's in the water.

Déjà Vu

'*Bonsang de clébard!*' Serge laughs as he extends his giant hand towards me, taking in my stomach – too big to miss. '*Bonjour! Félicitations!*'

I nod *Bonjour*, smiling – uneasy. I am watching the dog as it splashes about, wild and excited. I remember it was in winter, Serge's accident – so not now, not *yet*. There's still time.

'*Ca va?*' Marc reaches an arm across his friend's back.

I should go. I should leave them alone to talk. '*Je vous laisse,*' I tell them as I start back across the bridge.

Marc nods. He has understood. It will go differently now – for all of us.

Chapter *fifty*

I wake in the middle of the night. I am lying on my back, too big to turn over now. Marc is beside me, his form still but turned towards me. I have been dreaming about Lherm, about the *lavoir* again.

But this time, I was with Charlie.

I can't go back to sleep now – the dream has troubled me. I am thinking about a Sunday afternoon, not long after the thug and his headbutt. We were out for an afternoon stroll in Lherm, desperate for some action as Marc tried to fix a leak in one of the hot-water pipes. We could hear him cursing still – '*Putain, merde!*' – as we made our way towards the *lavoir*, some 50 metres up the road. Charlie's eyes flashed up at me, a half smile at his father's cursing.

'You know, Charlie,' I'd begun, 'if that kid even so much as *blinks* your way again, I want you to tell me.'

He shrugged. 'Whatever.'

'What's that supposed to mean? *Has* he been bugging you?'

'Maybe.'

'*Christ*, Charlie!'

Déjà Vu

I watched him clamber up on to the stone wall leading down to the *lavoir*, and walk along its edge, arms outspread to steady himself. At eleven he was quite small for his age, still just a kid. Marc had tried to reason with the thug's father, to no avail. He'd just been a bigger version of the son, and a cop, to boot.

'Charlie, why didn't you tell me about this?'

'Because...' He looked over at me, smiling. 'Pretty soon he won't be able to bug me any more.'

'Oh? How come?'

He jumped down by the side of the *lavoir*. 'Because.'

The water was still that day; fat worms twisting, wriggling in the water, their shadows reflected tenfold on the sludgy bottom.

'Because *what*?'

'*Because...*' He turned from me. 'I fixed it so he won't be able to.'

'What did you do?' I smiled. 'Take a contract out on him?'

'A *contact*?'

'*No*, a *contract*. Forget it. I'm just kidding.' I ran my hand through his sandy hair, glowing like gold in the sunlight as he squatted by the edge of the water. 'So how did you fix it, Shorty?'

He looked at me then, screwing up his lips – that *no way* look.

'Come on, Charlie.' I laughed. '*Tell me!* You're starting to worry me.'

He smiled. 'You *know*, Mum.'

I stared at him, confused. 'What?' I crouched down next to him. '*What* do I know?'

'*Come on*, Mum!' He was still smiling at me, his head cocked to the side, obviously convinced that I was in on it.

But I really had no idea. This time he had me stumped. I'd have to fish.

'Can you give me a hint?' He used to always like that game.

'Well… It's what *you're* good at.'

'*Me?*'

He nodded.

'I'm good at most things, so that's not much of a hint! Give me another one.'

His eyes met mine, solemn. 'You told me your grandma was good at it too.'

So then I knew.

'You made a wish?' My heart was pounding, anxious – anxious that he should be so upset by that little thug that he should have to resort to this.

'Yep.'

'What did you wish for, Charlie?'

'*No way*, Mum!' He was shaking his head at me as he reached over for a worm wriggling our way. 'You know I can't tell you that. Otherwise it won't come true.'

So I left it. But I think I might know *now*: what he'd wished for, how he'd 'fixed' it. He'd wanted out of Lherm as much as me. So he'd wished and wished *and wished*…

And that was it – our last Sunday together.

Chapter
fifty-one

I wait. It'll be any day now.

I am in the middle of painting the second bedroom in our Paris apartment. White, pure white – a whitewash. I run the roller over the walls, ambivalent, dipping it into the paint tray, straining it against the metal grill to squeeze out the excess liquid, but droplets fall on to my swollen belly anyway. My mind is elsewhere.

I remember that last Sunday before Charlie was born. He was ten days overdue and, sick of waiting, I had gone for a walk with Marc in Centennial Park, round and round the bike track, up and over the rocks, through and past the shady flat where the pine trees leave their cones scattered. It was a fine spring day, September in Australia. I had walked and walked, willing him to come, to get it over with. And that night as I lay in bed, exhausted, tired of myself, my feet raised, bloated like giant goldfish, I wondered if he ever would. I cursed him. *Why won't you bloody come?*

And then finally, at midnight, the very last minute, he made his move when I'd given up and drifted off, taking me unawares – that wonderful unpredictability, even then.

It happens now, when I least expect it, even though the baby is ten days overdue, when I am only halfway through the second coat of paint. It is 4 o'clock in the afternoon, midnight in Sydney.

'Midnight, you say?' Marc says, smiling and raising an eyebrow. 'Maybe…'

'Rubbish. Pure coincidence,' I growl as he cuts a path through the peak-hour traffic, honking, banging on the wheel – the typical Frenchman. 'Psychosomatic,' I say. 'Mind over matter, the past controlling the chemistry of my hormones. The timing has nothing to do with *this* baby, nothing to do with Charlie, *my* Charlie.'

I am lying on my back in the labour ward, in the first throes. But I am still thinking about him, about his first cry, about his shoulders ripping me apart as he forced his way into the world, pushing through my skin, making it tear, determined. 'They're Marc's shoulders!' I'd growled at the time, cursing them both, the father and *his* child.

I am breathing slowly, feeling the pain, the unbearable pain of my thoughts.

I will not love this baby.

'*Quoi?*' Marc's face is over mine, anxious. 'What did you say, Annie?'

I realise I have said it out loud. *I will not love this baby* – words full of fear and anger.

The pain of it hits me as another contraction shoots through my body like lightning cracking me open. I have heard them before, these tough words, seen them written in my mother's face.

They ask me if I want an epidural. *Yeah*, give me anything. I don't care. But it won't take the pain away, the *real* pain.

With Charlie, I was determined to do it without any help. 'No drugs, nothing,' I had growled through gritted teeth, cursing them all, cursing Marc, cursing my mother for not telling me about this *god-awful* unnatural pain, with just my stupid pride to see me through it.

Now I will accept any help I can get. It doesn't matter.

This is not my first, Mum, I have told her. *This is not my first baby, my first love!*

Be strong, Annie. You will love this baby.

I won't, Mum! I can't forget Charlie!

My Charlie!

The rest is in the past, Annie.

But it's not. He's with me always. He is my present – my every waking moment.

It is over, at last, in the early hours of the morning – 3 a.m. I remember Charlie was born at 11 a.m. 'Congratulations,' they had said, right on the dot. 'You have a lovely baby boy.'

Marc smiles. 'It's 11 a.m. in Sydney.'

I close my eyes and shake my head at him, tears escaping, running down my cheeks. No, it is 3 a.m. *now*, end of story.

I am too tired to look, to ask if it is a boy or a girl. I don't care. I just want to sleep, to wake up and find *him* again, my Charlie. Marc is coming towards me, holding the foreign bundle, swaddled in their hospital wrap. I close my eyes again as he leans over me. I will not look.

I feel it lying across my chest, the weight of it, the incredible weight. Marc has taken my hand, forcing my fist open. *I will not* touch it.

I hear him whispering in my ear. 'Annie, *s'il te plaît.*'

'No, Marc!'

Don't make the mistake I did, Annie.

'*Tu ne veux pas*, Annie?'

You will love this baby.

As you loved me?

I hear the midwife hovering, her anxious mutterings. '*On va la laisser dormir, non?*' We should let her sleep.

Yeah, let me sleep, I think. Just let me sleep.

'*Ouvre tes yeux! Please* look. Don't you want to see?'

His fingers are threaded through mine, forcing them open. But he can't make me look. I hear the midwife hovering behind him. She wants to take the baby off my chest.

'*Non,*' says Marc, firm.

Déjà Vu

That's right, Annie, as I loved you – just as I have always loved you.

And then I feel it – the tiny head. Not a perfectly rounded little head, *no*. I wrap my hand around it, rubbing it softly round and round, feeling it in the palm of my hand, and I smile, crying out loud – for the sheer ecstasy. It is there, as it was.

The bump. That wonderful bump.

LISTEN

Kate Veitch

Rosemarie leaned her weight on the big kitchen knife with blind efficiency. No one wanted to know the real secrets, not the really big ones. And, she thought emphatically, I don't want anyone to know mine!

On Christmas Eve in 1967, a London woman unhappily transplanted to the Australian suburbs makes a decision that will change forever the lives of her four young children.

Forty years on, those children are adept at concealing their shared pain. Deborah has a demanding political career, James is a successful artist, Robert a respected school principal. Only Meredith, the baby of the family, seems stuck. But as their father begins to lose his grip on reality, they find themselves floundering in an unfamiliar sea. And their past is about to reach into the present in ways that will shock and challenge them all...

A spellbinding contemporary novel, *Listen* draws us deep into the intensely private world of family life and brilliantly illuminates the joys, sorrows and sustaining comfort that we find there.

THE UNEXPECTED ELEMENTS OF LOVE

Kate Legge

Climate is what you expect and weather is what you get.

Janet is a TV weather presenter. Sometimes she'll admit to liking the adrenalin and modest celebrity of the nightly news. Other times she wonders if her job justifies the time away from family – after all, she's hardly curing cancer.

But now the weather seems to be invading her home. Her young son, Harry, is increasingly terrified by storms and endlessly distracted at school: everyone but Janet wants to put him on medication. And her husband complains that their marriage is slowly drying up. Like the content of her forecasts, Janet's life feels beyond her control.

Roy is scared of the weather, too. An acclaimed sculptor and father of Janet's oldest friend, he is working on the biggest commission of his life. When he feels the first splinterings of dementia he knows the creation will be his last. He's got to make it count. After almost fifty years of devoted marriage, Beth can't bear to witness his deterioration. Is Roy producing a masterpiece or a monstrosity? What can she do in the face of the darkening clouds?

Kate Legge's first novel beautifully traces the shifting connections between people as they encounter the high pressure zones of youth and old age. *The Unexpected Elements of Love* is a wonderfully insightful, tender and engrossing portrait of how we live now, under a common sky.

THE LOVE CHILD

Fran Cusworth

Is there life with children?
Is there life without them?

Serena gave up a career she loved to care for her two small children, and now she's going stir-crazy. With a workaholic husband, a motley crew from mothers' group for companions, and the awful possibility that she's pregnant again, she's fighting the temptation to run.

Ana, child-free, is aiming to be senior columnist at the *Morning Star*, searching for Mr Right, and dealing with a mother who's rewriting her past. Does she really need to learn to Wiggledance as well?

Both women believe they're free to shape their own destinies. That's until the mysterious tides of life and death come flooding in, changing everything.

A funny, touching, bittersweet story about two friends struggling to reconcile their once-lofty expectations with the messy reality of their adult lives.